Prodigals in Provence

Book One

Kyle Hunter

Monceau Publishing

Cover design by Erika Alyana Sañga Duran.

ISBN 978-0-9906246-9-1

More romance by Kyle Hunter that will take you places

Circle Back Around

One December

Provence Series

Prodigals in Provence

A Promise in Provence

The Second Chance Series

Marissa Rewritten

Julia Redesigned

Chapter One

Bree Sorenson's parched throat felt like rough burlap and her face prickled with heat. If she could dive into the carafe of water that beckoned from the podium, she'd do it. She eyed it before returning her attention to her audience.

"For those of you who dream of a Provence cooking tour, we have one scheduled later this fall, where world-class chefs will teach you French recipes in small groups." The microphone gave her voice a strength she didn't feel. The metal felt slick in her hand as she relaxed her grip. She panned a friendly gaze around the ballroom, making eye contact with the scattered few attendees seated in the first four rows. If the Coastal Cove Gracious Retirement Community had given her a smaller room in which to do her presentation, it might not have been so brazenly obvious how few people had shown up.

"Our May trip will be to the magical Luberon mountain region, well-known for having the loveliest villages in France." Rivulets of perspiration traced a path down her spine beneath her spring linen jacket and blouse despite the air conditioning flowing through the room. If only she'd taken the *unseasonably warm* forecast more seriously.

Several wizened residents nodded. Others fidgeted in their chairs, faces blank, probably wondering why she was wasting their time. She took a deep gulp of water and forced the corners of her lips upward, trying to keep her expression enthusiastic. "When you travel with Le Bon Voyage, you'll be part of a small, exclusive group of no more than ten people, for a more personalized experience."

Stay upbeat! Smile! The mental reminders flowed countercurrent to the weight pulling inside her. If she didn't fill this trip with a minimum number of travelers, the company's profit would be almost non-existent for the second trip in a row. They have to plunge again into their reserves.

Bree glanced around the room. The elegant five-star details—the carved molding on the coffered ceiling, the plush patterned carpet underfoot, the impressionist-style paintings on the walls—spoke of the financial means of the residents. But that didn't guarantee they'd be open to European travel on short notice.

If anything would convince these would-be travelers to sign up for the nine-day Provence excursion scheduled for the following month, her photos would. They'd plant in her audience a burning need to go. That need had been like breathing for Bree, ever since she first lived in France as a college exchange student. But such a passion was difficult to communicate in a few short minutes to a fidgety crowd whose minds were likely on the dinner menu or tomorrow's bridge game.

She started the slideshow and adjusted the focus. A vibrant purple panorama of lavender fields lit up the screen on the wall behind her, and she was rewarded by ooh and ahhs around the room. The pink-hued buildings of Roussillon, the fountains of Aix-en-Provence surrounded by colorful café awnings, stretches of gnarly grapevines in neat rows, medieval walled villages perched on hilltops. She clicked through the photos, one by one and watched the expressions on the faces in her audience. The final photo of an elevated sun-swept terrace shaded by overhanging grape vines expanded on the screen then faded from view. She loved ending with that one, the most dramatic *and* most likely to trigger a decision to sign up.

"After each day's adventures, you'll return to a private villa where you'll be able to take a swim, then dine on the terrace under the stars." Bree proffered a handful of brochures to each row. Her eyes roved to a clock on the opposite wall of the room. Only ten minutes left to convince them. "The brochure highlights our current trip. We still have space and I'd love to have you among us for our tour. If you can't come in May, be sure to sign up for one in the future."

Thirty minutes later Bree stepped through the sliding glass doors from the cool air onto the baking sidewalk. She trudged away from the main building, which resembled a large Caribbean villa, and passed the smaller patio homes on the way back to her car. Her shoulders sagged from a laptop case on one side and a canvas bag of brochures on the other.

It was late April and the property was already fully landscaped with cloudbanks of impatiens in red, white, and pink framed by pale green ferns. A balmy breeze, carrying a scent of new plants and fresh mulch tickled her neck and filled her lungs. Spring in northern Virginia never failed to revive her spirits, though that particular day she fought her dark thoughts and what-ifs and their tag-along emotions.

Bree moved her jaws, stiff from an hour of eager smiling. More like pitiful pleading. She may as well have said, "Please, I need another warm body in order to make my bottom line!" Maybe the low numbers were the result of the economy or insufficient marketing. Whatever the case, Le Bon Voyage was in trouble.

Once her tired body slid into the gully of her Honda's hot bucket seat, she sighed and ran her fingers through her hair. How long could she keep doing this? The last-minute tension, the fear that important details would fall apart at the wrong time . . . Sometimes the stress was unbearable. Each trip held the inherent challenges of weaving together an excursion on foreign soil. She always double and triple checked dozens of lists and computer files, as well as stacks of folders and notebooks piled on her office desk, just to make sure she hadn't neglected any detail. Despite this, something could still slip past her obsessively watchful eye. And that didn't even take into account the possibility of random events, such as vendors in Europe who had misplaced requests, gone on strike, or double-booked a service she needed.

The phone beeped in her purse. Maybe it was Lauren, her business partner and best friend. Glancing at the screen, she saw the name Mariah, her friend from church. Bree could use a friendly voice, even as she sweated in the car. Mariah was studying counseling and got a lot of practical experience with Bree. She turned on the ignition and flipped the air conditioner to max before responding. "Hi, Mariah."

"Hey, Bree. How did your presentation go today?"

Bree sighed. "The presentation went well enough, but I'm afraid the timing is too tight for most people. We should have done this kind of promotion months ago, but I kept thinking the trip would fill up."

"Don't you think you'll have enough people?" Mariah's voice held a layer of concern which calmed and reassured Bree. It was good to have a friend who wasn't annoyed by Bree's anxious nature.

"It's hard to tell. We still have six weeks, but usually people reserve months in advance." Bree let out a glum sigh. "It's been three years, Mariah, and Le Bon Voyage still takes two steps forward then one step back. All we need is two more tours that are under-filled and that'll be the end of us. We're just a razor's edge from disaster."

"It might still work out, though." Mariah's voice turned soothing, but Bree knew her friend she didn't have answers either. "It takes time to get a business established." That part was proven true daily.

"I know." A message flashed across Bree's phone indicating a call. "Oh, I wonder if I should get that."

"You have another call?"

Bree stuffed down a sigh. "I'll call them back. I might as well tell you and please keep this to yourself. I've quietly made some inquiries into other travel companies just in case—you know. In case we go under. One of them just called back." Maybe she should never have contacted them. Would she be ready for their response if it were positive?

Mariah drew in a quick breath. "Are things that bad?"

"If we have a good summer, we can get back into the black. If not—well, it never hurts to make a plan."

"What about Lauren? What would she do?"

"She's dating Mark and they're pretty serious, so I think she's all set. But I'll have no place to go if the business folds." She couldn't return to her mother in Minnesota. She'd never be content with small-town life. No, Bree would have to fend for herself if everything went up in smoke. So, she prepared for the worst, plotting her leap from the burning building before it actually caught fire.

"Oh. I see. Don't worry, I won't say a word to Lauren or anyone else. Maybe it will work out. Just take one day at a time."

Sound advice, if Bree could only do it. She hung up with Mariah and listened to the voicemail. It was from Horizon Tours, one of the companies where she'd sent her resume.

She listened to the raspy male voice. They didn't need her, not right now. The company's current interest was Asia, although they might expand into Europe within the coming two years. They'd keep her posted.

And in the meantime, she'd pray the bottom would not fall out of her fragile business.

ભ   ભ   ભ

Travis Jefferies planted his hands on his knees and leaned over to catch his breath after a rigorous climb up the Huckabee Trail. He lifted his head and squinted, making out the edges of Wilson Mountain in the distance. All of Sedona sat at his feet. The savage, quirky wilderness and the pointed red rocks that jutted up into the crystal blue expanse above soothed him to a standstill. He had no choice but to stare at the grandeur. This was pure majesty in dry, rocky form . . . hushed, pristine, natural.

Such a jarring contrast to his sterile apartment back in Portland and his filming projects across the globe. Of course, he thrived on the kaleidoscope of people, tastes, cultures. But sooner or later, he ought to stop. Rest.

Not his best skill.

Footsteps crunched on dry, crumbly gravel. Travis turned. More hikers, a couple in colorful spandex and chunky hiking boots, approached. He smiled, nodded, then turned back to the panorama before him. The couple, too, was silenced by the scene painted in bold colors as the cliff dropped away.

"Wow," said the woman. "I could stand here all day." She grinned at her companion and included Travis in her gaze. "You found a great lookout. I hear there's a creek at the bottom that's really something to see."

Travis nodded. He'd been on the trail before, one of the more rigorous in the national park. He knew what awaited him once he reached the final portion of the trail—along the fresh, clear waters of Oak Creek two hundred feet below.

"Hey, I know you." The woman had turned back to face him. "You're on TV, aren't you? Travis something? What was it . . . *Planet Discovery*. That was it. We just saw the latest one in—" She turned to the man. "Do you remember, Rick?"

"Nepal, or Bhutan or someplace in Asia."

"Nepal and Kashmir," Travis said. Wasn't too often that someone recognized him from his programs, which aired four times per year. Certainly unexpected, out here in the middle of a desert trail. He was usually able to keep his privacy intact. Fortunately.

"We love your program." The woman shielded her eyes from the sun with one hand. "I especially like the interviews."

Travis grinned and took a sip from the water bottle on a string over one shoulder. "That's one of my favorite parts to do. I enjoy introducing viewers to new places, but it's the people who live there that make it memorable, I think."

"Every show gives us new ideas for places to go," the man said with a smile.

"You guys on vacation?"

"Yes, we hike all over the U.S." The man slid his sunglasses to the top of his head. "This is our second time in Arizona. You?"

Travis's gaze slipped to the trail that beckoned him. He could almost feel the cool water of the creek on his feet. He planned on wading barefoot as soon as he could get down there. He drew his attention back to the couple. "We just finished shooting in Serbia and Croatia for a special that'll air in midsummer. Just taking a few days to rest."

11

"If you can call this resting." The man chuckled then wiped perspiration from his brow.

Travis moved toward the trail.

"We'll look for the program later in the year. Good to meet you, Travis."

Travis waved and stepped through a narrow space between two boulders. He felt a thread of satisfaction from the encounter. For that couple, at least, he'd helped open the world a little bit wider. He loved helping viewers discover other cultures and ways of life. And plan their vacations.

Being on vacation himself, however, was another story. Having time off left too much room for memories to bounce around inside his skull. So, he stayed on the move. Once in a while, though not very often, he'd pause to take a breath. This was one of those times. He'd stopped to visit his mother in Sedona, Arizona before heading home to Portland.

Two hours later, Travis parked his rental car in the driveway at his mother's house. He glanced at his watch. She wouldn't be home from church yet. He circled the house and slipped through a low, painted fence onto the patio. It looked mellow and inviting, though in a couple months it would be like a hibachi grill out here. The scents of bougainvillea and of jasmine from star-petaled carissa flower wafted toward him. The plants shared space in tidy beds with red yuccas and hibiscus bushes. Stucco ranch houses of the retirement community, all similar to his mother's, lined the curve of the street like neatly-placed dominos, the expanse of beige and muted pinks broken by the turquoise of swimming pools visible over the row of fences.

When he heard the garage door mechanism groan, Travis slipped from the patio into the cool kitchen. His mother was just closing the door to the garage behind her. She looked up and met his smile. Her lined face, framed by close-cut gray hair, was lit with intelligent blue eyes.

"There you are." She set her purse on the kitchen table. "Did you sleep well?"

Travis grinned. She always asked that question in the morning, ever since he was a kid. "I always sleep well when I come here." Far from the pressures he'd created with his travel business, which had exploded with success in the last couple years. The pressures he'd return to in just a couple of days.

"You're with family. You can let your hair down." His mother reached up to his shoulder and tugged playfully at the shaggy curls that hung below his ears. She opened the fridge and pulled out a glass casserole pan covered with foil. "I marinated these all night, so we'll stick them in the oven and see what we get."

She turned on the oven to preheat. "They were asking about you today. Ellie and Sheryl, you know, my old friends. They know you're in town and wanted to say hi."

Travis avoided his mother's gaze. He'd told her last night that he'd let her know if he'd be attending church with her today. But early that morning he'd left a note for her on the counter and slipped out to the trails. "I don't mind going to church, it's just that your friends give me those sad eyes, as if to say, 'Isn't he over that thing yet?'"

"They just miss seeing you, that's all." His mother's voice was quiet. "It's been five years since 'that thing'. They figure you've gone on with your life. Recovered. I'm the only one who knows," she shrugged one shoulder, "maybe you haven't."

"Of course, I've have, Mom." He pushed down the note of adolescent defensiveness in his voice. Maybe she had a point. "I'm fine now, really. Lexi made her choices, I went on with my life. I know you'd like me to find another girl, but I'm okay."

13

Compassion etched his mother's face. She cupped his cheek with one hand. "Finding someone else will take care of itself, in time. But I know my son. You aren't the same zealous Travis you once were. Well, you're zealous for other things. Your documentaries all over the world, your books. Yes, zealous and maybe even a bit driven. Not that I'm not proud of you. Of course, I am. But it's not the same."

He sighed. No, he wasn't the same. He'd gotten wiser, more wary. He'd learned a lot from being kicked in the head by life. By Lexi. Maybe even by God. But he'd poured his hurt and anger into his work. At least he'd had a productive outlet. He wasn't angry anymore. It just didn't matter.

His mother leaned back against the counter. "You know, you don't have to work so hard when you come to visit Gray and me. I saw all the junk you put out on the curb. Thank you for cleaning the garage. And the grill, and the storage bins."

"Just wanted to help. I may as well be useful while I'm here. It'll save you two the trouble, since you're not spring chickens anymore." He grinned at her, and she laughed.

"I want you to be able to unwind here after your trips around the world. It couldn't have been too relaxing over there in—where were you again?"

"Serbia and Croatia. It *was* kind of a grueling schedule." He had to admit, he thrived on the pace. For nearly two months on location, he'd slept in places ranging from comfortable to primitive, eaten strange and sometimes delicious food, and negotiated with locals having little vocabulary in common. He loved his work, doing the research, preparing scripts, filming, interviewing nationals.

Lately, though, something had been missing. He was still struggling to figure out what it was. What would he do if he lost his passion for his work?

"Once you get back home you won't ever relax, I'm guessing."

"Probably not." Travis pulled an apple out of a bowl on the counter and bit into the crisp flesh. "That's why I come here, to see you guys and to get away." True, getting out of town to someplace where he wasn't doing a program was the only way to recharge his batteries. "Besides, in Sedona it's drier, sunnier, *and* warmer than Portland."

"Plus, you have your mom's TLC and coconut pie."

"That too." He'd already eaten more than he should have during his visit. His gaze found hers. "Are we going to see Gray today?"

"Yes, we'll eat lunch then go," she said. "That'll give him time to get his nurse's visits out of the way and have his lunch." She flashed a sudden grin. "He wanted me to smuggle some snacks in for him. I guess the hospital food is living down to its reputation."

"I've got him covered." Travis pulled a box of cheese crackers, a bag of chocolate-covered yogurt balls, and cinnamon graham cookies from the cupboard and tossed them on the counter.

"That was sweet. You always did remember our little cravings. Seems the older we get, the more we have."

Gray certainly had his cravings. After shoving a few cheese crackers into his mouth, he stuck the box out to Travis and his mom and even the nurses, so they could all help themselves. "Travis bought the good ones, not those knockoff crackers no one likes." Gray's color had improved in the last few days since his hip replacement. He still floated among sheets and pillows as he leaned against the upward-tilted end of the hospital bed.

"Only the best for you, Gray." Travis grinned back at his stepfather and closed his fist around some crackers in the depth of the box. "So, one hip replacement out of the way. What's next?"

Gray rolled his eyes, deepening the lines around them. "One down, three to go."

"Three more hips? No wonder you were in pain."

Gray's laughter barreled through the room. He winced, then sputtered, "One more hip, two knees. By the time they're done with me, I'll be new like Barbie, plastic parts from the waist down."

Travis secretly wished he could get a few of those plastic parts for his heart and his brain. At least plastic didn't hurt or ask questions. "So, how's that going to work for the Provence trip? Will you be able to walk around okay? Climb castle walls, browse in tourist shops?"

A lengthy silence followed. Gray's tightened lips worked around, as if he needed to say something, but didn't dare begin. His eyes met his wife's, a plaintive shadow behind them. "Honey, I know this is your dream. I can try, but don't know how much good I'll be. Think I can get a hold of a wheel chair once we get there?"

Travis's mother laid a hand on Gray's arm. "No, Gray. I'll cancel tomorrow. Provence isn't going anywhere. Maybe we can go next year."

"I don't want you to miss this chance, Marcia. You've waited ten years to do this. I—I thought I'd be okay to travel, but the hips went faster than I expected. You need to go. I want you to."

"I don't want to go alone." Her voice was quiet. She arranged the salmon-colored carnation blooms that spilled from a clear glass vase on the bedside table.

"There must be other ladies going," Gray said. "Widow ladies who are used to traveling alone."

Her lips tightened and she gazed across the room away from her husband. Travis' mother seemed drained of her usual energy, despite forced cheerfulness. She'd had to know that Gray wouldn't be ready for an overseas trip for at least a year, maybe even two, considering how many surgeries he needed. And Gray had confided to Travis that he hadn't wanted to go on the trip in the first place. He'd only agreed for his wife's sake.

His mother looked back at her husband brightly. "It's not that important. I'll go another time."

Gray leaned back and scowled. "My lower half hurts, but they say I'll be good as new. That is, until the next operation." He settled a tired gaze on Travis. "Why don't you go to France in my place, Travis?"

Travis' eyes widened. "I . . . uh . . ." He swallowed. For one thing, he was about fifty years too young.

"It's already been paid for and you love to travel. Only this time, you won't be working. You'll just enjoy the trip, like everyone else. Seeing the world from the traveler's perspective might even help you with your work." From his cloud of pillows, Gray stared at him. Travis thought he saw pleading in the man's eyes.

Travis waited for his mother to intervene and save him from having to respond. Instead she turned a direct gaze on him, her eyes slicing him in two. "You'd enjoy it, Travis. Not everyone is elderly. You could gather some new ideas about traveling, couldn't you?"

Travis squirmed under his mother's hopeful gaze. "Uh, I don't know. I guess I can have a look at my schedule and see, but don't set your heart on me, Mom."

Accompanying his mother to France was not on his itinerary.

Later on, he'd tell her he'd checked his schedule and it was out of the question. His mother would understand and find a friend to go. She might find someone among her numerous friends at church or in the weekly Bible study she led.

Once back at his mother's house, Travis rummaged in his canvas bag for his calendar. He preferred the old-fashioned paper kind. He never had to charge its batteries or worry about it being stolen. His chicken scratch was the only disadvantage. He thumbed pages forward and checked the nine-day period when the Provence trip was scheduled. He checked it a second time and frowned. Wide open. For the two weeks prior, he'd be in Copenhagen and the weeks after, in the Italian Lakes region. He had a full ten days completely free between the two . . . and he was already going to be in Europe.

He'd have to find another excuse and do it fast.

Chapter Two

The heat wave dropped off over the weekend and temperatures returned to normal. By Monday morning, mild breezes tumbled through an open window, playfully shifting a stack of papers on Bree's desk. Outside, delicate fuchsia blooms on the redbud tree competed with ivory puffs on dogwoods, drawing her gaze. How she loved spring.

Or, she *would* love it, if everything were nailed down for the Provence trip. Then she could simply soak in the mellow sunshine with a tranquil mind. Only a month left. Maybe there would be mail in her inbox expressing interest, a result of her presentation the previous week.

To get to work, she only had to take a few steps from her kitchen. Her second bedroom was the office for Le Bon Voyage. Three years earlier when she and Lauren began the company, Bree moved from her native Minnesota to D.C., gladly escaping the small town and arctic winters, and found this two-bedroom apartment.

She didn't mind housing the office, though she reminded herself continually of the importance of dividing work from the rest of her life. It was tempting to creep in at all hours of the evening to take care of *one last detail* that came to mind.

Bree neatened the piles of paper, multicolored post-its, and pens on her desk. She scanned her inbox. From the Coastal Cove Retirement Community, only one inquiry. Then the name Marcia Stephens caught her eye. Marcia and her husband, Gray, had registered for the coming tour. A few weeks earlier Marcia had informed Bree that her husband, Gray, was only a "maybe", due to his worsening health issues. When Bree read the words, "I'm so sorry to tell you—", her hopes plummeted. Biting her lip, she scanned the rest of Marcia's email. Gray had just had hip surgery and was not ready to travel. So, Marcia wouldn't go either. Two cancellations at once.

She fell back against her chair, tears pricking her eyes. The trip was in just over a month. How would they recruit even one person, let alone two, to fill the Stephens' reservation? She and Lauren wouldn't cancel the trip, which meant they'd have to take the loss out of their dwindling margin.

Bree swiped a tear that trailed down her cheek as the front door squeaked open.

"It's me," Lauren called. "What a lovely day it is outside." She entered the office wearing a light green cardigan. Her chestnut-brown hair was pulled back into a French braid, and long silver earrings dangled, glinting in reflected sunlight. Seeing Bree's face, she halted in the doorway and frowned. "What is it?"

"Two cancellations." Bree scowled and blinked at her tears, feeling foolish. "The Stephens. I told you that the husband was iffy. Health problems." When Lauren was silent, Bree diverted her teary gaze out the window to the fluffy, white blooms on the dogwood.

Lauren set her purse and a canvas tote on her desk. She leaned back against the edge of it and crossed her arms. "Maybe we'll still be okay. Remember, I found that vineyard that was cheaper, so that's a savings. Then the villa didn't increase its rent from last time.

We'll still have a smaller margin with fewer people, but something could happen between now and then. You never know."

Bree needed her calm and optimistic business partner to balance her own rising panic. "We could cut something out," she suggested with a tilt of her head, though a heaviness sagged inside her. "Maybe an excursion or two. I just hate to overpromise and under-deliver."

Lauren chewed on her lower lip. "When did Marcia write to you?"

Bree peered at the screen. "Early last evening." Her eyes rose to Lauren's. "This is vaguely reminiscent of the last trip, remember? This eleventh-hour turmoil?"

Lauren sat down in her desk chair and gently spun it around to face Bree. "But we ended up with enough people and had a great trip. Hopefully you remember that part too."

"*Barely* enough people. I know it worked out, but it's so hard to deal with all the uncertainty that leads up to it. I'd be able to relax more if we had a bigger margin."

"That would help, no question about it. And that'll come. We're still pretty new at this." Lauren stared at her a moment then added, "Uncertainty is part of this business, Bree, on both sides of the ocean."

Of course, Lauren was right. Maybe Bree was in the wrong business, given her desire, or rather, her *need* to avoid mishaps. To protect herself.

Lauren shot her a look that was both serene and playful then turned back to her desk.

A thread of irritation needled Bree. How could Lauren not worry even a bit? Bree wished she knew Lauren's secret for taking life in stride, bumps and all. Sometimes her partner was almost too relaxed. Bree felt enough stress for both of them, but her worry wasn't going to rescue them from disaster.

For the rest of the morning Bree buried herself in preparations. Would the linens be delivered on time to the villa? Had a cleaning crew been engaged and given check-in and check-out dates? Were the van and car rentals confirmed? These tasks pushed Bree's fears to the corners of her mind. Nevertheless, their presence was felt, like a filmy shadow taunting her.

A few feet away, Lauren quietly worked at her desk. Her occasional comments throughout the morning reflected no more urgency than if there were still four months to prepare instead of only one. Bree would love to have just a bit of that calm assurance.

Just before noon another email arrived from Marcia Stephens. Bree sighed. The woman probably wanted to inquire about her refund. When Bree opened the message and read the first lines, she squealed. "Lauren, you were right, it's all going to work out."

"Told you it would work out. What happened?" A wily smile crept up Lauren's face and she pulled her chair toward Bree.

"Let's see . . ." Bree finished skimming Marcia's message. "She writes that her adult son has agreed to come in Gray's place. So, we'll still have eight guests, plus us."

"Oh, thank you, Lord! See, Bree, it doesn't do any good to worry."

Bree gave her a crooked smile. "It's not like I think it's strategic, or anything." Her voice softened. "I just can't *help* myself sometimes. I really want this business to work."

Lauren squeezed Bree's arm. "Me too. That's nice that the son wanted to come with his mother. I imagine she was disappointed, so the son offered to come in his dad's place."

"Whatever the sweet story is, I'm just glad he's coming. Not just for the financial end. I think it's more fun when there is a larger group."

Lauren clapped her hands once and stood up. "Why don't we break for lunch? We've put in a good morning."

"And we worked all weekend too." In fact, Lauren and Bree had worked late too many days in a row, typical in the month before a trip.

Bree turned out the small desk lamp and stood. She stretched her back, feeling as if a hundred-pound weight had been lifted from her shoulders. "What a great way to end the morning. I have some chicken breasts thawed and can make us stir-fry."

"How can I refuse such an offer? I'll help."

In the kitchen, Bree pulled a plate of half-thawed chicken breasts, broccoli, scallions, carrots, and soy sauce from the fridge. On impulse, she added a handful of cashews from a bag in the freezer. "You're the gourmet, not me, so please don't expect anything exotic."

Since the start of Le Bon Voyage, Lauren had been the cuisine and wine guru for the Provence tours whenever the group ate in. Bree's special role was detail police, the best job for a perfectionist.

"After lunch I need to do a few errands," Lauren said. "You'll have the place to yourself for a couple of hours."

"No problem."

Lauren settled onto a stool at the kitchen bar and crossed her arms. "Anything I can do?"

Bree leaned inside the cupboard to search for the wok. "In a minute I'll have you cut up some vegetables." She grabbed a frying pan. "This'll do."

"I meant to tell you I have the latest issue of Wide World, if you want to read it later." Lauren reached for the travel magazine that sat on the room divider and thumbed idly through its pages. "Hmm. Looks like a good issue. Here's an article on northern France you'd like. Normandy and Picardy. Good photos of the cliffs of Étretat, there's Honfleur. Love that. So beautiful. Oh, and here's a column by that guy, Travis, you know, your favorite travel critic."

Bree grimaced. "Who's he tearing apart this time? I wish he'd just go sell insurance or something and leave the tour companies alone." She began to cut the chilled chicken into tiny cubes. "He calls himself a travel writer, but you'd swear his goal is to scare everyone away from it. Like that book he wrote. What was it called? *The Dreams and Scams of Travel*, or something like that."

Lauren seemed absorbed in the magazine. "His article gives tips for picking a good restaurant in Asia and ways to avoid getting sick there. What to do if you *are* sick. That's helpful. I think he's done some documentaries on public TV too, but I haven't seen them."

"I might have seen one a couple years ago, but I confuse him with the other travel guy, Sean or something."

Lauren read silently for a moment. "Hmm, here's his picture at the end of the article. Oh. He's kind of cute." Lauren tossed the magazine back onto the kitchen table.

"I'm sure there are terrorists and serial killers who are 'kind of cute' too." Bree almost cut her finger. Who did he think he was, warning the world about imperfect travel packages, when people were only trying to make a living? And as Lauren herself had said, the nature of overseas travel had too many variables for a business to have complete control.

Bree rinsed and dried her hands. "Here, let me see him." She reached for the magazine to cast a withering glance at the photo of her nemesis, Travis Jefferies. Sandy brown hair, curly and stuffed under a visor. A camera hung around his neck. The man had a clear blue gaze. A startling gaze. She flinched and shook off the feeling that he was staring straight at her. "Hmmph. Good looks to camouflage an evil heart."

Lauren smirked then she and Bree burst into laughter.

An hour later Lauren slipped back into her cardigan and grabbed her purse. "Be back in a couple of hours. No stress, now. Deal?"

"Deal." Bree's heart did feel lighter. She sang, "I'm floating in a sea of tranquility."

Lauren pulled the door closed behind her. Bree returned to the office and sat at her desk, determined to be focused and productive. She'd write back to Marcia first. Bree took a deep sip from a tall glass of iced tea then turned on her computer, scanning her inbox for Marcia's email. She found it and clicked.

Bree reread the email, in which Marcia expressed her gratitude at not having to cancel her trip, since she'd dreamed of going to Provence ever since reading Peter Mayle's book, *A Year in Provence.* Bree leaned over her desk to jot a reminder to herself to include that reference in future promotional materials. She returned to the message. Apparently, Marcia's son was also in the travel industry and would already be in Europe. She'd attached the man's contact information and profile.

Bree liked Marcia already, feeling the woman's warmth seep through her message. And a son in the travel industry . . . what a small world.

She opened the attached information sheet on Marcia's son and leaned forward to read it. First name, Travis. Address, Portland, Oregon. He'd take a train to Avignon from wherever he was in Europe, but that should be no problem, as long as he was able to join the group the same day they arrived.

Bree read further and went still. A chill washed over her as she reread the first line. She shook her head. Couldn't be. "Travis *Jefferies?*" she said aloud into the quiet office. "This must be a joke."

Shock gave way to a sting of tears and a wash of frustration. Cancellations were bad enough, but why play a cruel prank on her? Marcia had certainly not seemed the type to go along with a scheme like this. Bree slowly read the entire application. No health problems, age thirty-four, profession given: journalist. She skipped ahead to the second page, and there was his photo, not the same one she'd seen in the magazine, the one that had incited a maelstrom of ridicule only two hours earlier. Sure enough, it was the same Travis Jefferies, and this photograph had the same effect, clear blue eyes that seemed to look directly at her, almost taunting her. And he was just as handsome, with a strong jaw and an outdoorsy camper look that suggested he'd be at home—and annoyingly self-assured— anywhere he went.

Bree cringed. Travis Jefferies the travel critic had chosen *their* company to embed himself as a regular guest, in order to gather enough data to expose their faults to the world. Le Bon Voyage was still in its infancy and could hardly compete with other tour groups run by corporations or a large multinational staff. To whom would he compare them? What would he think? It would be the end of Le Bon Voyage.

She had to stop him from coming. It would mean two fewer guests and that would be financially precarious, but it was better than the alternative, being torn to shreds publicly in print or hidden camera by Travis Jefferies.

It would be a shame for Marcia not to come. Or was she part of the ruse? If Bree could keep Travis from coming but still have his mother, that would only be one guest fewer. They could still stay afloat. And Marcia could fulfill her dream.

Before Bree could stop herself, she clicked the man's email address and began composing a message. *Dear Mr. Jefferies, I have received your application to travel in your step-father's place and, although your gesture is much appreciated, I'm afraid it is too late to honor your request.* She stopped, as a twinge of guilt scuttled by. An outright lie. Yet she had to stop him. What reason could she give?

The French authorities are strict with the hospitality industry and will consider it too late to make the change in reservation details. Your mother's application, however, is in order and will not pose a problem. We hope you will be able to join us on another excursion. Best regards, Bree Sorensen.

She paused again. Travis Jefferies worked in the travel industry. He would know she was lying. What kind of involvement could the French government possibly have in a private tour on the backside of a mountain in Provence? As a television personality, he might even know the French president personally.

It was a chance she had to take, to protect her company.

Her finger hovered over the 'send' button for several seconds, while a battle inside pulled her one way then the other, one moment with crushing guilt over her lie, the next determination to protect Le Bon Voyage, at any cost.

Finally, she clicked the button on her screen. As soon as she did, another wave slid over her, this time, molten hot, though a cool breeze wafted in through the open window. What if he used her refusal as a pretext for publicly criticizing the company? That could be worse than having allowed him to come in the first place. Lauren would blame her forever.

Bree covered her face with her hands, feeling the old panic seeping back. Aside from periodic twinges, she hadn't felt it this strong in years. Her breath came out too quickly. She slowed it down as her counselor had taught her when she was a teenager. Shame pricked at her. She mumbled into her fingers, "Lord, Lord. I'm sorry, I messed up. I was worried, but I lied to the guy. I lied. Please make everything okay."

But it was too late.

CR CR CR

"That'll be seven eighty-five," said the pimpled young man at the Gotta Pizza stand at the Phoenix airport food court. Travis pocketed his change and took the warm cardboard box and soft drink. A dinner likely to settle like lead in his empty stomach, but he knew for sure he didn't have anything edible in his refrigerator in Portland. The layover before his flight wasn't long, and he was antsy to return home after nearly two months on the road.

The near-constant echo of garbled flight announcements floated through the air as he milled among the passengers on the way to his gate. He settled into an empty seat close to the wall of windows overlooking the tarmac. Balancing the pizza box on his knees, he smiled at a beleaguered woman next to him who alternately hissed after two rowdy preschool children and shushed a fussy infant on her lap.

People-watching had always been a favorite activity, and this crowd didn't disappoint him. He was sufficiently entertained while he ate, observing every style from flip-flops to full-length gowns, travelers in all shapes and sizes. Finally, he heard the first boarding call for his flight.

Judging from the clog of passengers waiting to board, he had time to check his email one last time. Looked like there was a response from the Bon Voyage company, with whom his mother had blackmailed him into traveling the following month. Not overtly, of course. Her downtrodden expression wasn't likely a demonstration of theatrics. She was genuinely disappointed to miss the trip to Provence. When he reluctantly agreed to take Gray's place (on the condition that he pay his own way), he was rewarded with generous smiles and visible relief from both of them. He'd decided to take the positive angle. Being on the tourist side of the travel industry might give him new insight and might also spark life into his flagging motivation.

His eyes fell on the first lines of the email from Le Bon Voyage. Refused? He furrowed his brow and shook his head, perplexed. The French government? What kind of reasoning was this? A thread of irritation lodged inside, alongside a surprising wave of disappointment. He'd started to look forward to it, he had to admit. Still, he could use this email as his out, if it weren't so fishy.

"Final boarding for flight 439 to Portland . . ." He stood up, tabling his annoyance. He'd deal with Le Bon Voyage tomorrow.

Hours later he stood in the silent hallway in front of his apartment door. The clink of his key in the lock rang a forlorn echo. Travis pushed into the darkened room and flipped on a lamp, thankful to be home.

Only it didn't feel that much like home. More like a shelter where he slept and ate between projects. For years that hadn't bothered him, since the adrenaline of his work filled the empty spaces left behind by the wreckage of the past. Lately, the travel-high was a less effective anesthetic and he found himself longing for something other than a few walls and Spartan décor surrounding him. He'd forgotten what it was like to be welcomed home by a warm, human . . . woman.

Travis pushed the thought from his mind. No point going there. The next day he'd call a few friends and let them know he was back. That might buffer his solitary return. He opened his duffel and dumped the contents on the bed. Nothing to throw into the wash, thanks to Mom. The dust on every surface of his dwelling was another story.

That reminded him. He pulled out his phone and speed-dialed his mother. After the beep he said, "Just wanted to let you know I got here safely. Knew you'd worry." Though he was over thirty and made his living traveling around the planet, his mom appreciated knowing his flight had arrived.

He'd gotten into the habit of keeping an eye on her after his dad died of a heart attack thirteen years earlier. He felt almost like an only son, since his brother Josh, who lived in Manhattan, hadn't visited their mother often, even in the days prior to acquiring two children and a stunning investment career. So, Travis had always taken care of Mom, but she'd been there for Travis, too, especially when his world caved in five years earlier. His marriage and ministry, gone like a morning mist.

He felt like a different person now. Funny how those memories came back in random splotches on his mind, even after so many years. Whenever he slowed his whirlwind, it was just long enough for flashbacks to emerge from where they normally hid in carefully sealed mental storage bins.

Travis opened the vertical blinds wide, just in time to see the final sigh of a mauve and indigo sunset bleed into deep blue on the horizon. He stood still for a moment, watching the lights glow in a checkerboard pattern from the nearby office buildings. Tomorrow he'd regroup for the next program, maybe work on the book he'd started writing before leaving for Serbia, and squeeze in the long editing schedule for the filming just completed.

Tonight, he'd just grab a beer and catch up on the news. Or maybe relax with some music, if that would keep his thoughts anchored in the present. But first he'd jot a quick note to Le Bon Voyage. They might not budge on their policy, but at least he could tell them what he thought of it.

Chapter Three

Tuesday morning when the coffee machine sputtered a loud finale, Bree was ready with two empty mugs and the fixings on the countertop. The front door squealed open and clacked shut, but Lauren didn't sing out her usual greeting. "Good morning. Coffee is fresh," Bree called. No response. Her scalp prickled. Maybe it wasn't Lauren.

Bree leaned out the doorway toward the living room and saw Lauren slipping out of her hooded blue sweat shirt. "Lauren? Are you okay?"

Lauren turned and her green eyes impaled Bree. Without a word she whirled around and stormed into the office. Bree scuttled behind her and hovered in the threshold. "What is it?"

Lauren rounded on Bree. "You *cancelled* Marcia's son. Tell me, Bree, exactly *what* were you thinking?"

A hot flush washed down Bree's face and neck. Her mouth tasted like cotton. She'd wanted to hide her actions from Lauren, hoping it would look like a simple cancellation. Deceptive, yes. Seemed justified at the time, but the look on Lauren's face weighed a stack of doubts onto Bree's chest.

"Lauren, it's Travis *Jefferies*. Do you realize what kind of damage he could do?"

Lauren's face was closed, pinched. "So, you took it on yourself to tell him he couldn't come. He emailed a complaint to the info address, and I received it this morning. I can't believe you didn't talk to me about this, Bree. I thought we were a team." Her last phrase betrayed hurt mixed with anger.

Bree swallowed. "I'm sorry. After you left yesterday, I looked at his profile and realized who he was. If he comes— it will be the end of our company."

"Why are you assuming he'll find something wrong? When he writes bad reviews on a company, it's because they are doing something shoddy. Our standards are way above that, so why do you think he'd criticize us? There's no *reason*."

Bree considered the question, started to answer and stopped. She had no answer. "I guess . . . I thought . . ." Her voice was quiet. Lauren was right. But given his reputation, what else could she think?

Lauren let out a strangled sound of exasperation. "You are always worried, always expecting the worst. Where is your faith, Bree? You should have told me about it, then we could have decided together."

"You're right, I should have told you. I panicked." Bree's voice was quiet.

"Big surprise. The Panic Queen."

Bree bit her lip. Shame swilled through her, and she bowed her head. "I'm sorry," she said again. "What do you want me to do?"

"Contact him." Lauren spoke without hesitation. "Apologize and tell him you made an error and we'd be happy to have him accompany his mother."

Bree nodded and swallowed. Her throat ached. They'd rarely argued, including in matters of their business. It burned a hole in her gut. "I'll email him. I'll do it now."

Lauren turned to her then, her lips tight, her eyes grave, as she slowly shook her head. "This can't happen, Bree. We're a team." She crossed the room toward the door. "I'm going out for a while."

After the front door slammed shut, Bree stood still for several moments in the silent apartment, a leaden weight of guilt and regret pulling down inside her. She'd never seen Lauren so angry. They'd disagreed before, but never had Lauren stormed out. Never. And she was right. Bree had committed treason against their friendship and their business.

She trudged back to her desk and slid behind her computer, staring for a moment at the darkened screen. Pressing the power button, she mentally composed her apology to Travis Jefferies. He would join the tour, posing as a regular guest. He would spy on them all, write his report, expose their faults to the world, and there was nothing she could do about it, except watch Le Bon Voyage slowly disintegrate.

She fought a mounting wave of panic and breathed deeply, then squared her shoulders and opened a new email document. She squeezed her eyes shut for an instant, murmuring a brief prayer, then began typing. *Dear Mr. Jefferies, Yesterday I mistakenly informed you that it was not possible for you to come in your stepfather's place. This was an error. I apologize for this miscommunication and take full responsibility. On behalf of Le Bon Voyage, I would like to extend a sincere invitation for you to join us on the upcoming Provence trip.*

Should she offer him a five percent discount as an apology? She didn't know if they could afford that, but it might go a long way to favorably preparing Mr. Jefferies to join them next month. She couldn't make that decision without consulting Lauren. Bree would likely get herself into even greater trouble. She signed the note and pushed *send.*

She felt hollowed-out, empty. No matter what she did—and her efforts were unremitting—it didn't do any good. She was like a hamster on a wheel, running faster and faster. All she got for it was fatigue. Maybe she wasn't cut out for this business. She did love travel, especially to France, but couldn't figure out how to deal with the near-constant anxiety over the details, the outcome. She'd never outrun or outsmart the control that random events and other people had over her. Would she be forever subject to the fickle, heartless nature of chance?

Even worse, would she always be bested by the self-centered cunning of others, even those who didn't know her? Travis's handsome face rose up in her mind. She shook her head to dislodge the image. Bree couldn't shield herself from any of it. She could only do her best and brace for the catastrophe when it came.

Her eyes fell on a small, smooth stone she always kept on her desk. She stared at it for a moment then reached out and snatched it into her palm. She rolled it in her hand and closed her eyes as she thumbed its coolness. When she opened her eyes, she read the inscription etched into the rock, silently at first, then repeating the phrase aloud into the silent room. "Nothing will happen today that you and I can't handle together. –God."

She blinked and bit her lip, waiting for a breeze of comfort to dilute her panic. "Please, Father. Handle this. Handle *me*."

❧ ❧ ❧

The coffee shop emptied of noisy customers little by little, returning the volume to a calm purr. The nutty smell of ground beans filled the air, weaving in with the comfortable, earthy wood paneling and hand-woven banners on the wall. Travis had already started sipping his Ethiopian espresso, since he knew that his buddy

Matt would probably be late for their appointment, likely ensnared in Friday afternoon traffic. The phone on the café table pinged. Travis glanced it to read the arriving text message. Yup, sure enough. His friend would be another ten minutes, at least.

Travis had known Matt since arriving in Portland four years earlier. He was one of the few people who knew Travis's turbulent backstory. Since Matt's recent marriage, their get-togethers were less frequent, though they still managed to catch up on the rare occasions when Travis was in town.

A different tone on his phone signaled the arrival of an email. A brief scan of the grudging apology from Le Bon Voyage founder brought a smile of gratified amusement to his lips. A frown quickly followed. He couldn't get out of the trip now.

Travis sighed. He'd have to reorganize his schedule for the following month. Again. The France trip would last only a week, after all. Then he could go back to his preferred style of travel . . . yakking it up with the locals, learning their customs and favorite things, and planning the best way to highlight all of those in a documentary.

Travis had spent several hours already that day cooped up in the film studio with Seth, his editor, going through all the Serbia footage, the order of shots, placement of B-roll, and cutting or rearranging scenes that blocked the flow. He'd needed a break to clear out his head. Besides that, it might be the last time he'd see Matt before the next trip, another long one. Denmark first, to scout, meet local contacts, plan the flow and do some filming. Then he'd meet up with his mother in Provence. After that he'd travel northeast to the Italian Lakes. The Serbia project would have to be wrapped up and in the can before he got onto another airplane.

For the coming program, at least his executive producer, Clay, hadn't insisted that he follow the exposé style of travel journalism for which he'd gained a reputation in magazine columns. It hadn't been Travis's intent, of course, to be labeled as the voice of warning to hapless travelers. It all started with an abysmal trip to Jamaica. He hadn't wanted to whitewash the truth, using travel superlatives like lush or enchanting. And though there *were* places like that in Jamaica, the spot where *he'd* landed had teemed with cockroaches and other freakish-looking creatures, filth, and noise, not to mention a few unsavory practices involving drugs and women. He'd been mad enough to want to protect other people. The response to that article was so positive that the editors wanted something similar, leading to a series, then a column. Eventually he had enough experiences, ranging from unexpected to downright awful, to write his book *Travel Dreams, Travel Scams.*

He was typecast, and it was beginning to feel as comfortable as a straitjacket.

Gradually—and he didn't know exactly when—Travis started to chafe against the association people made between Travis Jefferies and travel warnings. He longed to once again unveil the joyful discovery of other cultures to travelers, not just tell tales of worst-case disasters.

He planned to keep Provence out of Clay's line of vision, just so he wouldn't get any ideas. He'd let the old guy think he was sunning on a French beach on his own time.

As if summoned by thought waves, the phone rang and Clay's name popped up on the screen. Travis groaned. He had to answer his boss. "Hey, Clay. What's going on?"

"I was going to ask you that. How is the Serbia piece coming?"

Behind solicitous words lay a grainy, tight tone that set Travis on edge, a feeling that, lately, had increased in frequency. "Good. Seth and I have been putting in some long days." Just in case he'd wondered.

"It'll be done before you head out again?"

"That's the plan." Silence. Travis would offer nothing else. He thrummed the table with his fingertips, hoping the call would be short.

"And you're taking some vacation time over there too, right?"

Travis bristled. Where had he heard that? "I'll have a few days between Copenhagen and Italy. Couldn't work out the interviews in Italy any earlier." It was on the tip of his tongue to defend his right to a few days of vacation, but he wouldn't surrender his dignity by explaining something so obvious.

"You could use that time for additional research, couldn't you? Your mother would understand."

"My mother?" Travis's voice cracked a note higher. Now his blood was starting to heat up.

"Becky mentioned something about you helping your mother out."

Travis snorted. "I'll keep that in mind the next time I'm chatting with Becky." He couldn't keep the surly edge from creeping into his voice. "It's no one's business, but yes, I'm accompanying my elderly mother for a few days."

"On a tour?"

"Something like that."

"Perfect. You'll be in a great position to observe everything without being suspected. No one will think a thing."

"This is *personal* vacation time. It isn't work, and I am not going to spy on anyone. Don't you think I'm entitled to a regular vacation?" Travis leaned forward, one fist clenched. He glanced around and lowered his voice.

"Of course. But think of it as two benefits for the price of one. See what you can find out. Everyone cuts corners. And these small group tours probably do it even more. You won't even have to name the company."

"Leave my vacation alone."

"Just *observe* while you're there, that's all. Observe. You probably can't help yourself. You'll do it without thinking. Okay, gotta go."

After he'd hung up, the roiling heat continued in Travis's bloodstream for several minutes, almost clogging his throat. He wanted to strangle Becky, Clay's receptionist. Why had he said anything to her about Provence? She'd had a calendar over her desk with a photo of a lavender field. Must have sparked a comment from him. One propelled by poor judgment, apparently.

The clack-clack of a barista banging the espresso scoop accosted his nerves. The idea of furtively observing Le Bon Voyage— a company that was probably doing its best—for an exposé was just wrong. Clay's pressure on Travis to sniff out dirt was starting to sour a career that he'd once found exhilarating. But what if he opposed Clay's agenda too hard? Could he lose his place on the network?

How he longed to follow his own heart and passion . . . unveiling fascinating and little-known ways of life to the rest of the world. How many times had he returned from a trip awed by the courage, perseverance, and *differentness* of human beings around the planet? How opposite an objective from being the investigative reporter, uncovering the horrors of unfortunate travelers. If only he could escape the very thing that had placed him squarely on a television network.

He was startled from his reverie by the scrape of a chair as Matt plopped down across the table from him, looking road weary. A five o'clock shadow framed his jaw. "You look lost in thought."

"I just got off the phone with Clay. Never a pleasant experience."

Matt chuckled, dark eyes squinting behind metal frame glasses. "Yeah, you've complained about him before. Overbearing again?"

"Wants me to *observe* things on the Provence trip, to gather ideas for a program."

"You told him no, right? That's your own time."

Travis frowned. "Yeah, I told him. If I know in advance that a tour company isn't doing right, I feel an obligation to protect people, like I do in my magazine column. But to go in and *look* for things," he shook his head, "just doesn't feel good to me. I did *one* program on scams and now Clay wants them all to be the same." Though the executive producer had relented on the Denmark-Italy piece, he wouldn't likely be placated for very long. The man had a thirst to hear the sordid details of a vacation gone wrong.

Matt nodded. "Besides that, you have the right to go and enjoy yourself. I'm glad you'll be a guest this time. I think it'll give you a new perspective."

"I thought of that too. I've been feeling restless lately. This type of reporting doesn't fit me. My trip may be just what I need to get a fresh angle. I've never been to that region of France, so it might give me ideas for a show or a series." He shrugged. "Little medieval villages and small towns in the mountains. Should be nice." He was trying to convince himself, at any rate. "I almost wasn't able to go, even after I'd decided to do it."

"Why's that?"

"The company tried to stop me from going in my step-dad's place. Not sure why. But she just emailed today and said it was fine. So, I'm going."

Matt laughed. "The tour director must have read your book. But it looks like you charmed her into letting you come."

Travis harrumphed. "I wasn't very charming, I assure you. And I don't think that charm would have had much effect on the Dragon

Lady. That's what I started calling her. Mentally, of course. I know I'm not a typical tourist. Even if I'm not doing a piece, she might be afraid I'd be critical."

"Will you?"

"I'm expecting a pleasant trip. My mom will be happy, and she'll know I care about her. That's my only goal."

"You get points for being a good son."

Travis pushed his empty espresso cup aside and lodged a serious gaze at his friend. "Every time I do a program where I can plan the content myself, I come away convinced at the potential power it has to unite people in the world. Tear down walls, open up dialogue."

"I've never thought about that, but you're right. It's your personal contribution to world peace."

Travis smirked. "I don't know if I'll earned *that* reputation. But if I can do a high-quality program that leads people to understand each other just a little bit more, it's worth the effort. I'm not sure Provence will do all that. Might just be a lot of wine-tasting and lavender fields."

Matt grinned. "You'll have more peace with your mother, at least."

"Yeah, she was pretty happy I was willing to go." Travis couldn't help smiling as he remembered his mother's delight when he said he'd go with her.

"And who knows, maybe you'll meet someone there." Matt gave Travis a sly smirk.

Travis laughed out loud. Leave it to a happy newlywed to prescribe the same bliss to all of his single friends. "I always did like older women. Someone about seventy-five or eighty is sure to catch my eye."

Matt chuckled aloud. "You never know. Maybe she'll be French. Or British. Lot of Brits in that area, I've heard."

Travis eyed him. "Anything's possible."

Matt's suggestion was highly unlikely and not on the radar. Travis was only counting on doing his mom a favor then going on with his life, though he felt more than a stitch of discomfort as he considered what that life might look like, if Clay had his way.

Chapter Four

The ten-passenger van rumbled along the A7 highway between the Avignon train station and the hilly outskirts of Cavaillon. Dry foothills arose in the distance as Bree drove the same route she had many times before as she shuttled guests back and forth from the station to the rented villa. They'd been fortunate to be able to rent the same house for two years in a row. This shortened the long to-do list, if only slightly, and Bree was grateful.

She and Lauren had arrived at the villa two days earlier to make sure everything was lined-up and confirmed on site. That was usually the point when much of the stress evaporated for Bree, since the list that had hovered like a phantom for months was nearly all checked off. Being back in dry, sunny Provence buoyed her spirits, wrapping balm around her frayed nerves . . . except for the nagging dread of Travis Jefferies's arrival.

"Is everyone comfortable back there?" She called to her four passengers, Michael and Beverly Morrison, Sarah Berman, and Alan Hennessey. The Morrisons from California were celebrating forty years of marriage, to Bree's surprise, since they held hands and cuddled like newlyweds. Sarah had retired from teaching high school biology several years earlier and had already visited two new countries each year since then. "My bucket list is very long," she'd claimed, "so I figured I'd better get started."

Finally, there was Alan Hennessey, from outside Boston, a single man in his forties, also a teacher but at an exclusive prep school. Bree's mind must have wandered when he told her his subject, since she couldn't remember.

The travelers had disembarked that morning at the Avignon train station from various points in France. Lauren was on her way to the Aix-en-Provence station, almost the same distance to the southeast of the villa, to collect Marcia Stephens and the Grahams.

Apparently, Travis Jefferies would saunter in whenever it suited his schedule. Tension needled Bree's stomach. She'd brace for his daily presence and carry on with a smile. He'd never know the tempest that simmered just below the surface, nor would Lauren. Another week and it would all be behind her. She could deal with it for that long, making everything perfect, so he'd have nothing to report.

"How long have you and Lauren been doing these tours, Bree?" Dark-haired Sarah leaned forward from the seat just behind Bree. A canvas bag full of knitting supplies lay in her lap and her hands moved tirelessly and continuously during the ride. Her voice bore a trace New York accent.

"Just over three years," Bree called behind her. "We fell in love with this region about five or so years ago, and the idea of bringing groups evolved from there. It's not a hard place for people to love, as you'll see." She glanced back at the woman in the rear-view mirror. The tight knot inside eased by degrees as she reminded herself to focus on her passengers.

"The last time we were in Provence, we stayed down on the coast." Beverly Morrison raised her voice above the engine noise. In the rear-view mirror, Bree could see her blond head and large, brown eyes gleaming as she spoke.

"Nice, Antibes, and . . ." She turned to Michael. "What was the name of those other towns, do you remember, honey?"

Michael's strong male voice emerged. "Cannes and Monaco. No, it was St. Tropez and Monaco. Yes, I remember all the yachts at St. Tropez."

"And casinos in Monaco. Oh, and that beautiful port. So many yachts there, too. Provence will have a different flavor, but we know it'll be just as lovely. I've seen pictures and just had to come here."

Bree glanced in her mirror just in time to see Beverly lean against Michael and grin up at him, whispering something private. Ignoring a sharp twinge inside her, Bree squinted her gaze back to the road. "We're almost to the villa. When we get there, you'll have some time to get settled, then we'll have lunch together on the terrace."

"Are you cooking today? Or is there a chef on site?" Alan's thin voice reached her from the back row.

Bree wasn't sure how to interpret his comment, as mere curiosity or expectation. She pushed out a cheerful tone. "We have a catered cold meal for lunch today, since everyone is arriving at different times. Normally Lauren will cook on the days we eat in, and sometimes guests enjoy helping out with preparing the meal."

"They use a lot of garlic and olives in Provence cuisine," Alan stated. "Special preparations called aioli, from garlic, and tapenade, from olives, are particular to this region. Basil and rosemary are common as well."

Bree smiled at the authoritative tone in his voice. "You're right, Alan. I hope you like all of those."

"There's a lot of seafood in this area, though I'm allergic to some of it, and garlic. There's a stew called bouillabaisse made with

45

fish. I don't know if you've tasted that, but it's quite good. Aren't there truffles in this region too? Or is that only in the southwest part of the country? I wonder if they still use pigs to sniff them out."

"I think there are truffles both in this region and the southwest," Bree told him. "The pigs like to eat the truffles, so I believe they use dogs more often now. But you'll have to ask Lauren culinary questions once you meet her. She should arrive shortly after we get there." Bree turned the van down a narrow country road, lined on either side by tall pine trees. "And here we are, just around the next corner."

A miniature stone chateau came into view behind a clump of trees. Each wing of the villa stretched out under a sloping slate roof.

"Oooh, look at that." Beverly leaned toward the window. "How beautiful."

After a noisy disembarking, everyone gathered inside the villa, surrounded by baggage that stacked up and filled the hallway. The four travelers panned gazes all around and began wandering into the dining room and main room—the *salle de séjour*— gawking at the elegant furnishings, the layers of stonework on the chimney, and the panoramic view through a wide picture window of the lushly landscaped yard and pool area.

Bree oriented her charges to the floor and wing they'd occupy for the next week. Once the guests left the foyer to scout their rooms, she fell onto the couch, breathing in the silence. Seemed like a nice group, so far.

Several minutes later they re-convened in the *salle de séjour*. "What lovely rooms!" Sarah clasped her hands and looked around. "In fact, the whole place is straight out of a magazine." Bree rose from the couch, hoping everyone else had the same opinion.

About fifteen minutes later, the sound of a car motor outside the front door grew louder until it abruptly cut off. The large wooden entrance door creaked open and the new arrivals, a couple and a woman, piled into the front entryway. Finally, Lauren pushed through the door carrying bags and totes. "We didn't have any traffic today but I saw some going in the other direction. People heading to the market or the beach, I guess."

Bree's eyes landed on Marcia Stephens, easily recognizable from her application photo, and the fact that she was alone. "You must be Marcia. I'm Bree." Bree took Marcia's hands in a firm clasp. The women exchanged broad smiles. Something about Marcia warmed Bree from the start, as if she'd known her for a long time.

"Finally, we meet." Marcia's round cheeks and gentle smile were framed by a graying crop of short hair. Clear blue eyes were the same as her son's. Maybe she truly was Travis's mother, and not a *plant* in his scheme.

"This is Herb and Doris Graham." Lauren gestured to an older couple who could easily fit into a country club setting with their stylish clothing and tanned faces, which creased with smiles.

Bree shook their hands. "Welcome to Provence. I'm Bree, like the cheese." This drew a chuckle from them. "Did you have a good flight?"

Doris spoke up. "Yes, it was long but we were able to spend a couple of days in Paris before taking the TGV to Aix-en-Provence. We spent a couple more days there. Trying to cram everything in, aren't we, Herb?" She turned to her husband then back to Bree when he didn't respond, apart from a vague smile.

Lauren introduced herself and her passengers to the other guests then helped them find their rooms. Bree returned to the living room and found Sarah, to whom she'd taken an instant liking. She was perusing a row of hard-bound books on a built-in shelf in the living room.

She turned to Bree. "Have you seen Bayeux, in Normandy?"

Bree nodded but didn't have time to respond before Sarah continued.

"It's the place where they have that famous medieval tapestry. Or maybe it's in Brittany. I'm not sure. Well, one of my biology students went to France to see the Mont St. Michel but fell in love with the city of Bayeux, which is nearby, and ended up doing a semester there once he was in college. He'd changed his major from economics to French."

Bree chuckled. "France has that effect on a lot of people. Some just come and enjoy their visit. Others fall in love with it and it never leaves them, so they keep coming back, or end up moving here."

As she spoke, noise in the foyer caught her attention. The front door had opened and several voices echoed in the entryway. She heard Beverly exclaim, "Hi there! I saw you on TV a few months ago. Or else you look just like Travis Jefferies."

Oh no. He'd arrived.

Bree's stomach clenched and she breathed deeply, continuing to smile and nod toward Sarah, unable to keep up with the conversation. Maybe she could put off the inevitable moment by encouraging the woman to tell another lengthy story. But that wouldn't really solve anything. She'd have to face him sooner or later.

When Sarah said, "Oh, looks like someone else has arrived," her gaze strayed over Bree's head toward the hallway. Bree knew she couldn't ignore Travis any longer. She'd do her best to undo the way she'd begun with him. At least on the outside.

As Bree edged toward the entrance she heard Beverly ask, "Are you doing an episode about our tour here? Are we all going to be on your show?"

Still hovering in the doorway, she heard a warm male voice say, "I'm between projects. I'm here to accompany my mother. This is strictly vacation for me."

Yeah, right. Time would reveal the truth.

Bree heard more gushing from Beverly, then she emerged from the shadows of the hallway to introduce herself. He was speaking with Beverly and Michael. When she approached, his head lifted, almost as if he'd expected her. His clear blue gaze found hers, sending a jolt, just as it had each time she'd looked at his photo. He was taller than she'd imagined. Light brown hair curled below his ears, and his face bore a slight tan. A pair of sunglasses hung on a fabric string around his neck atop a long-sleeve T-shirt that bunched around his elbows. Adding cargo pants and Birkenstocks, he fit right in as a world traveler.

A world traveler who had just invaded *her* corner of paradise.

"You must be Travis." She extended her hand, forcing the warmest expression she could muster. His eyes held hers and a small smile played around his lips.

He grasped her hand quite firmly. "And *you* must be Bree Sorenson. Thanks for letting me come." Was he being sarcastic? Sincere? She had no idea.

"I didn't know we would have a celebrity among us!" Beverly clasped her hands together.

"Really, I'm just a regular guy in need of vacation, like everyone here." So far, he didn't act like a celebrity. He seemed embarrassed by the attention. But *of course,* he'd need vacation time, given his career of crisscrossing the planet several times per year. But was this the *real* motive of his visit to Provence? Bree highly doubted it.

"Did you travel by train all the way from Copenhagen? You must be exhausted." Bree flashed him a smile. Maybe he'd be fooled into thinking that she was concerned. If she talked logistics, maybe he wouldn't bring up the awkward incident. After all, she'd made it up to him and she'd been properly chastised by Lauren.

"I flew from Denmark to Paris yesterday then took the TGV to Avignon. It was a faster trip than I expected. I got a cab to bring me here." As he spoke, she felt he was sizing her up with his eyes, though his expression remained open and friendly.

"What were you doing in Copenhagen?" Michael asked.

Travis turned to Michael, ankles crossed in a relaxed stance as he leaned against a hall table. "My next program will cover Copenhagen and the Italian lakes district. They both have a lot of water, but that's about all they have in common, so it should be an interesting contrast. After this week, I'll head to Italy."

What would he find to criticize among the Danes and Italians?

"You have such an interesting career, doesn't he, Michael?" Beverly nudged Michael, who promptly agreed, while Travis shot a glance at Bree.

Lauren emerged from the shadowed hallway, looking relaxed and laid-back, as always. "You're Travis, aren't you? Welcome to Provence. I'm Lauren." She extended a hand and gave him a warm smile, looking genuinely glad to see him. Was she? Bree didn't know, but likely, Lauren would expect the best and overlook the hazards. And Bree would have to pick up the pieces.

"Travis, your room will be up this hallway," Bree said. "Second door on the right." She indicated the hallway with one hand, as if she were a flight attendant pointing to an exit.

In this case, she wished it were an exit. "Please let Lauren or me know if you need anything."

When Bree turned, she saw that the group had gathered in the hallway, curious to meet the newest guest. Lauren excused herself to the kitchen to get lunch organized.

"Everyone," Bree called out. "This is Travis, our last arrival. He is Marcia's son. You can all get more acquainted over lunch. We'll meet in thirty minutes, that's one o'clock, on the back terrace. For those of you who'd like to rest after your travels, you'll have some time after lunch to do that, or explore the grounds or the nearby area." She took a deep breath, feeling a sense of release, having faced Travis Jefferies.

ʘ   ʘ   ʘ

Travis sank down on the plush queen bed covered by a tufted white quilt and eased backward, a sudden wave of fatigue overtaking him. Though the trip from Denmark hadn't been difficult, only nine hours door to door, he'd ended up in an uncomfortable hotel bed in Avignon the previous night. He was still stiff, but dismissed it, since he frequently found himself in uncomfortable spaces.

His thoughts must have kept him awake as well as they shuffled through the transition in settings, from the pristine peninsula nation of Denmark, with its colorful, angular buildings reflected in the water surrounding it, to dry, hilly Provence with its rural village ambiance. He'd also been unsure of how he'd fit with this group as a fellow-tourist. For sure, this would be a first, being a guest rather than a host. He couldn't deny the usefulness of this experience to his career, even if he hadn't thought of it himself. And he wouldn't spend too much time interpreting Bree Sorenson's suspicious welcome. Rather, he'd try to appreciate the week for what it would be. That was the plan, in any case.

He glanced around the clean white walls that surrounded him. Wood beams protruding from the ceiling endowed the small

51

bedroom with rustic charm. A filmy white curtain puffed gently at an open window, slipping a silky breeze across his prone body.

A chuckle escaped his throat. Had he really referred to Bree Sorenson as the Dragon Lady? More like a five-foot-three blond bumble bee, flitting around seeing after everyone's welfare. He had to admit, he'd expected a huge, lanky volleyball player-type, not a small, rather pretty woman with an almost-mean blue-eyed glare that she tried unsuccessfully to mask.

His mother, on the other hand, had lit with pleasure when she'd emerged from a hallway and seen him standing in the foyer. She seemed to glow in anticipation of the week to come. That only confirmed the rightness of his decision to join the tour.

Travis glanced at his watch, its leather band worn and its face cracked from more global adventures than he could count. Time for lunch. He was slightly hungry, but even more, eager to see how the day would unfold.

He shut the door behind him just as another guest, Alan, was leaving the room next to his. The man lifted a watery gaze to Travis, his pale face bland and absent of warmth. A panel of black hair fell across his forehead in sharp contrast to the whiteness of his skin, giving him a menacing look in the dark hallway. He nodded to Travis. "Time for lunch." As he turned, he added, "How nice that you could go on vacation with your mother."

Travis narrowed his eyes. The man's voice sounded almost patronizing. "Yes, I don't see her a lot," Travis said before turning down the hall, with Alan steps behind him. They found their way to the terrace where the others had already gathered.

When Travis saw the lush, emerald green yard behind the villa, he knew he'd be spending a lot of time out there. That would keep him sane, no matter what else happened that week. It seemed a peaceful oasis for the alone time he'd surely need after spending the day with eight strangers. Large, irregular flagstones gave a rustic warmth to the terrace. Three of the five round wrought-iron tables shaded by lime green umbrellas were neatly prepared for the group, who idly stood or ambled around the terrace, waiting for lunch to be served.

Beyond the terrace and the neat row of red and white begonias fringing its edges, a carpet of satiny, thick grass rolled out toward a kidney-shaped pool. Nearby lavender plants unfurled in large purple tufts and released a tangy scent into the air. Encircling the pool, lawn chairs and cocktail tables invited him. Though Travis didn't necessarily care for swimming, the presence of water had always soothed him.

The guests began to settle around the tables of three or four, already adorned with matching place-settings. His mother gestured to him and he sat by her. Soon, one of the couples joined them. Lauren and Bree brought covered dishes out from the house. Soon they had elements of a French picnic in front of them—meats, cheeses, pâté, tiny pickles, smoked salmon slices, a variety of salads, fruit, and chunks of sliced baguettes. A gentle breeze rocked the overhead umbrella and the scent of wild thyme swept across the terrace.

"You are so fortunate to have your son on the trip with you, Marcia." Beverly's blond hair curled stylishly around her face. She rested her chin on folded, manicured hands. "I can't get our kids to do more than visit us at Christmas."

Marcia cast a fond glance at Travis. "He knew I didn't want to come alone. Always looking out for me." She returned her gaze to Beverly. "I know he'd rather be doing something else. I was lucky because usually he's so busy. He had an open spot in his schedule, so I grabbed it!"

"What made you want to come to Provence?" Travis was interested in the couple's response, but also eager to pull the conversation away from his presence on the trip.

"We really *love* France." Michael cut into a piece of pâté. "The Luberon was one area we'd heard about through some friends of ours who had gone on a barge cruise further south of here, so we decided to come. We've already been to the Côte d'Azur and to Paris."

The man appeared to be in his fifties. He was still in possession of a fair amount of dark hair, though it was streaked with gray. Travis surmised they were financially comfortable, probably some kind of businessman. Maybe self-employed.

"We'll keep working our way around the country." Beverly dabbed her mouth with a napkin. "This is our fortieth wedding anniversary, so we decided to celebrate by doing something spectacular."

"Forty years is quite an accomplishment." Travis reached for his water glass and swept a glance to the table where Bree sat. She was nodding politely to Alan, who spoke in a loud voice about his last trip to Egypt and Morocco. The other couple listened quietly, courteous smiles frozen on their faces, though the husband had a faraway look in his eyes.

Bree appeared to listen with effortless kindness to those at her table, people who probably ranged from boring to irritating. She asked questions and nodded attentively. Maybe there *was* softness somewhere underneath the crisp greeting she'd given him a while ago. He could see it as she listened with rapt attention to an older woman with reddish hair and too much eye makeup— Doris was her name. Bree leaned slightly forward, as if to catch every word. When her face lit with a smile of surprise at something Doris said, it was as if the sun had emerged from the clouds, transforming her face. It startled him. Were her interest and her smile just a part of her job, or were they real?

Lauren was attractive in her own way. More earthy. She struck him as reserved and task-oriented, ferrying platters in and out of the kitchen, refilling wine and water glasses, delivering baskets of sliced baguettes. She inquired about the meal and condiments but had left the task of welcoming each guest to Bree. He could see why. The woman was a natural.

So far, Bree Sorenson was a beguiling and complete . . . paradox.

Chapter Five

Bree shifted her weight in the passenger seat of the van, anxiety nipping at her nerves. They'd been circling the town of Isle-sur-la-Sorgue on the ring road for several minutes looking for a space to park the ten-passenger van. They'd wanted to leave earlier that day to avoid parking problems in the picturesque village about ten miles from the villa, but with so many people, that had been all but impossible.

She glanced at Lauren, who sat behind the wheel, jaw set and face flushed, whether with heat or frustration, Bree wasn't sure. Maybe it had been a mistake to come on Sunday, the day of the busiest antique and farmers market in the Luberon region. The village was a magnet for tourists, who were enchanted by the many canals and waterwheels. Bree scanned the faces of her passengers, looking for signs of irritation at the delay. Some chatted with the person beside them, others gazed out the window. Maybe she was over-reacting. It was their first full day and she so wanted everything to go perfectly. And not just for Travis Jefferies's sake.

Bree sat on the arm of a seat and faced the back of the van. "I did warn you this morning that the market today would likely be crowded." She glanced out the window and saw people pouring into the town from the parking lots and the ring road. Her stomach clenched again.

She kept her voice upbeat. "This is the town they call the Venice of Provence. It has the largest open market in the Luberon area. You'll have a memorable French market experience in a beautiful setting."

"I can see some canals from here. Looks lovely." Sarah leaned toward the window and peered out, though her hands continued to knit as if self-propelled.

"I don't think you'll be disappointed, Sarah." Maybe she should occupy them while Lauren circled again. "This town started out as a fishing village and the people often built their houses on stilts because it was marshy. The river surrounds it as though it's an island, which is where the name comes from."

"Is the Sorgue the name of the river?" Marcia shifted forward against the seat in front of her.

"Yes. Many towns in France have names that include 'on' with the name of a river. A lot of textile was manufactured here using local wool. Waterwheels were used back then for that purpose, and there are fifteen of them in this relatively small town, though there used to be seventy." This drew two or three gasps from the group.

"It seems a small town to have seventy waterwheels." Doris leaned closer to the window to get a better look. "I wonder where they used to put them all."

"In the middle ages," Bree said, "the town was under the control of the Vatican. Now it's mostly known for antiques and has the largest antiques market outside of Paris."

Alan's voice rang out, louder than necessary, as always. "In Avignon, where we arrived yesterday, which isn't very far from here, the pope actually lived during the period when there was a French pope. Then for about forty years there was conflict about where the papacy should be, Italy or France, so they had both. The papacy went back to Rome in 1417."

Bree nodded and smiled. "You must be a historian, Alan."

"I teach history and philosophy, as I told you yesterday."

"Yes, of course." Right. How could she have forgotten? She glanced at Travis, who stared fixedly through the window, unreadable. She'd had no conversation with him since yesterday, but at least he seemed to take initiative to chat with the other guests, blending easily in the group. That was one point in his favor.

The van slowed. Bree let out a heavy sigh when Lauren began to wedge into a narrow space. Lauren hadn't spoken much that day. Maybe she was simply concentrating on the task of driving hilly roads with a bulky vehicle.

Once the group had clambered down from the van, Bree called to them, "If we get separated, we'll meet back here at three o'clock." Essential to have a back-up plan. Once they entered the town and got absorbed in the multiplying crowds, it would be a miracle if they all stayed together.

"Oh, Bree," Doris said. "Herb has some medication he'll need to take in an hour. Should I take it with me, or will we be coming back here to the van?" Her worried gaze wandered to Herb then returned to Bree.

"We probably won't come back to the van until we leave, Doris. Do you have a place for it, or would you like me to carry it?"

"No, I'll take it." Doris climbed back inside the van. Herb stared after her. Bree watched the man, wondering if he had gotten motion sick on the ride. He turned and met her gaze without speaking, though he offered a timid smile. He'd hardly said a word since they'd arrived.

Once inside the village, the sound of flowing currents surrounded the group, as did canals . . . wide and narrow, calm and foamy, running between narrow streets. The airy sound of frothing water soothed Bree's tight nerves. The beauty and magic of her surroundings took hold and she relaxed, looking around her to rediscover the town. Pastel-colored petunias spilled from flower boxes hung on painted metal bridge railings. Lively pastel-painted shop fronts filled the horizon, accented by brightly-colored canvas umbrellas and awnings.

"The crowds aren't as thick as I feared." Sarah adjusted her wide-brim hat. "Look, the market tables are on the other side of that canal. And it looks like the market follows the flow of the river. Look up there. It just keeps going."

As the group crossed a bridge and approached the market stands, the rumble of voices increased, accented by cries of, "*Un kilo de tomates, trois euros! Les fraises fraîches! Cinq euros la barquette!*" Scents of fresh bread and pastry, roasted meat, cheese, and fish blended into the warm summer breeze. Soon Bree was squeezed among a throng of camera-clad tourists and French shoppers with canvas bags, baskets, and grocery sacks on wheels.

"I'm so relieved you got that parking space when you did," she told Lauren, who'd regained her peaceful countenance. She bit back the words, *I was beginning to worry*, which would only remind Lauren of her wound-up nature. Bree had battled her fears for so long, often it was easier to give in. She knew she should address it but didn't have the time or extra income to see a counselor. Besides that, she'd invested two years in counseling as a teen, at her mother's insistence. She could function now. Which wasn't saying much, since tension still ate away at her nerves each day.

"Things usually work out," Lauren answered calmly.

While the group members browsed the stands of produce, flowers, artwork, kitchen gadgets, and everything from spices to prepared food, Bree leaned against a metal railing and watched the activity around her and surveyed the group members for a moment. Marcia seemed to have struck up a friendship with Sarah. Doris spent as much time hovering over Herb as she did sampling the market, and Travis took photos. Continuously. Every time she cast a glance his way, he was snapping photos with a professional-looking camera equipped with a long telephoto lens. She spied Lauren on the other side of the canal scrutinizing something in a bin. An ordinary gesture, yet not normal for Lauren, for usually on the first full day of a tour she and Bree would both be surveying the group for any needs or issues.

"Are we going to do the waterwheel circuit?" Alan's voice surprised her from behind and she turned. His pale face ended in an angular jaw that made her think of a scarecrow. She couldn't picture him in a straw hat, though. More like a high cleric's collar or a tall, black hat, like the guards wore at Buckingham Palace.

She glanced away, fearful that he'd misinterpret her observation. She stemmed the random flow of her thoughts and said, "We certainly can. They're scattered around the perimeter of the city, so we'll pass many of them as we walk." She hitched her bag on her other shoulder and joined the others on the opposite side of the bridge as Alan walked alongside her.

"The oldest one is from the early fifteen-hundreds." His voice emerged in a bland monotone, though he gave her a smile.

"Imagine that," she said.

Bree increased her pace and fell into step beside Lauren. "It's just as beautiful as I remember." They'd added the village to their itinerary the year before, and it had been well-appreciated by the guests. When Lauren didn't respond, Bree added, "Are you okay, Lauren? You seem preoccupied today."

Lauren gave her a faint smile that didn't reach her eyes. "Just thinking of tonight's meal, wondering if I need to stop for anything after we drop everyone off. And I didn't sleep well, either. First night, you know."

Lauren had overcome her anger at Bree for cancelling Travis, but there was still a trace of chill between them. Or was it her imagination? Maybe Lauren had some tension with her long-term boyfriend, Mark, or something else unrelated to Bree or the trip. As a trained chef, Lauren planned the menus and did the cooking when the groups were at the villa. It was a sizeable responsibility and could easily account for her distraction. Bree hoped the meal was the only thing bothering her.

The sound of rushing water grew louder as they approached the first waterwheel. Travis was already planted in front of it, staring at the wide, wooden spokes encased in slimy strands of algae. He'd taken several photos by the time Lauren and Bree reached it. He looked up and smiled.

Before she could stop herself Bree blurted, "Will you write an article about the crowds and the parking problems? Or maybe you found pollution or pesticides in the water." She instantly regretted her words, but it was too late.

She felt a sharp jab from Lauren's elbow. Travis had an amused glint in his eyes, as well as a trace of wariness. "Haven't seen any pollution. If there is any, it's probably just centuries of residue from peoples' lives. Kind of interesting, I think." He turned back and adjusted his lens then snapped more photos.

Lauren pulled on Bree's elbow until they were out of Travis's earshot. She hissed, "You need to change your attitude *now* about Travis. He's one of our guests and he deserves the same courtesy as everyone else."

Bree nodded, humiliated. For the second time in a month, anger blazed from Lauren's eyes, burning Bree to the core. She lowered her gaze. Again, Lauren had taken Travis's side. Though he'd done nothing antagonistic, Bree still wondered what he wrote in his notebook, what photos he was taking and what he'd do with them, what data he would gather in the days to come. She knew she was judging him on what she feared and little else, but she couldn't help herself.

Lauren's harsh expression softened then she shook her head in exasperation. "Loosen up, Bree. You'll enjoy your week much more, and so will our guests."

Lauren abruptly turned and walked back to where Travis stood. She started chatting with him and he responded with a warm smile. Loosen up, she'd told Bree. Bree should have those words tattooed onto her forehead.

Herb, Doris, and the Morrisons joined them in front of the slowly spinning waterwheel. The water slush-slushed as the stream dropped from one spoke to the next. Silently Bree walked alongside Marcia and Sarah as they continued on the worn path toward the church of Notre Dame des Anges.

Once inside the church, the cool air refreshed Bree's sagging spirits. Her eyes widened at the ornate splendor of the Baroque design, the painted scenes in the overhead dome, and the bright blue arches on each side, which were surrounded by gilded scrollwork. She stared for a moment then remembered to take a quick head count. When she reached Travis, his eyes locked with hers. Heat rose to her face, despite the chill emanating from the centuries-old stone walls. She returned a tight-lipped apologetic smile. He gave a slight nod, his lips quirked faintly in what appeared to be amusement.

She rejoined the women and walked solemnly around the perimeter of the cathedral, observing the alcoves where statues silently told the story of Christ. A hush floated in the cavernous spaces, sliced by the echo of a voice here or there. Bree felt a presence beside her. She turned to find Marcia gazing up at a marble statue of Christ. "It's so lovely." She blinked misty eyes.

"Yes," Bree agreed. "The statues are beautiful, but a daily relationship is even more so. I feel God more alive than in these statues."

Marcia turned back to Bree. "You're a believer, Bree?"

Bree nodded and smiled. "He is my anchor every day." And boy, did she need one.

"That's so nice to know. Is Lauren also a believer?"

"Yes. We both felt God leading us to start this business. We don't talk a lot about our faith here, since people are from different backgrounds, but we hope somehow peace and faith come across." As she spoke, Bree knew she was failing miserably on both counts.

After lunch under a sprawling red umbrella in front of a cheerful bistro, the group resumed their stroll past the waterwheels. The market merchants gradually took down their stands and repacked their wares into vans. Beverly said, "Michael and I want to visit a couple of antique shops. We'll meet you back at the van at three." They were immediately swallowed by the surging crowd.

Several minutes later Bree heard Doris shriek, "Herb, where are you? Herb?"

Everyone turned to Doris, whose face was pale and twisted with panic. "He was just here a minute ago."

"He's probably in a shop." Lauren spoke in a soothing tone, touching Doris's arm. "He couldn't be very far."

"You don't understand." Tears sprang into her eyes. "He's—he's got dementia. The beginning symptoms, anyway."

Bree turned to her, compassion mixed with frustration. "Did you mention this in your application? I don't remember that."

Doris shook her head. "No, I'm sorry. I didn't think it was bad enough to mention it. And it comes and goes, but I knew he was getting worse." Her voice broke. "This was going to be our last trip together. I didn't think he was bad enough to just wander off like that." Tears slid down her tanned cheeks, streaking mascara into dark creases.

Bree slipped an arm around her. Her voice softened. "We'll find him. It's possible he's in a store nearby." She called to the others. "Let's all look through the crowds and in the shops. Remember, if we're separated, meet at the van at three." She turned back to Doris. "Of course, we won't leave without Herb."

Doris looked only slightly relieved. Already Lauren, Sarah, Marcia, and Alan were scoping the crowds and calling Herb's name. Where was Travis? Bree bit her lip. Probably taking photos, but she could really use his help right now.

She turned back to Doris. "Do you have a photo of Herb? I speak French, so I can ask in the shops and among the vendors."

"That's a good idea." She rummaged in her purse and found her wallet, then pulled out a photo of the two of them together. "Here, this one is pretty recent."

Bree called, "Let's meet back here in fifteen minutes," but nearly everyone in the group had already gone to look for Herb. She turned to Doris. "We'll stick together, okay?"

Doris gave her a weak smile and nodded. For the next ten minutes Bree asked vendors and shopkeepers if they'd seen Herb, showing them his picture. Vendor after vendor shook their heads head. Bree took a deep breath as a flutter of panic took root deep inside.

She and Doris didn't go far from the spot where Herb went missing, since he hadn't been gone very long. She scanned the crowd, up and down, left and right, until she felt dizzy. Lauren approached them, but she was alone. When Bree spied Sarah and

Marcia returning from across the bridge without Herb, her spirits sagged. Then she heard a male voice shout, "Got him!"

She and Doris looked toward the voice and saw Travis weaving through the crowd, waving to them with one arm. The other arm was linked with Herb's. As they walked Travis spoke to Herb, who looked bewildered.

"Oh, thank God!" Doris pushed through the crowd and threw her arms around Herb's neck. "I was so worried about you!" She turned to Travis and hugged him too. "Thank you so much, Travis." She began to weep again, but a smile broke through.

"Good work, Travis." Lauren grinned at him. "Where was he?"

Travis looked winded and his skin glistened with perspiration. "He was a couple streets over, past that bridge, watching a chalk artist. He was glued to it, so it was easy to spot him. It was hard to get him away, though." Travis laughed. "You like watching the picture appear on the sidewalk, don't you, old fellow?"

Bree felt strangely touched by the way Travis looked with affection at the older man, who beamed back at him. Herb hadn't shown that much expression since his arrival. A few stones from her defensive wall tumbled down.

The ride home was solemn, whether due to exhaustion or the day's near-crisis, Bree didn't know. She felt bone-weary, though she'd enjoyed the day until the crisis. She'd enjoyed it aside from her resident stress, that is. *Please, let it be smoother after this.* She prayed silently all the way back to the villa.

ଔ   ଔ   ଔ

Travis stretched out on the chaise lounge next to the pool, thankful that he was the only one there. Overall, he liked the people who had come on the trip. That was a relief, since they were all more or less stuck with each other for the week. But he wasn't used to being in a crowd twenty-four-seven, so savored the quiet moments. The others had likely collapsed in their rooms from fatigue. His agenda was the same as theirs, but he'd take his relaxation alongside the gently shifting waters of the swimming pool.

The first day was nearly over. So far . . . well, he wasn't exactly sure. Today's debacle seemed unavoidable, given Herb's condition. Travis had known there was something off about the man but hadn't been able to pinpoint it. They'd all have to keep a close eye on him until the end of the trip if they were to evade an even worse disaster.

Aside from that, Bree had remained prickly most of the morning, then seemed to mellow in the afternoon. Once he retrieved Herb, she looked downright grateful. He should have taken a photo of *that*, since it would likely be a rare event. He hoped she didn't remain chilly for the rest of the trip. Even if they never became friends, he preferred getting along with everyone.

An unbidden thought entered his mind, startling him. What *could* have happened, if Herb hadn't been found? That would certainly have upended the entire week. "Oh, thanks, Lord for letting us find him." The words still slipped easily from his lips when it was undeniable that God had stepped in at just the right moment. He certainly had that day, even though Travis wasn't necessarily the Almighty's favorite person.

How had he gotten to this distant place, so far from Him? First it was hurt, then anger, over all that happened in Brno and all that happened with Lexi, and the blinding agony that saturated his days afterward. He'd been paralyzed with pain for so long that apathy had been the only means of survival. Then apathy became habit, and busyness took over from there. Yet deep inside some hidden place he forgot he still had, a haunting echo sometimes beckoned and reminded him.

Maybe one day he should return to the Czech Republic, walk the same streets, stroll around the University, finish his healing process by facing it all. But his life was satisfying now. Why jeopardize that contentment by digging up the past?

Yet something inside sometimes called him to find his way back to God. His faith didn't have to look exactly like it had before. In fact, he couldn't go back to the same place if he wanted to. But would God be patient with him while he muddled through and figured it out? Was it too late to even ask that question?

Travis sighed. It was hard to imagine returning to the rah-rah and easy answers so often given to him by the people he used to know. *Just have faith. Everything happens for a reason.* Life wasn't a path of easy answers, even with faith. Maybe he'd been surprised by this harsh and unexpected truth. That may have been why he'd felt abandoned when the bottom had fallen out of his life.

It hadn't all been Lexi's fault. She wasn't completely to blame for falling into Varoslav's arms. It took Travis years to admit to his own part, that he'd treated her like a ministry partner instead of a cherished, beloved wife. He'd loved the fact that they shared a calling. Yet as he ran after it, he lost *her*.

How had his mind gone down that uneasy path? His stomach rumbled. The tiny salad he'd eaten at lunch wasn't food for a grown man, and dinner wouldn't be served for another two hours. He pulled himself up and ambled into the villa.

The kitchen was empty. He stood for a moment, observing its refined yet rustic details before locating the fridge, a tall burnished silver door embedded in the stone wall. After examining the contents of the shelf at eye level, he squeezed off a chunk from a block of cheese. He popped it into his mouth just as Bree walked in. He tucked the cheese into his jaw and murmured, "You caught me."

Her mouth curved up just slightly and she blinked once, twice. "Thanks for helping with Herb today." Her voice was soft, yet a cool distance remained in her eyes. Her blond hair tumbled in gleaming ribbons around her shoulders, mussed as if she'd been lying down. Of all people, she had reason to need a nap. On top of all of the drama of the day, he had the impression she stayed wound up like a spool of wire at all times. Even with the tension she exuded, she was pretty . . . he'd even say beautiful, with smooth, pale skin and large blue eyes.

"I was glad to help." His statement brought nothing further from her, so he decided to risk speaking his mind. "Bree, it seems like we got off on the wrong foot somehow. Is there something I've done to upset you?" There. The nagging question was out.

She paled. Swallowed. "I'm—sorry I, uh. I'm so sorry I come across that way to you." Her words edged out. She hadn't really answered his question, though in his gut he already knew her answer.

He thought she'd say no more, but then her tight bands of control seemed to fray before his eyes and fall away. "It's just—" she took a breath. Grimaced. "People like Lauren and me, we just want to have a good business, good tours that people enjoy. We do our best, we work long hours for months and months, but people like you don't seem to care about that. You just look for everything wrong. Maybe that builds *your* career, so you get known as the one who tells all the awful stories. So instead of helping people enjoy traveling and encouraging your fellow colleagues in the industry, what do you do? You damage their efforts by scaring travelers away. You give people dozens of reasons not to go *anywhere*, and we both know that the last thing people need is to stay huddled and fearful in their houses. The world is too big a place to not discover it."

Color rose in her cheeks as her eyes flashed and became more luminous. Passion. Yes, she had passion for travel, like he did. Something stirred, warmed inside him. He blinked and took two steps toward her. His voice was low as he said, "First, Bree, I feel exactly the way you do. I want people to discover the world and not just stay in their provincial lives. Second, I did not come here to do an undercover program on your company. I came to help my mother, who didn't want to come alone nor miss the trip. I wanted to come for her sake."

They stared at each other for a moment, silent. She seemed to be deciding whether or not to believe him, then finally huffed, "You have a reputation, so I was understandably afraid of what you'd do."

Travis winced. That reputation again. "I know, and I'm not really surprised by your feelings. I'm trying to change my reputation and my direction, actually. My first exposé piece went over so well I guess it became my brand."

She narrowed her eyes. "Really? You didn't intend any of that? You wrote a book about it, so I can hardly believe you just stumbled into this type of journalism by accident."

That was fair. "You have a point. My goal was to *prepare* people, not only warn them. Usually trips go just fine. But once in a while they don't, and I wanted people to be able to be flexible. Have you read it?"

She shook her head. "I've read some of your magazine columns. I think I saw one of your shows a year or so ago."

"When we get back to the States, I'll send you a copy of the book. You'll see that it's not all critical. I try to be helpful to travelers. And most of my TV programs don't cover scams or rip offs."

Bree crossed her arms, her lips tight. With a deep breath she lifted her head. Finally, she said in a voice that sounded defeated,

"Okay. I apologize." She lowered her eyes. "For everything. I didn't welcome you very well, and I'm sorry."

He frowned. "No need to apologize, Bree. I hope you understand I'm about more than just warning people. I really want them to discover the joy of travel. Same as you."

He waited a moment for her to respond, for the clouds to clear away from her countenance. She shrugged. "Okay, I guess you can stay." She gave him a reserved half-smile.

He stuck out his hand. "Friends?"

She rolled her eyes, but her small smile had grown almost to a grin. Again, when she smiled, he had the impression of the sun pushing out through clouds, reflecting off of water-soaked leaves.

Bree grasped his hand in hers, warm and soft. Maybe they could be friends after all.

Chapter Six

Fully awake and dressed, Bree strode into the kitchen the next morning, expecting Lauren to be slicing baguettes and bustling with the breakfast beverages. She found the room empty. She leaned through the doorway to the dining room. The table, glazed by bands of bold sunlight from a tall set of windows, had already been set with white porcelain dishes and cheerful yellow cloth napkins. Fresh sunflowers leaned out of a cornflower blue vase in the center of the table. On the sideboard, coffee and hot water carafes released translucent spires of steam. Baskets of teabags in metallic wrappers, drink condiments, jams, and glass canisters of cereals sat like dominos along the buffet. But no bread and no Lauren.

Bree glanced at her watch. She must be out buying baguettes. The guests would be coming down for breakfast within fifteen or twenty minutes, so she'd have just enough time.

Bree peered out the front window. The van and car were still there. Bree frowned. There wasn't a *boulangerie* within walking distance, so how would Lauren get the baguettes? She dashed down the hall but Lauren's door was open, the room empty. She returned to the kitchen, aware of minutes slipping away.

Bree grabbed her keys and headed to the car. The roads were empty and silent, not unusual for Monday morning, since in France many stores were closed Mondays. As she pulled up in front of the bakery she noted that it, too, was closed. She remembered another one a few blocks further. She drove there and dashed inside.

"Bonjour, Madame." She felt breathless. "I'll take five baguettes and a dozen croissants *au beurre*."

Minutes later Bree pushed her way into the foyer, arms loaded with bags of bread. She went into the kitchen and saw Lauren at the counter. "Lauren, where were you? I just got the baguettes." She chided herself for her irritation.

Lauren looked up from slicing baguettes, her face impassive. "I have baguettes."

"You do? I came down a half hour ago and there were no baguettes, and no Lauren."

"I arranged to have them delivered. I must have been at the side gate getting them when you came looking for me. Sorry, I should have told you, but it didn't occur to me that there would be any reason to do that."

Bree sighed. "No reason . . . it's just me . . ." She shook her head. *Just me being neurotic again.* She left the baguettes on the counter and returned to her room to collapse on her bed. The day just couldn't start this way. It just couldn't.

She stared up at the ceiling. "Lord," she whispered into the empty room. Sighed deeply. "I know this needs to stop. I'm a control freak. I torture myself every step I take. Please, help me to let go. *Please.*"

She blew out a sigh. Why didn't she let Lauren take care of breakfast, since that was *her* responsibility? If only Bree hadn't come down to check, she'd have been serene instead of in a flutter. But she'd done it again, taken over out of fear.

By the time she returned downstairs, wicker baskets on the table overflowed with baguette slices and croissants stacked ten inches high. At least there'd be enough food.

"Good morning!" She forced a cheerful lilt into her voice and spread a grin as she made eye contact with Beverly and Michael, Sarah, and Alan, who were already seated.

Alan lit up and boomed a cheerful, "Good morning," which seemed forced, though Bree didn't know the man well enough after just a day. When he stared at her too long, her eyes darted away. Oh, no.

She slid into the upholstered chair at the end of the long dining table just as the others came in and sat down. Greetings spun out around the table.

"So, what's the plan today, ladies?" Beverly dabbed her lips with a paper napkin and looked back and forth between Bree and Lauren.

"Today we'll be visiting a village very close by called St. Rémy-de-Provence." Bree reached for a croissant. "It's smaller than the town we were in yesterday and it should be less crowded, because it's not a market day." She sent a subtle glance at Doris to reassure her. "It's a charming town. Vincent Van Gogh lived there for a while. Nearby there are some Roman ruins for anyone who's interested."

"Did you say Van Gogh?" Alan perked up and straightened his shoulders. "That was when he committed himself into the asylum. But he painted over a hundred pictures during that time."

"Oh, that's quite a lot," Doris said. "Painting could be therapeutic."

"It wasn't in his case. He shot himself two months later." Alan reached for the cream, his face pale and expressionless.

"Oh, dear," murmured Beverly.

Bree pressed her lips together. Maybe she should be grateful for Alan's assistance, though she wasn't sure about that. "Unfortunately, there aren't any Van Gogh paintings to look at, since most of them were sent to bigger cities and museums. But there are reproductions around the town in the various places where he painted them."

"That's nice, an outdoor gallery." Sarah smiled and looked around the table.

"It's also the birthplace of Nostradamus." Alan again. "Sixteenth century."

"Yes, it was." Bree had been on the verge of mentioning Nostradamus. Alan surveyed her furtively, possibly to test her or assure himself that she was sufficiently impressed. Travis, dressed in a faded denim shirt and khaki cargo pants, also appeared to be watching her, though she couldn't interpret his expression. She was relieved that they seemed to have made a truce the day before.

Later that morning, they arrived in the small town of St. Rémy-de-Provence. After entering the town through the arched Porte St. Paul, the group joined the flow of crowds strolling down Rue de la Commune.

The morning seeped away under the shade of linden and plane trees, pruned to knobby ends where summer foliage burst out like bouquets. Three-story pastel buildings with contrasting shutters lined each side of the narrow street. Petunias and geraniums tumbled from flowerboxes at each window, and at ground floor boutiques, cafés, and art galleries beckoned those passing by.

After exploring the fourteenth century wall, its arched doorways, and the maze of narrow streets inside, Bree and Lauren led the group back to Place Favier. There they all gratefully collapsed at two large terrace tables beneath café umbrellas to have lunch. Bree shared a table with the Morrisons and the Grahams. At the other table sat Travis, engrossed in lively conversation with his mother and Sarah, while Lauren and Alan studied the menu.

"Let me see if I can read this." Michael opened the menu and squinted at it. He attempted and slaughtered a French pronunciation. Bree and Beverly couldn't stifle a laugh, which sparked laughter among everyone at both tables. Fortunately, Michael laughed along while Beverly nudged him playfully.

"These are appetizers." Bree pointed to the left side of the menu. "We Americans call the main course an 'entrée', but in France the entrée is the appetizer, like the entrance to the meal. The main course is called a *plat*." She helped them decipher the menu until the waiter arrived, clad in black with a white starched apron reaching nearly to his toes.

Toward the end of the meal Lauren announced loudly enough to be heard at both tables, "Hey, everyone, just need your attention for a minute. This afternoon I can take a group to the Roman ruins nearby, if anyone is interested. It's a settlement not very far from here, called Glanum. Those who don't wish to go can continue to visit the town here."

"I'll be staying here, if anyone is not going with Lauren," Bree said.

"Me too," Marcia said. "I prefer this cute town to old ruins."

After everyone had finished dessert, Alan, the Morrisons, and the Grahams left in the van with Lauren. Once the group had diminished Sarah stood. "I'd like to get some of that pretty pottery we saw. It would make good gifts. Would you like to go, Marcia?" Marcia pushed her chair back. "We'll meet you here a little later, okay?"

Once the women had left, Travis got up from the other table, ambled over, and sat down across from Bree. "Looks like we've been deserted. What would you like to do, Bree?"

She looked across the small table at him and her heart started to thump. Her mind darted to possible responses, but honesty won out. "Right now, I'd love a café au lait."

"Go for it." He held her gaze in his just a second too long and a warm swirl began deep inside her. Until a couple of days ago she'd considered him her nemesis, but here he was at close range with a lazy smile. She wasn't sure how she felt about spending the next hour or so with him. Actually, if she were honest with herself, the thought wasn't unpleasant.

The waiter came to the table and took her order. He turned to Travis. "*Pour vous, Monsieur?*"

"I'll take more water, please," he answered in French. The waiter nodded and turned away.

Bree raised her eyebrows. "You speak French?"

"Not a lot. I know enough to feed myself. I can eat in eight or nine languages." He leaned back in the café chair. "Tell me how you got interested in this business."

Her sudden bolt of anxiety must have shown on her face, because he added, "It's not an interview, I promise." He held up his hands. "See? I don't have any recording devices or hidden cameras. Not taking notes. Just want to get to know you a little more. As a friend."

Bree laughed. "I guess I don't have a choice but to trust you. Especially with that disclaimer." She linked her fingers across her stomach. "Okay, let's see. The first time I traveled anywhere was to summer camp in Canada. I know that doesn't sound exotic, but it opened my eyes to a different experience." She lifted her eyebrows at him. "*That* was only the beginning. In college I minored in French and spent my junior year in Tours, up in the Loire Valley. That's where I met Lauren. Years after, when small group tours were becoming popular, we came up with the idea for Le Bon Voyage. It seemed manageable for just the two of us, since it was designed for smaller groups, and we knew the area pretty well."

"Do you only work in Provence?"

"For now, yes."

"How long have you been doing tours?"

"We started about three years ago. It was slow in the beginning, but we're getting good reviews now." She was tempted to recite all the accolades they'd received and all they'd accomplished, but she bit her words back. She had nothing to prove to Travis Jefferies.

He nodded, his interest likely springing only from courtesy. He was on television and had been to exotic places around the world, so her business probably seemed small-time to him.

"It takes courage to start a venture like this." His words surprised her and his tone bore no trace of derision. "Two women pulling all this together," he gestured with his hands outstretched. "Must take an enormous amount of planning."

"How did you know?" She threw him a wry smile. The waiter arrived with a steaming cup of café au lait and a frosted carafe of water.

A mild breeze rustled the leaves of the plane trees overhead and a low murmur of conversation swirled in the periphery. "What about you, how did you get into televised travel programs?"

He poured water from the carafe for both of them and took a long sip. "I was working as a journalist for a newspaper in Portland. One day the guy responsible for the travel column had a bad accident and was laid up for a few months. I'd had some overseas experience, so they asked me to fill in. It was a good fit. First the column, then the book. After that a public network wanted to try a program." He shrugged. "It worked. People seemed to like it."

Most people wouldn't shrug off an accomplishment like that. Was his humility genuine? "What do you love most about what you do?" Now she felt like the interviewer, but she was curious and couldn't stop herself.

"I've never been the guy who'll sit in an office all day. I'd rather travel the world than have a big house or bank account. I love seeing the different ways people around the world live, their daily routines, their traditions, their foods, holidays. By doing these programs, it feels like I'm helping people around the world to understand other cultures that are different from their own. There's so much variety on this planet."

"I seem to remember one program where you were sampling monkey meat. You acted like it was delicious." They laughed.

"It wasn't my favorite, but I couldn't say so on air. That was my Asian series a couple of years ago, when I was just getting started in public television. I'm glad you saw it." He paused and added, "You see that I'm not all about tearing tours apart."

"No, I guess not. I got paranoid. I couldn't think of why else you would come." She sipped a frothy layer from her coffee. "You seem close with your mom."

He nodded. "I'm glad to be here for her sake, but as you can see, she would have been absolutely fine on her own."

"I noticed that she and Sarah have become inseparable."

"I'm glad for her. But I'm not at all in the habit of just touring without some other useful role. I feel a bit useless. You'd be doing me a big favor if you'd let me be helpful in some way. Would you, Bree?"

His words surprised her, which was becoming a habit with him. The intensity in his gaze showed he was serious. "Um, maybe I could use your help. You could keep an eye on Herb, for one."

"It'd be my pleasure. He's gotten attached to me anyway, since I rescued him from the street artists."

Bree laughed. She *had* noticed Herb following Travis around, his new best friend.

"If you need help fetching things from the store, lifting boxes, whatever. I need to be useful."

"I'll look for ways you can help. Shouldn't be too hard." Might be a relief for her . . . and a might even be a pleasure to have him hanging around. Only because he was nicer than she'd expected. Yeah, mainly that.

"Want to walk, if you are finished?" He drained the remaining liquid from his water glass and moved his chair back.

"Yes, I'd love to." She rose to join him.

They walked in silence for a few moments, browsing in boutiques and storefronts decked in front with carts and shelves filled with pottery, post cards, dried herbs, and other tourist knick-knacks. He strolled beside her in a relaxed gait, seeming at home with himself. Maybe some of that calm attitude would seep onto her.

"Bree Sorenson. That's a Scandinavian name. So, if you're Scandinavian, how'd you get so short?"

"Someone must have stepped on me when I was born." Bree grinned and shrugged. "My mom is short."

"Either that or you didn't eat enough pickled herring and smoked salmon while you were growing up." He grinned at her.

She laughed. "Yeah, that's it."

When they passed the dolphin fountain near the city hall, Travis stopped and stared into the water a moment then continued walking. The intermittent silence was comfortable, but Bree found herself curious to learn more about him.

They rounded a corner and encountered another fountain. This time the upper part was a carved image of a man who stared back at them. Travis looked down at Bree. "I love fountains. Do you mind if we stop for a minute? This one is a bust of Nostradamus."

He approached the semi-circular stone basin and examined the statue. Thin streams of water spouted from three openings below the stone sculpture into a basin below. Bree loved fountains too. The music of the water soothed her already.

He took several photos then gestured toward a dry space on the circular ledge. They sat down on a dry section of the concrete.

"What plans do you have for your tours in the future?" he asked her.

That didn't take much thought, since it was always in her mind. "I'd like to have a consistent number of guests, maybe ten or twelve, and five or six trips a year, as a first step. I could live here a couple months or so at a time, to avoid multiple trips back and forth. Then we could expand to other parts of France, maybe a wine tour in Bordeaux or Bourgogne, or a castle tour in the Loire Valley. If we had more staff, they could handle more of the details while Lauren and I scout out new locations." She would toss the same question back to him. "What about you?"

"I'd do straight travel shows instead of covering scams. In a lot of ways, I'm already living my dream. But—"

She perked to attention.

"It can be lonely sometimes. I see tons of people, though not always the same ones." He watched the swirling water over one shoulder. "There's my camera crew, audio people, editors. But the trips are a revolving door of relationships. It would be nice to have someone who is always there." He looked back at her and tossed a half-smile with a shrug.

He was allowing her a glimpse into his heart. Any remaining defenses against him crumbled right then. She shouldn't ask him this. "Have you—ever been married?"

"Yes, years ago." He spoke quietly but offered nothing further. "You?"

She swallowed and shook her head. "I date from time to time, but I think I scare men away with my, um, intensity. I tend to worry." Not to mention that some of them scared her, too.

"They must have been pretty wimpy." Softly he added, "Seems that a real man would calm your fears, not run away from them."

Their eyes locked together as his words caressed a hidden bruise. A hum began in a cavern deep inside. She looked away, praying he wouldn't see it on her face. "Yeah, I agree with that."

"You seem relaxed now. You're different here than when we're at the villa. There you're the Tour Director Extraordinaire."

"There's so much to think about. I'm good with details, but I'm always afraid things will go wrong." Bree gave him a rueful smile.

"Then what will happen?"

She shrugged. "Maybe people won't come on the tours, leave bad reviews. I don't know. I imagine the worst."

"Makes me wonder *why* you imagine the worst. Must have been something scary in the past. A bad experience, maybe."

Bree felt beads of perspiration break out on her back. She said lightly, "Why would you say that?"

"I don't know. It's often the case when someone worries too much."

He saved her from feeling the need to answer when he said, "Ready to walk?"

She nodded and rose. "How do you decide what to do for a program?" She'd steer the conversation back to safer ground.

He cocked his head to one side. "Usually I pick what I think is an interesting destination but try to dig up tidbits viewers wouldn't ordinarily know."

"Has this trip given you ideas of new places you'd like to film?"

81

"Well, funny you should ask. I was just thinking it might be fun to do a sort of reality-style program in a small group tour."

Bree's eyes widened. "Really? Hmm. I can see that might work. You'd have to invent all kinds of typical problems that would happen, people having conflict, things like that, wouldn't you? That's how reality shows are, it seems."

"But then there would be resolutions at the end. That's my goal when I warn people what can go wrong, so they'll be prepared with a backup plan and still be able to enjoy their trip."

Bree frowned. Her own approach was simply to try to control every aspect, so that nothing *could* go wrong. And her method was exhausting. "A reality show seems perfect for you, since you highlight things that can go wrong."

"Exactly." Travis smirked. He pulled his shoulders up and his voice brightened as if the thrill of a new idea inflated him with fresh energy. "So, when the group arrives at the destination and they find that their villa has already been rented to someone else, what do they do? Does it wreck their whole trip and they go home? Of course not. The tour leaders put their heads together, bring in a couple of locals to help them, and they all come up with plan B."

She nodded. "I think that could be a good show. You'd have to select a few disasters and plan how you'll resolve them, bring in characters with different backgrounds—some of them could be obnoxious. *That* could be entertaining." Sounded appealing for a television program, but she sure didn't want her trip to mirror that experience. Even if it already did.

"You've got it." He seemed lost in thought for several seconds and turned to face her. "Would you be open to *thinking* about doing a joint venture?"

She stopped walking. "*Me?*" To her ears her voice sounded almost shrill. "Let me see if I understand. You want to create a reality program based on one of *our* trips?"

"Doesn't have to be yours. But then, why not? The public would become aware of your company, so you'd benefit there. But of course, viewers would know that it's a program. They wouldn't expect things to go wrong on a *real* trip."

"Hmm. Not so sure about that. It could backfire. People might assume we're not well-organized."

"We wouldn't have to name your company. But we'll find a way to make sure it benefits from publicity in a positive way."

She eyed him without speaking. Was this a trap? Or could she somehow promote her company through his idea?

"Bree, I would make *sure* that you had good exposure that would promote your company. Besides, it might be fun to do a project together."

Together? She fought a wave of suspicion. What was his real angle? Part of his idea appealed to her. But he wanted her to collaborate on the program, work together with *him*? She opened her mouth to say something but wasn't sure what.

"Just think about it. I know it's not what you're used to doing, but you'd be in an excellent position to give a realistic scenario for the show. You know the local culture. I know how to put a program together."

Bree started walking again. "Why would you want to do a program with me? You don't even know me very well." Besides the fact that he knew she hadn't been thrilled that he came.

He waved the air dismissively. "I have an instinct. But you're still suspicious about me." He shot her a knowing smile which warmed the edges of her distrust.

"Even if we didn't do the show, I'll still have to convince you I'm not planning to criticize your company and digging for dirt isn't my interest." He watched her a moment as if waiting for her reaction. A smile tugged at his lips. "Besides that, I like your passion for travel. That's why it would be fun."

She hooked her thumbs into her pants pockets. "I'll think about it as an idea for the future. I like the concept, but I don't know yet how much I'll want to be involved. I have a lot on my plate right now."

The look on his face was calm yet open, inviting her. "No rush. If you're ever ready to consider it, we can talk more about it then."

Bree realized he was serious and didn't know what to say. She heard a voice call, "There you are." Looking up she saw Marcia and Sarah walking toward them, arms laden with plastic bags. She felt a wave of let-down at the interruption.

"Looks like you did some shopping." Travis approached his mother and peered into one of her plastic bags.

Marcia grinned at both of them. "I'd better pace myself if I don't want too much to take back to the States after the trip." She pulled a green and yellow ceramic pitcher from one bag. "Isn't this pretty? I also got some bags of herbes de Provence in cute little Provençal bags for my Bible study ladies."

"Good thing we ran into you. It's almost time to meet the others." Once again Bree was the tour-leader. Her privileged moments with Travis were over. She slipped a glance at him as they walked back toward the Place Favre. He was adjusting something on his camera. It was as if he'd quickly slipped to a private place out of reach.

Bree felt a stab of disappointment. She had to admit she'd enjoyed being with him and it had ended too soon. The afternoon at St. Rémy-de-Provence had been entirely unexpected . . . and confusing. She was too drawn to Travis Jefferies, to his relaxed, unassuming way, his outdoorsy good looks and the way he looked at her, as if he really saw her on the inside. Like a starving animal, she'd lapped it up, his concern and attention, which seemed genuine. To top it off, they shared the same passion for helping travelers discover the cultures and peoples of the world.

This was *not* a good idea. He likely wasn't a Christian, and shared faith was important to her. It would be too easy to let her heart lead where it already wanted to run ahead. She'd never been one to let things slip through the cracks.

She wasn't about to start now.

Chapter Seven

The van bumped along the narrow road up the Mont de Vaucluse toward Tuesday's destination, Roussillon, a medieval village perched on a mountainside. *Day three*, Travis wrote in his journal next to the date. As the van inched higher and higher, he could already see patchwork shades of green stretching across the gentle fields of the valley below. The van chugged more slowly with each hairpin turn. This time Bree was at the wheel.

Bree the mystery. She seemed to slip back and forth between a tense program director and an honest, approachable woman. The previous afternoon he'd had a glimpse behind the mirror at the real Bree, vulnerable, passionate, questioning. It had been a long time since he'd been that comfortable with a woman. Okay, he hadn't really spent time with *any* woman in a while. His half-focused efforts at dating over the last three years had been an afterthought, complying with what his well-meaning friends all thought he should do.

Had he really suggested a reality show to her? He'd even surprised himself with that idea, though it seemed like a fun project, completely off track from what he usually did. But he suspected he'd been trying to invent some way they could work together. He'd love to see her in a different context, one where she didn't feel this crushing burden to control the outcome. Unless he'd misread her, she hadn't been completely closed to the idea.

The van slowed and came to a halt. Travis squinted through the front window. A blockade and a small sign indicated road work, though no workers were visible anywhere. He heard, "Oh, dear," from the driver's seat. Bree sat still for a moment then turned to Lauren. "Wish I had the GPS right now. Do you have the map, Lauren? Maybe we can find another route to the village."

When she turned to reach for the map he saw her lips set in a grim line, her jaw firm. Though her outward demeanor was calm, he could guess that turmoil roiled inside. He fought a powerful urge to gather her in his arms and tell her not to worry. Instead he leaped from his seat and stumbled along the side aisle to the front of the van.

"Is there anything I can do, Bree?" Kind of stupid, really. What could he do that Bree and Lauren weren't already doing? At least Bree would know that, true to his word, he wanted to help.

Her smoky blue eyes found his and sure enough a shadow hung there. She gave him a tiny, grateful smile. "I don't think so. The road is closed but no detour is suggested. We'll have to circle around somehow. At least it isn't too far from here."

Lauren poured over the map. "Here are several departmental roads that make a ring around the area. That might work. There should be another access, especially since it's a touristy town."

"Why don't we take the D2?" Bree pointed at the map. "Looks like it gets close then connects with this smaller road here. We'll get off schedule." She seemed resigned, her lips sagging into a worried frown.

"Bree." Travis waited until he had her attention again. Her eyes met his and he lowered his voice almost to a whisper. "No one knows how long it is supposed to take, so we're not off schedule. They don't know so they don't mind."

She seemed to relax slightly. She panned a glance over the passengers, as if needing to verify his words. "You're right."

He turned to see the other passengers, who didn't seem concerned or even aware of a kink in the plans. Rather, they looked out the window or talked quietly. Sarah, of course, was knitting and seemed content, regardless of any delay.

The van arrived only twenty minutes off schedule, having found a tiny farm route which then led to larger roads. Bree had handled that well, at least outwardly.

As much as the pastoral calm of the valley had drawn his eyes, the view up ahead was nothing short of spectacular. The village of Roussillon adorned the top of pine-covered red cliffs like a crown. Time-worn red, orange, and yellow buildings were capped by clay tile roofs, and looked as though they'd been tossed haphazardly, remaining for centuries where they'd landed.

Alan announced, "Lots of artists and writers came here to paint and write. And that yellow stone surrounding the village has a lot of iron in it. I believe it's called ochre, like the color."

Bree had apparently given up humoring Alan. Travis noticed that Alan furtively observed her, but his commentary seemed to have little effect, aside from what he guessed was annoyance, which she masked with a bland smile.

"What is ochre?" asked Sarah. "Is it some kind of mineral?"

Lauren nodded, looking back from the passenger seat in the front of the van. "Yes, it's a pigment whose minerals give the color. Iron oxide gives it the yellow or red color. This town sits on one of the largest ochre deposits in the world."

Marcia snapped a picture. "I guess back when they built these houses, they didn't need to paint them, since their materials were already so colorful."

Like the other villages Travis had seen, closely-spaced and connected buildings huddled together in the narrow stone-paved streets. The difference lay in the variety of reds, yellows, and pinks, which gave a rosy, candied glow to the town. Bright shutters and doors decorated the pastel facades.

Once they had descended from the van and entered the village, the group stayed together for most of the morning. They shuffled through the maze of cobbled paths not wide enough for a car. Travis kept an eye out for the elderly guests in case anyone had a problem or needed anything. Herb was never far from his field of vision.

Bree chatted, organized, directed, and explained, but otherwise kept her distance from him. He'd caught her eye once or twice, and she only smiled. Why was she avoiding him now? Did she regret talking to him about the reality show idea? She hadn't committed to it. Maybe she thought she'd revealed too much about herself. Maybe she didn't like the part of her that *wasn't* in control and regulating everyone's leisure.

Didn't matter. He was almost halfway through this service to his mother. There were worse things than wandering around medieval French villages for a week. Soon he'd head east to Italy, back to his comfort zone. Back to being in charge of himself instead of being led around like a kid on a kindergarten field trip.

By early afternoon the group had seen the entire village, had lunch, and begun a stroll through the adjoining nature path in a park of ochre cliffs and rock formations. The deep red hue of the jagged cliffs reminded Travis of the Sedona rocks near his mother's house. Savoring a few minutes of solitude, he stood and gazed out over the grotesquely beautiful ancient rocks, which displayed centuries of scars from weather as well as man's exploitation. Despite this, the rocks spoke of strength and eternity. *He alone is my rock and my salvation.* The phrase leaped from a cavern of the past into his mind. He felt a stirring. *I want to find you again, God. But I don't know the way back. It's been too long.*

The pine trees returned a melancholy sign, matching the sudden hollow ache that filled him just then. He felt a presence beside him and glanced over. His mother stood silently, looking out where the embankment dropped off and a surreal splendor filled the valley as far as they could see.

"It shows the glory of God, doesn't it?" Her voice was soft with awe.

"I was thinking the same thing. After everything and all the years gone by, He is still my rock."

She turned to him. "He's still rooted inside you, Travis, despite all that's happened. He promised never to leave, just like any good parent would. Regardless."

Travis grimaced. "He's there, but I'm in a place I don't recognize. It's like I can't find my way back."

She laid a hand on his arm. "You don't need to go back. Start where you are and go forward. You don't have to be exactly what you were before. He knows where you've been and He understands. He's creating something new for your future. Just take it a day at a time and let Him into your day. That's all. It's not hard. It's just daily. He will lead you from there."

Travis nodded, and turned his gaze on a pine tree growing horizontally from a cliff. There was a time he wouldn't have listened to her this long. He would have closed off, sure she didn't understand his pain, the comfort of his apathy. But it was time to let it go. Start from where he was? Yes, maybe he could do that.

He gave her a small smile. "Thanks, Mom."

Travis and his mother joined the travelers on the path and walked in silence. As they approached the end of the trail, Lauren got their attention. "It's two-thirty now. We can either go to another village called Gordes, only about six miles from here, or we can stay and visit the ochre museum. Another option is a Cotes de Provence wine tasting experience."

Travis leaned toward his mother and muttered, "Now we have to wait for ten people to come to an agreement." He shot a grin at her and added, "I'd just as soon stay here on this cliff."

The majority voted to visit Gordes, so they piled back into the van and arrived shortly after three. As they visited yet another picturesque mountain village, Alan filled everyone in on the involvement of Gordes residents in the French Resistance during the Second World War. Turns out that Sarah also knew a thing or two about history, and a minor dispute ensued between the two teachers.

Travis half-listened, watching Bree's reaction to Alan's historical commentary. This time she didn't respond to him, but instead seemed to be observing Lauren, who chatted with Doris. Ever the people-watcher, this drew Travis's interest. Was there friend trouble between the two Bon Voyage founders? Lauren seemed apt to roll with whatever happened, pacing herself through her tasks, not given to emotional peaks or valleys. A stark contrast to Bree.

Bree's emotional landscape was fascinating to him, one minute relaxed and unassuming, the next, striving frenetically to orchestrate the day. He wondered about the cause of her anxiety. If only she'd learn to kick back and flow with events, if she'd smile more, learn to laugh at herself, take more risks, care less about, well, everything . . . he would probably never leave her side.

Now, where had *that* thought come from? He shook his head to dislodge the unbidden idea. *Get a grip, Travis.* Bree Sorenson was about as cuddly as a porcupine. If he valued his skin, he'd stay far away from her.

℞   ℞   ℞

"I guess visiting the winery was too much at the end of such a long day." Bree leaned back in the passenger seat and watched through the side window as the sun melted into the horizon, staining the sky with swaths of purples and pinks. Lauren looked straight ahead through the windshield, appearing not to have heard. "Don't you think so?" Bree asked her.

Lauren spoke quietly. "Yes, it was too much. I know you want to give everyone a full experience, but most of our guests are older and probably tire more quickly. Two villages and a wine-tasting were an awful lot for one day. It's not your fault, though, we both agreed."

"We'll learn for next time." At least Lauren hadn't blamed her. Or had she? Bree frowned, unsure. A tasting at Châteauneuf-du-Pape, a famous vineyard not very far from Gordes, had been on the itinerary, but they'd run out of time. Not wanting to disappoint anyone, when they passed a small vineyard offering Côte du Luberon wines, Bree suggested stopping for a tasting, hoping they'd be satisfied by the last-minute substitution. She'd explained it would be just as valuable an experience, since Provence rosés were well-known, and supplied most of the rosé wine for the entire country. The tasting wasn't supposed to take too long. But their little group had tasted Provence wine samples so freely, and even ordered extra glasses, that the Grahams and Morrisons got tipsy.

Fortunately, an adjoining café provided a light meal, which balanced the alcohol and freed Lauren from her evening cooking duties. But it would be almost dark before they arrived at the villa.

Bree looked at Lauren, who'd fallen silent. She had, in fact, been silent most of the day, aside from snippets of conversations with their travelers. Gone was the complicit feeling Bree had always had with her friend. What *else* had Bree done wrong? She was at a loss to even guess.

"Have you talked to Mark?" Bree's voice slid again through the silence, as she sought to reach into the tangle that lay between them. Despite the dusk, Bree thought she saw Lauren stiffen. Lauren and Mark were a committed couple, weren't they? Maybe they'd had a disagreement and that was why Lauren had been withdrawn. But Bree was her best friend. Why had she said nothing?

"Not yet." Lauren's gaze was frozen ahead. "He knows how busy I get while I'm here, but I'll call him half-way through the trip." In a softer voice she added, "Probably."

Bree stared at Lauren, feeling as though an ocean separated them, then pressed down the sharp twist inside her as they lapsed back into silence. She turned her head to watch through the window as the light purple band in the sky darkened.

Several minutes of silence passed. Then Travis's voice rang out. "Herb, I don't think you need to go anywhere right now." Bree turned and saw Herb standing, ducking his head against the ceiling of the van, although they were still moving. Travis stood a row behind him, his hands on the older man's shoulders. "We're almost there, Buddy. Why don't you have a seat?"

Herb, swaying from the wine and motion of the van, looked back at Travis then fell back into his seat.

A shrill giggle broke out in the next row as Beverly covered her face and leaned against Michael. They'd both drunk quite a lot and, despite the food, were still enjoying the effects. At least Lauren was the one at the wheel. Bree smiled, in spite of her sadness and fatigue. The Morrisons knew how to savor each moment and enjoy each other too. A stab of envy reached the void inside. She turned away and stared again out the window at the now blackened landscape

In the reflection from the darkened window, Bree saw that Travis was seated again, staring woodenly out the window. What was he thinking? Maybe he was wondering why she'd avoided him most of the day. She hadn't wanted to encourage him by seeking him out. At least that was what she told herself. If she were honest, she didn't know what to do with her attraction to him. Best to just keep her distance until the trip ended.

Once the van pulled up in front of the villa, Bree helped Beverly and Michael stumble onto firm gravel. "I'm sad that we didn't go to Chateauveus, I mean Chateauwiss . . . that place we were gonna go." Beverly tripped, fell into Michael, and burst out laughing.

Bree winced.

Sarah, who had overheard, came alongside Bree and murmured, "You cannot please everyone. I thought it was a very pleasant day."

Bree smiled gratefully. And Sarah was right. Bree knew one of her problems was desperately wanting to please everyone at every moment. Did she live for the applause of men instead of God? Or was she just afraid He could not protect her in the face of their disapproval? *Lord, please help me live for Your approval. Help me stop trying so hard to protect myself.*

An hour later the Grahams and Morrisons, sufficiently sobered-up, Sarah, and Marcia, gathered in the living room to sample some of the board games that were stocked in one of the cupboards of the main room. Bree glanced through the picture window and saw Travis by the pool, his back facing the house. Another pang of guilt stabbed her. She'd cut him off cold that day, with no explanation. He couldn't know she was trying to protect her feelings. To him she probably just seemed fickle or rude, considering the time they'd spent together the previous day.

She slipped out the back door into the deepening twilight and stepped gingerly across the cool, spongy grass. The evening was still balmy but held a trace of chill just beginning. A faint tang of lavender flowers and pine spiced the summer air. As she approached the pool she saw that he was writing in a journal. She tensed, then chided herself. He'd told her he wasn't writing an article about them, so she should believe him. Then *let go*.

She stopped by the lawn chair next to him. He looked up, surprise on his face.

"I wanted to tell you they're playing board games inside, if you'd care to join." It had been a perfect pretext to come talk to him, to break down any barrier she'd erected that day.

"Thanks, I'll pass." He closed his journal.

"What's that you're writing?" She sat on the lawn chair next to him.

"I'm just finishing an article. Would you like to hear it?" He reopened the journal and read in a narrative tone. "Le Bon Voyage encourages alcoholism among its elderly patrons, as if they don't have enough problems already. In addition, the excessive cuteness of every destination only sets people up for disappointment when they return to their ordinary lives." He watched her face.

"Excessive *cuteness*?" Bree lifted her brows and couldn't stifle laughter.

Travis grinned. "I'm just playing with you."

"You're taking a risk, considering how I nearly booted you off the tour a few weeks back." She smiled then paused, lowering her eyes. "I don't take things lightly. Ever."

The night breeze flicked his hair. "What can we do about that? Life is zooming by and you're missing all the fun."

She let out a belly-deep sigh. "I'd like to have more fun."

"Maybe I can—help you?" he offered.

Despite lengthening shadows of dusk almost covering his face, she could see an openness there, raised eyebrows, telling her he might be sincere. There he was again, reaching out to her when she'd only been cold to him. It surprised and touched her.

"How?"

He paused. "Not sure yet. I could remind you of the big picture when you're about to freak out."

"Like you did this morning in the van."

"Something like that, yes." He shrugged. "Maybe I'll create a crisis and bring you along for the ride, so you'll have practice handling it. Or even an adventure."

His words held an intriguing promise. Was he teasing her? The twinkle in his eyes made her unsure but caused heat to puddle inside her. She hoped she hadn't made a mistake in joining him by the pool, going against her commitment to protect her rogue emotions.

She probably owed him some kind of explanation, to help him understand the anxiety that stayed with her like a low-grade fever. Aside from that, something about him made it easy to open up, to say everything she was thinking. "I—I had a difficult childhood. There were a lot of times when I felt completely helpless." She tilted her head to one side. "Hence, control freak as an adult. In some ways I have the perfect profession. I get to organize tons of details, which I like, and travel too, which I love."

He pulled himself up and leaned his elbows on his knees, squinting with compassion. "So, you protect yourself by trying to control everything." He nodded, as if understanding her for the first time. "You know, you also have the worst profession, since you can't control people or other cultures. You'd be better off in an office with paper and pens. They're pretty predictable."

She eyed him. "Yuk. I'd just shoot myself, then. I'm not made to be cooped up." She encircled her knees with her arms and settled back against the lounge chair. "Okay, Travis. Tell me. You work in the same field as I do, but you go to places that are primitive, unpredictable, and sometimes war-torn or else about to explode into civil war. How do you handle the unknowns?"

"I lean in." At her lifted eyebrows, he chuckled. "I lean into the experience, like being on a surfboard. I *know* I don't have control, and I assume things won't work out perfectly, so I do what I can and let the rest happen. It usually works out fine. If it doesn't, it's still usually okay by the end. After all these years it doesn't catch me off guard. I expect it."

"You aren't ever afraid of being in danger or getting hurt?"

"No, not really. There's always a way out. So far." He grinned.

Could she learn that attitude? Of all people, she should learn to 'lean in'. Lean into God. If Travis wasn't a Christian, why should he have this peaceful attitude when she herself did not? Why had it always eluded her, despite the faith she professed?

A chill threaded through the summer evening. Bree shivered and crossed her arms.

"Here, take this." Travis pulled off his sweatshirt before she could protest and handed it to her.

"You don't need it?"

"I'm fine."

"Thanks." She smiled at him and slipped it over her head and shoulders. It was still warm from his body and scented with mellowed cologne and maleness. Of course, she could have just gone inside, but she didn't want to. Not at all.

He laughed. "You're swimming in that thing, but I hope it warms you up."

"Yes, it helps." She leaned back in the chair, pulling the extra fabric of the sweatshirt into her palms. Tilting her head back, she stared at the stars stippling the inky sky, feeling peaceful. "Is there anything about your work that you have trouble with or find difficult?"

"There is one stubborn thing." His deep voice wove into the murky dark of the poolside. "I make a huge effort to be organized. I manage and do okay with the bigger things. The little ones, though—retrieval, especially. Little pieces of paper that I can't find. Computer documents, sometimes in duplicate, that have been labeled in such a way that I don't remember where they are, lots of hard-to-read notes in my paper agenda."

Bree laughed. "I should come work for you, then. I'm great at all that organizing stuff. That's bliss for a neurotic perfectionist."

He gazed at her in silence for a moment, holding her eyes as a smile hovered on his lips. "I'm not sure it would be bliss working for me, but it might be fun."

There was something vaguely sensual in his tone, nearly flirtatious. She felt heat rise to her face, hoping it was dark enough to hide it. Had he taken her comment the wrong way?

Her voice was light. "Maybe so."

She turned toward the pool, still as glass. It mirrored a slice of the moon, cold and bright, its reflection barely moving on the glistening surface of the water.

Silence settled between them. A burst of laughter and a gleeful shout floated from the open windows of the villa, swirling up into the quiet night. Crickets chirped pinpricks of sound into the velvety dusk and the redolent scent of cut grass hovered around the pool.

His approach to the unexpected fit him. Travis, the maverick, the adventurer. Could she ever adopt that attitude for herself? If he could guide her, she'd learn. But could she learn it by herself? She'd have to learn it by herself, somehow, before she destroyed her own life.

Chapter Eight

The Cours Mirabeau in the center of Aix-en-Provence appeared to be the Champs-Elysées of Provence, surging with people who strolled or hurried, and those who surveyed the flow from their perches behind tiny round café tables. Bree could feel a spike in energy radiating from the wide avenues and shady sidewalks as she strolled alongside Doris. So different from the sleepy cliffside villages they'd visited the day before.

She stopped in front of a large, mossy hump that spouted a thin stream of water from the top, gurgling up from a hidden thermal spring. As a fountain, it had its own merits, though beauty wasn't one of them, unlike the many graceful fountains they'd seen in the city reputed to have a thousand of them.

Perhaps an exaggeration, but each one drew her with its babbling song of peace. In fact, she felt more tranquil that day than she had in a long time. Early that morning she'd decided to adopt Travis's concept of leaning in. She pictured herself leaning into God, being in His hand. The image soaked her soul in calm. She only hoped she could maintain it.

The members of the group moved more slowly that day, expressing less energy, perhaps due to the long schedule of the previous day. Bree and Lauren decided they'd return to the villa after lunch instead of staying all day in the city. That evening they'd celebrate Michael and Beverly's fortieth wedding anniversary. Lauren had already purchased most of the ingredients for a special meal.

Bree turned to Doris, who stood beside her. "This fountain is supplied by a natural hot spring, so the water ought to be warm. We'll see." Bree climbed up on the concrete base that supported the fountain. She stuck several fingers into the tiny spurt of water that rose from the moss-covered mass. "Yup. It's warm, alright."

"It's not pretty like the other ones." Doris glanced over her shoulder, ever watchful of her husband.

Bree saw her gesture. "How is Herb doing? He hasn't had any more trouble wandering." She fell into step beside the older woman as they continued walking.

Doris shrugged. "He hasn't gotten worse, that's one good thing. But he isn't the same man I married." Her voice broke. She shook her head and blinked several times. "We've been together for forty-six years and I'm losing him, one day at a time. He looks the same, but he's not. It's like he's ebbing away." Several tears squeezed out and rolled down her plump cheeks.

A lump throbbed in Bree's throat. She slipped an arm around Doris's shoulders, unsure of what to say. There was nothing she *could* say, as time and disease took their toll. "I'm so glad you've had forty-six years together. Think of those, Doris. Herb would want you to remember those times."

Doris nodded. "That's true. They've been happy years." After a few more tears fell she reached into her purse for a tissue. "I know he hasn't talked a lot on the trip. He *can* talk, but he forgets a lot of words, then feels embarrassed about it. I didn't want you to think he wasn't social."

"I understand. I hope he is enjoying himself." Bree couldn't really tell if he was or not. She scanned the crowd and saw Herb leafing through some post cards on a nearby stand. Several other members of their group were beside him also surveying merchandise, while Marcia and Sarah fingered Provençal tablecloths with tiny flower designs in bright colors. Alan stood talking to the Morrisons, likely educating them about King René who'd made Aix-en-Provence into a powerful town. She didn't see Lauren, who had probably slipped into a shop to browse or buy something.

Travis was taking photos of the avenue, the fountains, and she didn't know what else. He must be in heaven, with all the fountains he had to enjoy in Aix. Twice she'd approached a fountain only to see him on the other side, staring down at the tumbling water and its reflections, as if searching for solace. He'd looked up and smiled at her. She'd felt a kinship with him then, especially after their conversation by the pool.

A half-hour later, Lauren still hadn't rejoined the group. Maybe she'd gotten caught up in a purchase and couldn't find them. Bree checked her phone. No message from her. Tension needled her stomach. "Lean, lean," she murmured to herself. At least Lauren was familiar enough with Aix-en-Provence and France to find her way back alone if she needed to. But would she have just wandered away and left Bree alone to lead the group? Something must have happened. An emergency? Maybe just an inconvenience.

Bree would have enjoyed having a full day without her new peaceful attitude being tested. Not just yet, anyway. It looked like there wasn't much chance of that.

"You're looking awfully serious." Travis had sidled up beside her.

A wave of pleasure nudged her concern slightly to the corridor of her mind. She gave him a wan smile. "Just wondering where my partner is. She's disappeared, it seems. But I'm *leaning*, can't you tell?"

He laughed. "Yes, I can. In fact, you seem relaxed today."

"I *was*."

She felt her phone buzz in her pocket. "Oh, good. This must be Lauren." She pulled the phone out and scanned the screen. Just a message from the agency that had rented them the villa. What could *they* want? She pushed away the possibility that there could be an additional annoyance she'd have to handle. She shook her head. "Nope. Not Lauren."

"Remember, keep leaning. It usually turns out just fine. Almost always."

His voice was smooth and reassuring. He walked close beside her and continued speaking softly, pointing out things they passed along the narrow but busy street. Occasionally he'd stop to take a photo and twice he took hers, usually when she was unprepared. She wouldn't read anything into that, since he'd snapped photos continually of everything and everyone since arriving.

He probably meant only to be reassuring and friendly, but she found herself wildly distracted by his closeness, by the smell of him. She'd begun to recognize his cologne and his unique male scent. All of her senses were alert and the mental voices grew louder, shouting opposing directives, toward him, away from him. She needed to get a grip on herself, instead of wondering what it might be like to run her fingers through his thick, curly hair.

Bree's eyes lifted to meet his as she returned a tight smile.

His gaze wandered to her mouth before darting away. He stepped slightly away from her as if warning himself away from danger, but he stayed alongside her through alleys and streets overshadowed by two-story pastel-painted buildings. In each one busy storefronts occupied the street level and apartments adorned with bloom-laden window boxes stacked up all the way to the terracotta tiled roofs. He stopped every few steps to take more photos. His nearness was a comfort. And a distraction.

They were seated for lunch beneath a wide canvas umbrella in the shade of towering plane trees when Bree's phone buzzed in her pocket. Lauren had finally texted, apologizing but not offering much in the way of explanation, except to say that she'd been "tied up". Bree texted back the name of the restaurant and Lauren, flush-faced, arrived several minutes later. Though she chatted with the others, she avoided Bree's gaze. A formless dread took root in Bree's stomach and spread its tentacles. Maybe Lauren was only embarrassed that she'd deserted Bree. Or maybe it was something more.

Throughout the meal Bree struggled to maintain a peaceful attitude. *God, I'm trying. Please help me!* She'd almost finished mopping up the creamy Normande sauce with a chunk of baguette when Beverly cried, "My purse! Where is my purse?"

Travis leaped up, bumping the table so the silverware and glasses clanged, and took off running before anyone could speak. Beverly turned to Bree, tears in her eyes. "You told us not to put our purses on the back of the chair, but I forgot. It's such a habit."

"We're an easy target, being so numerous and seated outside." Lauren leaned toward Beverly. "What did you have in your purse? A passport? Credit cards?"

Bree rummaged in her purse and fished out a clean tissue. "It'll be okay, Beverly." She repeated the sentiment silently to herself as she proffered the tissue to Beverly, who had spread her hands across her face. Michael encircled her shoulder with his arm and patted it.

"Maybe Travis saw the guy or is hoping to spot a man with a purse." Alan pushed away his plate. "Should we go and look for it?"

"I'm not sure that would help at this point. He'd be long gone." Bree grimaced. "Beverly, do you remember what was in the purse? Maybe you'll need to cancel some cards or something. Whoever took it likely only wants the cash, but you never know."

"Fortunately, I didn't have any cards with me. I did have some Euros, which I just withdrew yesterday, though Michael has the bulk of them. My passport is the main thing."

"That can be replaced," Michael said, "but we'd have to act fast, since we're leaving Sunday. Today is Wednesday."

Bree sighed. As Travis had said, no one could control things in a foreign country. Or anywhere else, for that matter. She was surprised that her anxiety, though present, had remained at a manageable rumble, whereas normally it would have been off the charts. They'd have to spend an afternoon at an embassy or consulate—not on the schedule— and she didn't know where the nearest one was.

Everyone fell silent until an aproned waiter appeared by their table. "*Désirez-vous un dessert?*" He glanced at each one, unaware of the drama that had occurred.

Bree looked around the table. "Does anyone want a chocolate mousse or anything else? Might make us feel better."

As the waiter disappeared with their dessert order, Travis suddenly reappeared and fell into his chair, breathing heavily. He tossed a small, red purse with a long strap onto the table in front of Beverly.

"This better be the right purse," he mumbled then grinned at the table's occupants, sitting in a state of startled pause.

Then everyone cried out at once and Beverly's voice trebled over the others. "You found it! Travis! How did you find it?"

Immediately she snatched open the flap to inspect the contents. "Looks like it's all here. The guy didn't have any time to take anything, thanks to Travis."

Bree stared at him, open-mouthed, then found her smile. Travis looked spent, perspiration dripping down his face. Dark splotches of sweat had seeped through his shirt. He'd done it again.

"You must have sprouted a red cape and gone flying through Provence to catch him." Alan looked unfazed as he reached for the water carafe.

Travis had finally recovered his air supply and responded to the stares and acclaim around the table. "A little while ago I spotted a guy who looked like he was casing us, so I watched him. He didn't seem to be a customer. Unfortunately, I took my eyes off him for just a couple minutes, and that's when he made his move. But at least I knew who I was looking for."

"Travis, you're brilliant!" exclaimed Doris, clasping her hands.

"Again, you saved the day." Alan leaned back to turn his attention to the dessert arriving on a large tray.

"You deserve a dessert, Travis," Sarah said.

Marcia touched his arm. "Are you okay, Travis?"

He nodded and suddenly seemed uneasy with the attention. "I could use some ice cream. Do they have that on the menu?"

"Yes, certainly. I saw it." Michael signaled for the waiter.

Bree fell backward against the rattan chair and breathed heavily. She shot a glance at Lauren, who smiled briefly, then looked away.

CR CR CR

It had been a blessed relief to see the stone villa come into view, even better to take another shower—after sweat had crawled over him during his pursuit through the streets of Aix-en-Provence. Travis pulled a faded blue T-shirt over his head and ran a hand through his wet, matted hair. If his goal had been helpfulness during his week in Provence, he guessed he'd gotten some gold stars that day. He'd have been satisfied enough toting cartons around or running to the market but was glad he'd helped the group avert disaster. And especially glad he'd been able to lift a new burden of concern off Bree's shoulders.

He sat on the foot of his bed and pulled on his sandals. Felt good to sit down for a few minutes. Not that wandering cobbled streets and chasing a thief had worn him out. If anything, the thief provided a good distraction for him, since he was getting restless with tourist visits, even if each destination surpassed the one before in beauty and quaintness.

Besides that, he'd had trouble sleeping. He kept thinking about his moments at the poolside with Bree, just the two of them, talking and laughing like old friends . . . and *not* like friends. He couldn't deny that seeing her in the twilight, mauve shadows covering her pale, smooth face, did something to the inside of him. Blond curls shone coppery in the moonlight, and her large, blue eyes became silvery gray. All her defenses, competence, control, all the masks she wore, were gone, and in their place an intriguing mixture of vulnerability, determination, and femininity. He knew he was getting lost, but he couldn't leave the poolside. Instead he'd fought a powerful urge to lean forward and take her in his arms, lowering her to the woven lawn chair, pressing into her soft lips.

Travis leaned back and blew out a breath. He'd need to rein himself in somehow. He'd couldn't exactly avoid her for the next three days and didn't wish to. So, he'd try to push all those confusing and inappropriate feelings aside and be helpful. That was his plan, anyway.

He pulled himself up and ambled downstairs. The villa was quiet, seeming empty, but several bedroom doors in his hallway were closed. He guessed the activity had tired everyone out. He knew his mother had retired to her bedroom with her Bible and a book, claiming to need some alone time. Travis glanced out to the pool where Doris sat under a large umbrella holding Herb's hand.

Unsure of what to do next, Travis entered the kitchen. Bree looked up from where she stood near the counter and smiled at him. She held a swatch of paper in one hand and looked so cute with her hair pulled back in a barrette on top of her head. She'd changed clothes and was wearing a short beige skirt, a green tank top, and pink flip flops.

"What's up?" he asked, motioning to the paper with a nod of his head.

"Lauren needs some things from the big grocery store. She's out doing some other errands for tonight. Apparently yesterday she broke a bottle of olive oil and really needs some for this evening, and there are a couple other things that I'll pick up at the same time." She looked up at him. "Want to come with me to the grocery store? It's in the next town, Cavaillon."

"Sure. Will we take the van?"

"No, there's a smaller car that we use for short trips. We'll take that."

Once in the car, he rolled down the window and let the late afternoon breeze waft in. His wish to be helpful was granted, but a trip to the store with Bree wasn't going to help him with his resolve. He noticed her lime green sparkly toenail polish and smiled. A bit of whimsy for the uptight Bree. Or formerly uptight. She looked relaxed behind the wheel just then, dark sunglasses perched on her face, one arm out the driver's window.

"You were a hero today." She stated it as a fact, but a smile had slid up her face.

"Wasn't my intent. Just pure impulse. I'd almost expected that to happen, but I was stupid enough to lose my attention at just the wrong moment." He stared out through the passenger window at the dry, scrubby vegetation along the roadside. Bree picked up speed as she pulled onto the highway. He rolled his window back up a couple of inches.

"Are you kidding me?" She shook her head, pushed her sunglasses up, and stared at him before turning her eyes back to the road. "You're really blaming yourself? Where's the lean-into-crisis-take-it-in-stride Travis?"

He laughed sheepishly. "No, I wasn't blaming myself, but I think I could have prevented it. In fact, it was on the tip of my tongue to remind Beverly to put her purse between her feet, like you told them that first day."

"So much for my helpful warnings. Anyway, it ended well, as you predicted." She smiled over at him returned her attention to the road. For a few seconds he couldn't look away from her as the humming inside grew louder. Oh boy. This could get dangerous. He figured it was probably too late. At least she was behind the wheel.

Bree pulled into a parking lot in front of an average-size one-story building emblazoned with the word, *Intermarché.* He clambered out and fell into step beside her as she walked briskly, list in hand.

"Okay, we need olive oil as first priority. A small basket should do."

Travis had grabbed a metal shopping cart and jerked it, but it didn't come out of the queue. He fumbled in his pocket and found a Euro then inserted it. "Forgot about the system. Here, this should be big enough even for a bit of impulse buying."

She grinned at him. "You'll get your Euro back when we return the cart. While we're here I'll get a couple kilos of vine tomatoes." She laughed with mock surprise. "Oh, we're in Provence! That's the only tomatoes they *have* here, straight from the vine! The produce is usually really good here, and in the open markets, everything is fresh and usually reasonable. You could eat fairly cheaply just by shopping there most of the time."

Travis liked seeing her relaxed and chatty, talking about veggies, tomatoes, such normal things. He enjoyed walking beside her pushing a grocery cart. Seemed so domestic, something that had been absent from his life for far too long. The grocery store and resembled the stores back in Portland.

"Hmm, let's get something for the apéritif. Cashews, maybe some goat cheese." She bustled past him to the next aisle. He followed along, letting her lead the way.

He held up a box of crackers. "I used to love these as a kid. I'm surprised they sell them here. Must be a universal craving."

She placed a can of cashews into the shopping cart. "You haven't said much about your childhood. Where did you grow up?"

"Outside of Denver. We could see the Rockies from our house."

She cocked her head. "Bet you skied every winter and hiked every summer. I can see you doing that."

"You got it. Did all that. Went camping, hiked, played team sports. It's sunny there most of the year. I have one brother and we were always outside, even in winter."

"That fits," she said, almost too quiet to hear. "I'm from Minnesota, which is lovely too, but colder. Much colder. Now I live outside of D.C., and it's a relief to get through the winters without having to dig out of several feet of snow."

Down another aisle she said, "Looking for the olives. Do you see them?"

"What color?"

"Black."

"Got 'em. Kalamatas okay?" He reached for a jar at eye-level and held it up for her to see before placing it into the cart.

"Perfect. Okay, I guess we're done," she said.

Travis felt a throb of disappointment.

As they waited to check out, he glanced through the large plate-glass window in front of the store. The sky had darkened to deep blue-gray. "Looks like we'll have some weather anytime now."

Bree was saying something in French to the cashier, a teenage boy. She smiled and charmed him as he counted out her change and said, "*Bonne journée, madame.*"

She turned back to Travis and scanned the sky over his head. "Oh." She frowned. "It's really dark. Rain showers were forecast for this afternoon, but they should blow over quickly."

They loaded the grocery bags into the trunk, dodging the first spitting raindrops. A fleecy, blackened sky hung a low scowl over them. Travis and Bree slipped into the car and slammed the doors shut just as the bottom fell out, pelting sheets of rain onto the windshield, nearly hiding the supermarket from view. Thunder clacked and a finger of white light zig-zagged across the gray horizon.

"I guess I didn't need that shower after my Miami Vice routine."

Bree chuckled. "Maybe not." She peered up at the sky then leaned back against the seat. "We'd better wait until it passes. Shouldn't take too long. I'd rather not drive in that."

Clearly it was a wise decision, and he wasn't complaining about having to spend time in this cozy vehicle with her while the elements hurled their fury against the car windows. She leaned back and watched as the sky brightened with intermittent strobe lights. The clack of thunder and pounding of rain on the roof and against the windshield filled the small car with a rumble of noise.

She turned toward him. "Are you—are you enjoying your time here? I mean, aside from rescuing Herb and rescuing Beverly and who *knows* who you'll rescue tomorrow—"

Travis laughed. "Yeah, I am. It's nice to be forced, more or less, into something new." He shrugged one shoulder. "Not that I was really forced, of course."

"What's been your favorite thing so far?"

Meeting you. Travis swallowed and shifted his eyes from hers to the gray wash on the window just beyond her head. He took a breath. "I liked Roussillon and Aix. They're different from each other, but I'd go back."

What a banal substitute for what he'd wanted to say. He stared back into her smoky, blue eyes and seemed to get caught there. She didn't look away. Her lips parted slightly. Maybe she was waiting for him to continue speaking. Or maybe she was as drawn to that moment of silence as he was.

He lowered his voice and said slowly, softly, "When you travel you just never know what you'll discover."

She couldn't know, could she, what he really meant in those words? She could take it at face value. The way she stared back at him with round blue eyes, he doubted she had. She swallowed. Blinked.

He knew it was a mistake. He knew she'd recoil, put him in his place, but he was helpless to stop himself. Travis leaned forward to gently pull her small shoulders toward him. Cradling her there, he angled his head and covered her lips with his.

She didn't push him away. Instead, she leaned forward and curled both arms around his neck, pressing into him, welcoming him with open lips. Soft lips, as soft as he'd imagined, tasted of surrender as she responded to him with a hunger that surprised and humbled him. She fit perfectly into the circle of his arms, nestled against his body, as much as the bucket seats of the car would allow. A gentle sound escaped her throat, and a heady scent of honeysuckle swirled from her velvet skin, almost making him forget where he was.

He was hungry, too, couldn't hold it back. It had been building since that day he'd first met her with her dukes up. He'd seen past her protective shell and discovered her, one lovely layer at a time.

As they pulled apart her eyes clung to his and a warm flicker of hope kindled inside him.

She drew away and leaned back against the seat. "That did not just happen." She stared forward, breathing heavily. The rain had stopped and a few mounds of blue sky pushed through the clouds. "That did not happen," she said again.

Travis frowned. The warm flicker turned to ice. He'd never before heard those words from a woman he'd just kissed. He grumbled, "Then it was the nicest hallucination I've ever had."

She smiled then and shook her head with an uncomfortable chuckle. She started the car and backed up without another word.

Chapter Nine

A dancing golden glow from the tapered candles reflected back from the wine glasses sitting on the elegantly-arranged dining room table. From a pottery vase, fresh carnations, lilies, and daisies scented the room. Bree's gaze panned around the table to each person, all dressed up for the special dinner in honor of Michael and Beverly's fortieth anniversary.

The afternoon naps must have restored their energy. Loud, animated conversation rumbled steadily around the table throughout the evening, punctuated regularly by laughter. Only Travis seemed quieter than usual. Bree avoided his eyes but had noticed he'd put on a nice button-down shirt for the occasion. Every so often he rose from the table to open a new bottle of wine or help Lauren fill glasses. Helping out seemed to be a reflex for him. Just before dinner from where she'd sat in the living room during a rare break, she'd seen him lugging in a case of wine from the car.

Her face burned when she remembered that afternoon at the supermarket. Not from embarrassment but from desire and confusion. Lots of confusion. Why had it been so difficult to pull away from him? Well, that was easy. Because she didn't want to, not at all. The bossy voice inside her had eventually won out over what every fiber in her body had demanded.

She felt ashamed of what she'd said to him afterward, as if she hadn't secretly welcomed his touch, the greedy fulfillment of the attraction that had brewed all day, more than just that day, whenever he was near. He'd felt it too. His actions were proof that he felt something for her. She hadn't wanted to make light of that moment, but she hadn't known what else to say. She wasn't ready to have *that* conversation.

The moment he'd leaned over and pulled her into his arms, it seemed the most natural, logical thing in the world to kiss him. Almost inevitable. She'd been surprised by her own response, an eager craving for him she almost couldn't stop. She'd been prepared to scorn him, tolerate him for a week. Instead, since the day he'd walked into the villa, a powerful force had pulled her toward him.

But where could it possibly lead? In a few days they would go their separate ways and he'd forget all about her. She'd be left with yet another scar to overcome. No, it would be wiser to protect herself before her feelings got too deep.

She sighed and sought a distraction. "Do you need help, Lauren?" She looked up as Lauren cleared away the small plates used for the first course, *flan au saumon*—smoked salmon custard with basil. Lauren had gone for elegance for each course, including the appetizer.

"No, don't worry, Bree. I've hired Sandrine to help me tonight."

Sandrine was a young woman from the neighboring village who frequently helped them with big meals. She materialized from the kitchen, her dark eyes and hair contrasting with the starched whiteness of her long apron. She carried a large platter with steaming pieces of chicken covered in sauce. "*Je vous sers le coq au vin.*" She smiled around the table at everyone.

"*Coq au vin* is a specialty in France," Bree told them. "It means chicken with wine. It's one of those recipes that has probably hundreds of versions, depending on the family and the region."

"Is it cooked in red wine or white?" asked Sarah. She sniffed the air as the platter approached. "Looks and smells delicious."

"Red, which might surprise you." Lauren came in and placed a tureen of gravy in the center. "Usually a good burgundy, sometimes a pinot noir can be substituted with good results. That's why the meat is a bit dark and almost purple. It's been stained by the wine as it simmers. Be sure to get some mushrooms and bacon. The flavors all go well together. There are little pearl onions too."

The conversation died down as the chicken was served. "Lauren, you've outdone yourself." Beverly said. "This is wonderful!"

"Beverly, Michael, since it's your anniversary, why don't you tell us your secret for staying in love this long." Marcia leaned forward. Everyone fixed their eyes on Michael and Beverly.

"Well, you might not believe this," Beverly began, "but five years ago we were in marital counseling as a last effort before the divorce."

"Oh, my," Sarah said. "You'd never guess that."

"I think we'd gotten so wrapped up in our own individual lives, we forgot we were a couple. Each one running in his own direction. That's not what a marriage is."

Michael spoke up. "Then someone from our church recommended we attend a marriage retreat. We were two steps away from splitting up. I was already looking for another place to live." This drew ohhs from those around the table. "So, we thought, what can it hurt? We went to the retreat and it transformed our marriage. We kept going to the counselor after that, but instead of going just to say we'd tried, we did it because we really wanted to stay together."

"What a turnaround," said Doris. "You seem like newlyweds. Good thing you took the chance to go to that retreat."

"We'd spent so long together, knew each other so well, it didn't make sense to just separate without trying everything," said Beverly. "It's always better to work things through, I think, if at all possible."

"It's like a long-term investment," Michael said. "When the market dips, that's not the right time to sell your stocks. It's worth the fight sometimes, then you get past the bad times."

"You can tell he's an investment banker." Sarah murmured with a grin.

Bree shot a glance at Travis, who seemed lost in thought. She remembered him saying he'd been married. How long ago? She wondered how this conversation was affecting him, if he was even listening. He glanced up and stared at her before she could look away. Heat rose to her face. He reached for his wine glass and downed the last sip.

Her gaze roved to Lauren, who looked pretty in an aqua dress that matched her eyes. She was speaking to Marcia but her usual attentive manner was missing. She looked almost haunted. Bree couldn't shake the feeling that Lauren was erecting an invisible barrier between them for the first time since they'd met ten years earlier.

"You look really nice tonight, Bree." Alan startled her from her thoughts. "Your dress brings out the blue color of your eyes."

"Well, thank you, Alan. Everyone does look really good this evening, all fixed up." It was a bland comment, not likely to encourage him. He'd made a point to sit next to her, giving her an uncharacteristic gummy smile. And he'd complimented her instead of educating her about French history and culture, which heightened her wariness. The last thing she needed was one more relationship stressor in her life. She made a mental note to avoid Alan.

As she considered Travis, Alan, and Lauren, she wanted to shut her eyes and scream, *I'm leaning, Lord, but today it's not helping!*

Normally, she'd love an evening such as this one. The sound of crickets punctuated the still summer night just outside the tall French windows, which hung slightly ajar. Nearly everyone around the table was in high spirits. Even Herb laughed and grinned often throughout the evening. Bree tried to shuck off the tension and partially succeeded, until she glanced back at Travis and recalled the feeling of his lips moving against hers, his arms locked around her, only a few hours ago. She grew warm again at the thought.

After the main course, Lauren brought out two platters of cheeses and placed them at opposite ends of the dining room table. "In France people often eat a cheese course after the main course," she explained. "Typically, there will be several types and varied textures on a platter. Some sharp and firm, others soft and mild or fruity, for example." She pointed to each one on the platter. "This tube-shaped one here is goat cheese. It's common in this part of France, because the terrain is so suitable to raising goats."

While she spoke, Sandrine distributed small plates and additional baskets of baguette slices around the table. "This one here is a very special cheese of the region, called Banon. It is also a type of goat cheese but is wrapped with chestnut leaves. That gives the cheese a darker color than you'd expect."

"I don't think I had any expectations of goat cheese, to be perfectly honest," said Michael. Several around the table laughed. "I think I'll remove the chestnut leaves. Might get stuck in my teeth."

After the cheese course Bree rose to help Lauren clear the dishes. Lauren gently shooed her away. "I have Sandrine to help me." She placed a hand on Bree's arm. "Go and socialize. That's important."

Of course. What had she been thinking? As one of the trip leaders, Bree was *on* until she went to bed each night, whether she felt social or not. Always smiling, always making sure everyone else felt good. Usually that was natural for her and she enjoyed it. That moment, however, she just wanted to go back to her room and shut everyone out.

ೞ   ೞ   ೞ

He'd been very close to saying goodnight right after the main course, but that would have looked awkward. Then of course, when Travis tasted the Charlotte au Chocolat that Lauren had made for dessert, he didn't regret staying. He'd socialize a bit, then scoot out at the first opportunity.

Bree had distracted him for the better part of a week. He'd neglected all of the details of the Italy trip, aside from the basic itinerary, fully falling into the tourist role as if that were all he had to do. Now he needed to pull his mind back onto his next project. *Italy*, not Bree Sorenson.

She'd made herself clear, hadn't she? Well, not really. He'd been surprised by the fervor of her response to him, then stung by her cool reaction afterward. Bound by rules and prescribed behaviors, she'd probably berated herself for her passion. She'd disregarded the moment that he still savored in his memory. In *that*, she'd been very clear.

She seemed uneasy that evening, not just because of the kiss they'd shared. There was something else. He observed her glancing surreptitiously at Lauren every few minutes, then back at him. He could almost feel her torment. Well, he couldn't help her now. He wasn't the answer to her emotional debris. Not when he had so much of his own.

Still, he watched her throughout the evening. Couldn't really help himself. The blue scoop-neck dress she wore with the dropped waist, a colorful cord encircling her hips . . . blond tendrils ribboning down from a wispy bun . . . To avoid gazing at her took more strength than he had, but he was discreet. And still annoyed.

"Want some more cake, Travis?" His mother's gentle voice interrupted the dismal flow of his thoughts.

"No, thanks. It was great, but one piece is plenty."

"You know, Lauren said this crust is made of little cookies. The mousse inside softens them up and makes it into a crust."

"Hmm. That's interesting." He made a bored sound in his throat and his mother laughed.

"I'm glad you came. I know that I've sort of left you on your own a lot, and I didn't mean to after you made the effort to join me. Looks like you've made a friend, though."

His head jerked up and he narrowed his eyes at her. "What do you mean?"

She shrugged and gave him a wily smile. "Your mom might be old, but she isn't blind, not yet. I'm thinking my son has a young lady on his mind tonight."

Travis groaned and leaned back against the chair. Fortunately, his mom had lowered her voice. "Don't get your hopes up, Mom. I'm not sure it goes both ways." No point in denying it. His mother knew him too well. He just hadn't realized she'd noticed.

"I like her. I think she'd be good for you." She licked chocolate mousse from her fork.

"You seem to forget, it takes two."

120

"Ah, but who could say no to you?"

He sighed. She didn't know the latest. Four more days. He would stay friendly. It was the only thing to do. And focus on his next project.

It was a shame. He could see himself with Bree, with their shared passion for travel. He enjoyed talking to her, hearing her unpretentious opinions and ideas. He loved her commitment to her work, loved watching her connect with each guest, loved watching her oversee the details like a pro.

Lauren . . . she was another story. Despite brave efforts to appear otherwise, she was—he could only describe her as detached. A spark was missing. And Travis had a feeling, in view of Bree's concerns, that Lauren's behavior was a recent change, though Lauren had certainly pulled dinner off to perfection.

He sent a tight smile to his mother then pulled away from the table. Some of the guests had already gotten up and were chatting in the living room. Bree was doing her best to fend off the sudden attentions of Alan. Travis ambled into the kitchen, where Sandrine and Lauren were loading the stainless-steel dishwasher. "That was a great dinner, Lauren."

She smiled up at him. "Thanks. This is the part I love."

Travis leaned against the counter and crossed his arms. When Sandrine had returned to the dining room he lowered his voice and asked, "If this is what you love, why aren't you working in a four-star restaurant somewhere? Or catering big affairs like this dinner?"

Lauren paled and grew still. "I, uh— Seems you've been reading my mail. Or my mind."

Uh-oh. He'd stumbled onto something. "Really? Meaning you are planning a . . . transition?"

Lauren dropped her head. "*Please* don't say anything to Bree. At this point I'm only considering options. I've been sort of restless this year. This is our third year, and it was fun, but it wasn't the same for me as it was for Bree. This is her dream job, and, well, it turns out that it's not mine."

"I see. I won't say anything. It wouldn't be my place." He paused. "You likely know her well enough to guess that she's stressed out. She knows something is up with you."

Lauren nodded miserably. For the first time he noticed the unique hazel-green color of her eyes.

"Yes." Her voice was soft. "I feel like a heel treating her like this. I just can't act like everything's the same. And there are other things going on I can't talk about. Anyway, it's not the right time to discuss my involvement in Le Bon Voyage with her. We'll be going to the coast after this week to scout out some new locations, and that won't be the right time either. Besides, I'm not absolutely sure of anything yet—what I want to do, the timing, any of it. I need clarity on that before I say anything."

"Your secret is safe with me."

She faced him then and looked straight into his eyes. "You're a good man, Travis. Bree and I were both nervous about your being here, but you've been really nice and helpful. I apologize for any negative attitudes I had before. It was ignorance and assumption."

That reputation again. He offered a crooked smile. "I understand. And no need to apologize. I only knew about Bree's attitude, since she didn't hide it very well." They both laughed.

"Seems you've gotten over that." Lauren smirked.

Travis sighed and frowned. Had *everyone* noticed his attraction to Bree Sorenson? "Not sure what to say. I do like her." He shrugged. "But . . . yeah, just don't know what to say at this point." And he didn't. Not to Lauren, not to his mother, not to himself.

The summer night beckoned him. He slipped out of the front door, welcomed by the caress of the breeze and the sweet scents of honeysuckle and lavender. His sandals crunched on the driveway rocks as he walked toward the street. A short stroll would do him good, especially after the heavy meal.

A wave of tension rolled off of his shoulders. The evening had been, or would have been, very pleasant, if only his mind hadn't been so preoccupied. He pulled out his phone, a tool neglected over the last forty-eight hours, but then shoved it back into his pocket. It could wait, whatever it was.

There wasn't much out there, just a lot of space between villas, with mellow light spilling out of each window. The sight of it spoke of home and family, and a stir of melancholy cut his breath. The cavern opened a little wider and his spirits drooped. If Lexi had been willing to go with him to counseling, if only she'd considered them worth fighting for, as the Morrisons had done. But it was water under the bridge, wasn't it? Except that he'd been running away from the fallout ever since.

"Lord." He spoke into the silent blackness. Swallowed. "Am I just running, all the time running? Running from the past, or maybe even running from You? Would You—" His eyes stung and he blinked. His voice now emerged in a whisper. "Is it too late for me to come back? I mean, I know all the right answers about grace, about never falling out of Your hands. Maybe You're waiting for me, or maybe You got tired of waiting. I've gone a long way from You."

His only answer was the scrape of the pine needles rustling together as they reached to the sky, and a lonely moon, hazy and cold. In the past he'd considered himself a committed Christian, then a dedicated missionary and husband. Then an angry prodigal, finding comfort in the world's answers. After that, he wasn't quite sure. Maybe it was time to make a move, as his mother had encouraged him, one day at a time. Just let Him in. Start small but start. Travis only hoped God would be there to welcome him back, that the grace period hadn't expired.

Travis looked around and realized he'd wandered a long way from the villa. He turned around and retraced his steps back to the familiar stone house. As he pushed open the front door he heard voices still ringing out from in the living room. He slipped back toward his room and passed Alan who was headed the other direction.

Travis nodded to the man then heard him mumble, "Guess I don't have a chance, with you around. Mr. *Celebrity*."

Travis stopped and turned. "Pardon me?" He'd heard clearly but wanted to be sure.

Alan stopped and sent him a cool gaze. "Nothing. I'm wasting my time."

"Probably." Travis shrugged. "But, go for it."

Alan's brow lifted for an instant before he turned and walked away.

That was mean, Travis knew, and felt somewhat guilty on Bree's behalf. What had possessed him to give Alan any encouragement, further complicating Bree's delicate balancing act? And just after his sincere prayer for renewal? But Bree didn't seem to know what she wanted. Maybe he didn't either.

Finding the solace of his bedroom, he kicked off his sandals and leaned back on the bed. He really should check his phone now. He turned it on and thumbed across the screen. Several email and phone messages from the team that would be joining him at the Italian Lakes popped up, one from Toby, his camera guy, who was coming Saturday or Sunday. Seth, back in Portland, had editing questions on the Serbia piece. And Clay. Travis frowned. He didn't want to hear anything from his executive editor that night. But he was his boss, and Travis had ignored his email for too long.

The email was dated yesterday. He skimmed it. *Travis, trust you are enjoying France. Please give me a preliminary outline on the new program as soon as you can, so we can get a head start. You can pull out some advantages and disadvantages of small-group travel that hopefully you have observed already on your trip. Focus on what can happen in a small group that might not happen in a larger one, things like that. Of course, these small companies don't have the budget and network that larger ones do, so naturally they'll run into more difficulties. That'll make good viewing.*

At first, Travis was confused. Which new program? Italy? No, Clay had mentioned small group tours. His eyes widened with understanding. Clay was targeting Provence. A fist tightened inside his stomach. The guy wouldn't let up. Sure, there were things he could talk about. Elderly tourists with health problems, inadequate infrastructure, relational problems on small teams, and so on. But he'd never tell Clay about that. What would be the point? Besides, he wouldn't betray Bree, regardless of her current behavior toward him. He considered the risk of not playing ball with Clay, doing things his way.

Possibly his job.

Chapter Ten

Travis pushed the phone closer to his ear to hear his messages despite the yowl of monsoon-like wind that whipped his hair in every direction. A swirling cloud of leaves and debris filled the streets of Avignon. The whole Provence chapter had reached its expiration. It was really time to move on, even though Avignon would be, under other circumstances, an intriguing place to explore. He shook his head and tightened his jaw, then grabbed his sunglasses as they nearly whirled off the top of his head. No use, he couldn't hear a thing in his phone. To avoid getting knocked over he grabbed the nearest street sign.

"What's this thing called again?" he shouted to Lauren.

"The Mistral." Lauren ducked into a doorway where the wind's shriek was more subdued. "It's a strong wind that blows through Provence in multiples of three, six, or nine days, though depending on conditions, it can be just one. It's more common in winter and spring. But at least Avignon offers a lot of inside activities."

His eyebrows lifted. "No way to predict it, so you don't have your hair done that day?"

Lauren laughed. "Not that I'm aware. It may only last for today. And we'll be leaving soon, at least."

Travis followed her glance to where the other women in the group were holding their coiffures and clothing in place. Hiding inside was the best plan. The enormous yet empty Palace of the Popes had been an interesting distraction from the elements and, thanks to Alan, Travis now knew more about the Great Schism of the Medieval Papacy than he had ever wanted to know.

Sarah was missing from the group, having gotten a sour stomach. She'd claimed it was the special Provence goat cheese they'd eaten the previous evening, but it could have been anything, perhaps even a virus. She'd stayed behind to rest. Then Michael and Beverly, despite verbal claims of marital bliss the night before, had apparently butted heads, cause unknown, and remained at a frosty distance from one another all afternoon. Not a stellar day in the Provence tour annals, with gale-force winds added into the mix.

"I will add," said Lauren, "that after a Mistral, often the weather gets really gorgeous. So, we have that to look forward to."

"Unless the thing lasts nine days, in which case we'll all be too far away to enjoy it."

She nudged him with her elbow. "Pessimist."

He laughed. His eyes sought Bree and saw her falling against his mother, struggling like the others to keep her balance. Unlike the other women, she made no effort to keep her hair in order, but instead let her blond waves fly freely in the maelstrom. It was a stirring sight, fit for a movie, a vision he'd tuck in his mind to savor long after Bree Sorenson was only a memory. Yeah, he was suddenly a pessimist, for the first time in years.

He and Lauren approached the others as the gale calmed to a whimper.

"Is it my imagination, or is the wind dying down?" asked Beverly, knotting a scarf under her chin.

"I think it is. Should be better this evening." Bree's voice was reassuring, though the look on her face expressed some doubt. Bree the tour director, soothing everyone's expectations. She turned just in time to catch his gaze and offer a weak smile.

Once she turned away again, he heard his mother's lowered voice beside him. "Don't know what you did, Travis, but you're crazy to let her get away. Not that it's any of my business."

He turned to her. "Why do you think *I* did something?"

She gave him a half-smile and shrugged. "Because you're a good catch, so that's all I can think of."

He chuckled. "Thanks for the old-fashioned compliment. I guess if it's supposed to happen, it will. And you're right, it isn't any of your business."

Was he crazy to let Bree get away? Probably. She was clearly attracted to him, so there had to be something else blocking her, holding him off. Maybe she was afraid of her own feelings for him. He'd probably never find out the reason.

Lauren called everyone back to the van. Good, an early end to the excursion. It was the only thing to do, in view of the fact that they'd visited everything that was available inside. The elements howled and the trees swept their branches back and forth, as if scouring the brooding sky. Bree would probably welcome a break from Alan hanging around her like a puppy. Everyone looked bedraggled and tired and seemed more than willing to return to the villa an hour or two in advance.

He hadn't decided yet how he should respond to Clay, though words and phrases, both diplomatic and sarcastic, had churned in his mind all day. He needed to tell the man something, but he didn't want to think about it yet. He settled on a brief email, which he sent just before mounting the van. *Hi Clay. Regarding your thoughts, it's too early to say. I'll be honest, there isn't a lot to report here,*

and I'm still on vacation, but we can talk more about ideas when I
return from Italy.

Was that vague enough? More like a cop out. Travis hadn't given Clay anything specific to sink his teeth into, yet he hadn't come out and refused either. Clay wouldn't be placated by such an evasion for very long. No, things would come to a showdown sooner or later between Travis and his boss. He'd probably be wise to begin thinking of his options . . . apart from public television.

ભ્ર   ભ્ર   ભ્ર

Bree trudged into the house, wanting only to lie down. It had been a trying day, with one new challenge after another—Sarah's sickness, the Morrisons argument, the Mistral. Often throughout the day she'd reminded herself to lean on God while praying for it to become a reflex.

Standing in the foyer, she glanced at the digital time displayed on her phone. Still an hour and a half before dinner, enough for a short rest before rounding up everyone for the next activity, which would be, if the weather cooperated, a terrace-side barbeque. Normally on day six or seven of a tour she became utterly exhausted and had to find a means of rallying a second wind until the end.

The phone blinked. A new message, a second one from the agency that had rented them the villa. She'd forgotten to call them back the day before. She listened to the message they'd left and groaned, sinking onto a bench in the hallway. The owner had decided to sell the villa, so Le Bon Voyage wouldn't be able to rent it again for their next tour. Perfect. Bree and Lauren would have to visit more villas before leaving France, which hadn't been in the schedule. Another layer of stress to the day she'd already had.

After a heavy sigh, Bree relaxed her tense shoulders, stood and went into the kitchen. Lauren was putting away snacks and drinks from their day's excursion. "Do you think we'll still be able to cook outside tonight? The wind seems to have calmed down."

Lauren looked up from the large canvas tote bag she had emptied onto the counter. "We'll try. That's one great thing about the villa—the valley protects us from the wind."

Yes, a great thing they would lose once the owners sold. No sense in bringing that up now.

"Sarah seems to be feeling better now," Bree said. "I saw her in the *salle de séjour* just now, talking with the Grahams. The Morrisons seem to have gotten over their tiff as well."

"I'm so glad. The last thing we need is food problems and relational tensions."

Relational tensions . . . One thing that they had not escaped, even if Lauren had chosen to ignore it. Bree flung a glance around the room and in the adjoining hall. No one was within earshot. Her heart began to thump but she had to know. Softly she said, "Lauren, I've noticed that you seem, um, different on this trip, maybe distracted. I wondered if you were angry with me or upset about something else. Usually we're able to talk about things, but I have the impression that you've been avoiding me." There, it was out.

Lauren stilled. After several seconds she turned and made eye contact. "You're right." Her voice emerged just above a whisper. She paused for what seemed like an hour, but it was only several seconds. "I—I met someone and I've been really confused about it."

Bree's eyes widened. "Really? When? Who?"

Lauren pressed her lips together and drew her arms across her chest. Her voice was low. "I didn't want to say anything, because it isn't likely to go anywhere. Just a few days ago I was at the Marché in St. Rémy getting provisions for the meal. There was a man at the seafood stand haggling over the quality of some mussels. Turns out he owns a restaurant in Cavaillon. We started to talk and there was this strong connection between us in just a few minutes. It was strange—" she splayed her hands and shook her head, "—and very disorienting. It was almost like he was a kind of soul mate I was supposed to meet. We talked about food, about restaurants. The conversation went on for nearly an hour. His name is Jean-Pierre."

Despite her bewilderment, Bree's mind began darting. "Did you run into him again that day we were in Aix-en-Provence? When you were missing?"

Lauren shook her head. "He doesn't live around there, though he frequents that Marché, since it's larger than Cavaillon. I was on the phone with him, though. He really wanted to talk to me again, so I'd given him my phone number."

Bree bit her lip, silent. She should probably be glad for Lauren, but instead she couldn't stop the *what if* that leaped into her mind as she considered the fate of Le Bon Voyage. "I thought of all kinds of issues that could have preoccupied you, but that wasn't one of them." She pushed both hands into her windblown hair, yanking her fingers through a few knots, though her eyes never left Lauren's face. "Have you stayed in touch with Mark?"

"I talked to him yesterday, but I felt like I was putting on an act in order to sound normal. Through all of this I've gotten confused about my commitment to him."

Bree measured her words. "Maybe when we leave France and you see Mark again you'll get perspective one way or the other. You've dated him for two years, but this Jean-Pierre is someone you don't really know."

"That's true. I have some other things on my mind too, but I won't bother you with them now. We'll have a chance to evaluate everything once we're home."

Alarm rippled down Bree's spine. "Evaluate everything? You mean the trip?"

Lauren gave her a dismissive wave. "We'll talk more when we get home. We can evaluate the trip like we always do, of course, and talk about . . . other things too. I don't really want to go into it now. I can't think. I'm tired and confused."

Her final statement closed a door, as did her facial expression. Maybe she only wanted to suggest they revamp the schedule. She knew that Lauren considered it too full. So now Bree would have something *else* to worry about for at least ten more days until they reached U.S. soil. Just great.

"Is something going on between you and Travis?"

Lauren's sudden question startled Bree. Her cheeks grew hot.

A grin broke out on Lauren's face. "I knew it. There *is* something going on. Your face is turning pink. You must like him. I noticed you sitting by the pool with him the other night."

Bree looked away. "I do like him. It's a surprise, isn't it, after what we used to think?" She'd refrain from mentioning that he had kissed her. "I don't think he's a Christian, though."

"Hmm. I think his mother might be."

"Yes, she is."

"Are you sure he isn't? If his mother is, maybe he is too. Just because we thought he was a creep—and found out we were wrong— doesn't mean he isn't a believer. Or that he's not open."

Bree squirmed. "Maybe you're right. But he probably has a girl in every country of Europe. Maybe I'm just his Provence fling."

"Think so?" Lauren laughed. "Well, why don't you ask him?"

"Besides that, it doesn't seem appropriate for me to strike up a romantic relationship with a guest. These are our clients. We provide a service to them. Just doesn't seem—" Bree searched for her words, but she'd made her point. Even if she wasn't completely convinced.

"Those are only semi-valid reasons. Despite your aversion to risk, Bree, don't close the door before being sure. *If* you like him, that is."

Bree looked up at her. It was more urgent to discuss Lauren's plans than Bree's momentary distraction with Travis. "What about Jean-Pierre? What'll you do?"

"I don't know. I'd like to see him again, to find out if there's any point keeping in touch. And I don't know what he believes."

Bree leaned against the counter and crossed her arms. Though the conversation had stirred up potential questions and problems, it had also brought a wave of comfort, since they were no longer maintaining a cordial surface relationship. But what could Lauren want to *evaluate*?

The way Lauren encouraged her toward Travis surprised her. A wave of guilt reminded Bree that she had again been rude to him by avoiding him.

On impulse Bree said, "Let me know if you need to spend an afternoon with Jean-Pierre, you know, to have clarity. I'll try to hold things together while you're gone."

Lauren gave her a grateful smile. "Bree, you're sweet. I will." She leaned forward and enfolded Bree in a hug, gripping her tightly for several seconds.

Bree's eyes stung. She had her friend back.

Fortunately, the wind had died down sufficiently to cook dinner on the barbeque grill. Tiny colored candle holders reflected dancing firelight on the patio tables. The sun had begun to melt mauve streaks across the sky, and pinpoints of starlight pierced shyly through.

The men were recruited to prepare the barbeques and supervise the cooking, which they all seemed to enjoy and consider their elite responsibility and privilege. Loud laughter and joking threaded through the meal preparation. Even Travis, who'd seemed detached for much of the day, joined the jovial banter.

When the meat was cooked, the men proudly presented the results of their labors— marinated kabobs of lamb, shrimp, and steak with chunks of onions, mushrooms, and tomatoes—on multi-colored platters. These were served at the small patio tables along with side dishes and salads Lauren had prepared that afternoon. Sarah and the Morrisons seemed back to normal and in good spirits, joining in the laughter and conversation that circled the terrace throughout the evening.

After Lauren had cleared away the dessert dishes, Sarah said, "I saw a guitar in the living room. Does anyone know how to play it?"

"Michael does. He plays at holidays and sometimes at church."

"I played the flute in junior high school a hundred years ago, but that's about it." Doris grinned.

"I used to play the—the—what's that little instrument called?" Herb leaned toward Doris.

"A harmonica."

He smiled fondly at a distant memory. "Har-monica." Doris squeezed his arm.

Beverly brought the guitar out to the terrace. For the next hour they tried various pop songs, searching for one that most of them would know. A few of the older songs, including some classics from musicals and country western hits, got most of them singing. The others listened and clapped along while a gentle flame leaped and glowed in the nearby fire pit.

Bree helped Lauren finish the dishes. A warm contentment filled her. Lauren seemed nearly back to normal, and their friendship appeared restored. Anything else they needed to discuss could wait. How bad could it be? They'd been friends for a decade. She'd handle it—she'd *lean*—with God's help—whatever it was. Even Jean-Pierre.

ભ   ભ   ભ

It had been a long time. Travis touched the cool, smooth wood on the curved side of the guitar and formed a chord on its neck with his left hand. With his other hand he strummed, and it all came back, a fragment at a time, that one song they used to sing in Brno almost every Sunday in the little church service. Another of their English students, Ludvik, would man the other guitar, and the two instruments nearly overwhelmed the miniscule meeting room and small number of participants. Lexi would smile at him across the room from where she sat intently listening as Darina translated the meeting into English. Neither of them ever mastered Czech. They weren't there long enough.

He never knew at what point he began losing her. At the time it had seemed sudden, but maybe she'd been silently telling him for months. He hadn't wanted to listen or hadn't been capable. They'd been so focused back then. Or he'd been the one with tunnel vision, as his marriage slid out of control, along with his spiritual life and pretty much everything else.

He looked up as Bree softly approached, somehow expecting her. "Hi." He leaned the guitar against a nearby lawn chair, glad for such a lovely excuse to escape the morbid flow of his thoughts. He was pleased she was no longer avoiding him.

135

She sat on the lawn chair next to him. She'd changed into jeans and a mid-sleeve pale blue cotton sweater. "Please don't stop on my account." At his shrug she added, "What language was that you were singing?"

"Czech. I spent some time in the Czech Republic after college. I picked up some of the language, but over the years it hasn't stuck." He tossed her a subdued grin. "It's not an easy language."

"I wouldn't think so." She smiled and they both fell silent.

He ached to discuss what had happened between them the day before, to assure her he was not just playing around with her, but he didn't know how to begin. He could just launch in with, "about *yesterday—*" but he lacked the assurance that it was the right timing, the best words. Diving head-first into the issue that sat between them like a boulder might just send her running. He wasn't ready to lose her company again.

"Have you been studying any Italian in preparation for your trip next week?" Her voice was sweet and light.

"How'd you know? *I piatti sono in cucina.*" He grinned at her. It was about the only thing he could say that sounded halfway intelligent. That was, of course, unless, one actually knew Italian.

"What does that mean?"

"The dishes are in the kitchen." They both laughed and his insides felt light, almost joyful.

"That's really profound," she said gravely, then smiled. "Think that will help you to eat while you're over there?"

"Not unless I do dishes to pay for my meal. I have trouble with the words birthday and breakfast. They're similar in Italian, and I keep confusing them."

"Happy breakfast to you, happy breakfast to you," Bree sang, and they both laughed again. "You might actually get some breakfast if you go into a trattoria and sing that."

136

Her eyes, darkened by the falling sunlight, held his. Her smile too, was fixed, then it fell slightly. It was as though she also wanted to say something, maybe talk about their relationship, but she remained silent. What a perfect moment, a perfect setting to kiss her, but he wouldn't do that again without an invitation.

"Were you—?" she paused, looking uncomfortable. "Were you young when you got married?"

He was surprised by her question, especially since he'd just been thinking about Lexi. He leaned back against the lawn chair. "I got married just out of college. College romance, pretty classic. We were together about seven years and—my wife was unfaithful. Left."

"I'm sorry."

He shrugged. "Me too. Or at least I was then. Makes you kind of revise your dreams and expectations."

"I'm sorry to bring it up. I thought of it when the Morrisons were talking yesterday about their marriage renewal."

"It's not a problem anymore. Life just does those things, doesn't it? Other people are free agents. They can start out one way but not stay the way they were when you met."

He looked at her intently. It occurred to him that she could fear the uncertainties another person could bring. Was that what held her back? Fear? He had a fair amount of that too. "Would you say that sometimes you fear that kind of risk in a relationship?" He felt like he was tip toeing across a fragile bridge. Would she feel pressure and clam up, or might she instead speak openly of her hesitancy about him, about them?

If she was shocked by the probing intimacy of his question, she hid it. "I think I'm afraid of every kind of risk." She uttered a hollow chuckle.

Something inside him squeezed, causing pain in a deep, hidden hollow. He waited.

"But I'm better than I used to be." Then she looked squarely at him with a firm set to her chin and a small challenge in her eyes, as if to say, *Here it is. Are you ready?* "My father was mentally ill and prone to—" She stopped. Swallowed. "Prone to violent outbursts."

Travis winced. He was afraid it had been something traumatic. His voice emerged in a ragged whisper. "He hurt you?"

She nodded. "My childhood was a kind of long, scary nightmare. But my mom tried to protect me. She had him arrested a couple of times, hospitalized once. He'd come back a changed man, a model father, for a few weeks. Then it would all start again. Finally, she sent me away to a summer camp in Canada. I was nine. The day she picked me up at the end of the camp, she told me we'd be going back to a different house in another city. I remember being confused. I asked her if I'd see my room again, and my friends. I didn't even ask about my father." She gave him a small, sad smile. "I never saw my father again."

Travis let out a long breath and squeezed his eyes shut against the mental image of a little, blond girl with large blue eyes staring in fear at the man who was supposed to love and protect her. How could anyone—?

"Please don't feel sorry for me. I've gotten strong through it all. In fact, my time in Canada was the beginning of my love for travel." Her voice held an edge. A survivor's edge.

"It's not pity. I see what a strong woman you are, Bree. Strong, but still so full of warmth and love for other people. But back then— you deserved to be loved. You still do." It was on the tip of his tongue. *I love you, Bree.*

Wait, was that true? Could he really have fallen in love with Bree Sorenson in just a matter of days? Was that even *possible*? For the last five years he'd protected his heart, meticulously maintained the layers of steel beneath his affable smile. Was it possible she could break through it so easily, this petite, determined woman? If it wasn't, then what else could explain his burgeoning need to be *with* her, to hear her thoughts and her story, to touch her, to protect her, to plan a future—

He longed to tell her. But he kept silent. She wouldn't welcome such news, which was news to him as well.

She grinned suddenly and swatted his arm. "Let's not get all morbid, okay? We're both survivors. We're okay because God looks out for us."

Her words surprised and warmed him. Could he one day share some of his own story with her? He'd have to tell her the whole tangled thing, how he'd abandoned his faith for a while, how he'd become a man of the world. He wasn't ready to give her or anyone else the gory details, not until he pulled himself together and was fully back on God's side.

Assuming, of course, that God would even fully take him back.

Chapter Eleven

"It's hard to think about going home in just a couple of days." Beverly cast a wistful smile toward Bree then looked back across the multicolored awnings covering two blocks of fruit and vegetable stands at the Lourmarin open market. She picked up a cantaloupe and sniffed it.

"Then, don't think about it, dear." Michael squeezed her with one arm around her shoulders. "We'll get there when we get there. Enjoy right now. Look, there's the flower stand you were looking for earlier."

She placed the melon back. "What I mean is, it's been such a treat to be in beautiful places, and so far outside of our normal environment, with the strip malls and subdivisions. Being here is almost like being in another world."

Bree shifted her woven basket full of produce to her other elbow. "That's why I love travel, and why I enjoy helping other people to love it too."

"It's a great career to have," Beverly said. "And you and Lauren have done an excellent job putting everything together for us. It'll be such a special memory."

Gratitude flooded Bree's mind, and her throat felt full of emotion. That week they'd had their share of unexpected bumps, but Beverly hadn't focused on them. Moments like this almost made it worth all of the endless preparation and stress. "Thanks, Beverly. That means a lot."

"I second that, Bree." Marcia laid a hand on Bree's arm and squeezed lightly.

"Maybe in the future," Alan said, "you girls could schedule more museums and history tours in churches. There's so much history in the area. That would be a great way to soak it up. In fact, before Provence belonged to France it was a sort of separate kingdom with lords who were like regional rulers. It's quite interesting. Someone should do a tour just on that topic."

Bree bristled but hid her reaction behind a tight smile. "It *is* interesting. The rich historical background adds so much depth to everything we see. But our goal for this trip was to provide an *overview* of Provence. If you'd enjoy a more historical emphasis, there are special tours that focus on that. I know that up in the Loire Valley, for example, there are thematic tours involving the castles and the kings who lived in them, along with the surrounding history."

"You could take a group of your students there, couldn't you, Alan?" Marcia fingered her straw tote bag.

"Then the school would pay for your trip, because you'd be chaperoning the students," suggested Michael.

Bree felt impatient and restless with the conversation and wished she could wander off by herself. She'd had almost no time alone for a week, and she wasn't likely to get any that day either. Lauren was meeting Jean-Pierre that morning while Bree went to the village of Lourmarin with those who wished to go. Bree couldn't help but wonder how the meeting was going, if Lauren felt any confirmation in that relationship, enough to jeopardize her long-term commitment to Mark . . . and her commitment to Le Bon Voyage and to Bree herself.

Only Marcia, Alan, the Morrisons, and Herb had come with her, and they wandered at an unhurried pace along the stalls and stands of the Marché, leafing through old books and kitchen gadgets and admiring a kaleidoscope of color at the flower stands and among the fruits and vegetables.

Bree noticed some fatigue building among the older travelers in the group. As for Travis, maybe he was simply tired of Provence and antsy to move on to his next adventure. At the thought of his departure, a wave of melancholy swept through her. Like a good friend, he seemed to truly understand her, compassionately, without judgment. Of course, his effect on her went miles beyond mere friendship. Last evening when they'd talked by the pool, he didn't volunteer any clues about his spiritual life, even after she'd suggested that God had looked out for them. Maybe there was nothing to tell.

"It seems that Albert Camus, the existential writer, lived in this town. He is buried here."

Bree returned a bland smile to Alan and didn't respond. She, too, was simply tired.

"I had to read one of his books in the eleventh grade," Michael said. "It was kind of depressing."

The curved, cobbled streets teemed with tourists, seeming to multiply with the passing minutes. Bree was thankful that Herb had joined them, even though Travis wasn't there to keep an eye on him. He seemed more sociable, making observations in short, simple phrases. She frequently asked him specific questions and had been delighted to hear him respond in a lucid and articulate way, even with simplified vocabulary.

"Hey, Herb, what do you think of this little pitcher? Do you like things like this?" Bree held up a red pottery pitcher when they'd stopped in front of a stand of Provence knick-knacks. Painted on the side was the word "Lourmarin" between small paintings of what looked like house flies or birds.

He took the ceramic pitcher and examined it on each side, then looked back at her with a sober expression. "No, I don't. It seems— it seems—" He paused as if probing his memory for the right word, then leveled a clear gaze back to her. "Tacky. That's the word. Some things here are very pretty, but not this one."

She grinned back at him. "I think so, too. But if you found a nice one that you like, would you want to take one home?"

He nodded. "Yes, I think so. We can serve wine from it, like they do here."

"That's a great idea. If you find one, it will always remind you of this trip."

He smiled and placed the pitcher back on the shelf.

As they walked she said, "You're talking more now than you did when you first got here. Is that because you feel more comfortable with everyone, since you've gotten to know them better?"

"Partly. Also, Doris often answers for me, so I just let her." He shrugged.

Bree laughed. "Oh, so you just sit back and let her do the communicating for you, eh? Maybe you should let her know that you still want to talk, like you did before."

"Well, maybe not quite as much as before. I still forget a lot. But she means well. She wants to be helpful." He paused. His lined face had become sober. "And I *am* getting worse."

He fell silent as they neared a different souvenir shop. He wandered toward a shelf filled with souvenirs and pottery and found another small pitcher. He held it up for her to see. "Here's one I like. I'll get this one." Before she could respond, he'd disappeared into the store to make his purchase.

Travis frequently invaded her thoughts, and though she sought to distract herself, the image of his handsome face, shaded in the twilight, rose up in her memory. She could see the clear blue of his eyes, surrounded by tiny laugh lines as he regarded her with a half-smile.

"You seem pensive today, Bree." She looked up and Marcia stood beside her, gentle eyes hooded with concern.

Just thinking about your son. Bree said, "I'm just a bit tired."

"It's a lot to organize and carry off. You and Lauren don't get to just relax and stroll around like we do. You have to plan, keep a watch over your people, maybe prepare other things in advance. I can imagine you might be exhausted."

Bree laughed. "You could say that. I love doing this, but yes, I get tired by the end of the week. I wouldn't trade it for anything, though." She hoped she was telling the truth and prayed she wouldn't be tested on that point.

"Do you have someone special waiting for you back home?" Marcia's question surprised Bree. "Sorry, maybe that's too personal. I just feel like I know you so well now, I permit myself to ask."

"Actually, I don't. Maybe it's because I'm too busy, or maybe I just haven't found the right person."

"What kind of person are you looking for?"

Bree imagined Travis, then forced her mind back to Marcia's question. "It would be nice to meet someone who loves to travel, of course." Funny how comfortable she was with Marcia. They seemed to have already developed a kind of kinship. "Someone kind and sensitive, but adventurous too. And of course, someone who shares my faith."

Marcia lifted her brows for a second, but then she smiled. "That's important, as is having similar values."

"Though it's no guarantee that someone I'd meet in church would be a good man. My last relationship showed me that. He was a jerk, but I'd met him in the church singles group." Though she wanted a man who shared the same beliefs, she had back then believed that every Christian man would be kind, treating her with gentleness and respect. She'd been shattered when she learned that even with a man who professed faith, there were no guarantees.

Bree fought the temptation to ask Marcia where Travis stood on spiritual matters. To come right out and ask would reveal far too much to his mother, and Marcia might not consider it her place to respond. The fact that Bree had even thought about it heated up her cheeks. She looked down at a handmade purse on a craft stand, hoping Marcia didn't notice. If she did, she'd likely read Bree's mind. At any rate, he'd as much as stated his position himself last night by the pool when he'd said nothing.

After a visit to the Renaissance Era Château de Lourmarin, nicknamed Villa Medici, Bree drove the group back to the villa. It was still early afternoon, enough time to help Lauren with some of her dinner tasks, and possibly take a swim. That might help perk up her drooping emotions.

Although it was too early, she'd get a few things in the kitchen prepared in advance so that Lauren could be organized for the meal, even if she had mentioned the possibility of going out instead. It might depend on how her day went. At least by doing small tasks to lighten Lauren's responsibilities, Bree could continue the positive trend in their relationship.

She hoisted her basket onto the kitchen counter and emptied it of the vegetables she'd bought at the Marché. She glanced at her watch and again wondered how things were going with Jean-Pierre. She'd have expected Lauren back before now.

No point thinking about it. She chided herself and shook her head, a grimace bending her lips. *Lord, let your will be done in Lauren's life.* She was determined to let go. If it killed her, she would learn to lean.

A scrap of paper lay on the counter tucked under a salt shaker. It was a to-do list that Lauren had left for herself. Bree skimmed the list. Lauren would need several cans and jars from the pantry and would probably be pleased if they were on the counter waiting for her when she returned.

Bree approached the pantry and pushed the door open. Along each wall were rows of thin cedar shelves lined with cans of tomatoes and vegetables, bottles of olive oils, vinegars, and jars of preserves and mustards. She stepped into the narrow room, which closed in like a small box around her. Her insides seized up as if a hand were squeezing her and a cold sweat beaded on her back. She breathed deeply through her mouth, then blew out puffs of air like her childhood counselor had taught her. She reached out to one of the shelves just above her head and took a can of olives. It wouldn't take long. She'd be okay.

"Are you alright, Bree? You look like you've seen a ghost." Travis filled the doorway but instead of feeling trapped, her panic drained away.

She gave him a weak smile. "I—I don't do well in closed-in places. My dad used to lock me in a closet when I was little, so they still make me uncomfortable."

Travis just shook his head with tightened lips, then his expression softened as he caught her gaze. "Understandable that you'd feel that way." He stepped aside to lean against the doorjamb, leaving the entrance unobstructed. "I missed you all today, but it was nice to rest and catch up on a few things." He glanced up the wall. "Can I do anything for you in here? You can come out of there and just tell me what you need, if that will make you feel better. Do you need me to get something down from the higher shelves?"

Bree nodded. "I feel better. And yes, thanks. Usually there's a step-ladder behind the door, but I'm not sure where Lauren put it." She looked down at the list. "Could you please get me the canned tomatoes up there on top?" She pointed, peering up several shelves. "Maybe four cans of them. Also, the capers, and uh . . ." She returned her gaze to the list Lauren had left. "Maybe some olives, dried shallots . . . look for a bottle there labeled *échalotes*. I don't know how she's fixed for olive oil, so better get some of that down too."

One by one he pulled down the items requested, reaching his long arms to almost the highest shelves, and placed them lower where she could reach them.

"Thank you."

He faced her, still in front of the doorway. "Feeling better?" His voice was gentle and his eyes cradled hers.

She nodded and managed a smile.

"No wonder you're afraid of being helpless. That was how you felt in that closet as a little girl."

She moistened her lips, which suddenly seemed dry. "Sometimes I waited for an hour before he'd either let me out or my mom would find me. That was his idea of discipline. Discipline for what, I never really knew. Punishment for being a kid, I guess. Like I said yesterday, he wasn't well."

Travis gave her a slow nod. "You also said through those kinds of experiences, you grew stronger."

"But not taller, unfortunately." She forced a chuckle and glanced again at the top shelf, hoping to lighten the moment.

"That's what guys like me are for. To help when it's needed and cheer you on when it's not." He looked back at her in the dim light of the small room, a smile hovering on his lips.

She returned a muted smile as silence fell between them. When he didn't speak, she knew she should. She ought to explain why she'd held him at arm's length for most of the trip, despite her habit of seeking him out at other times. She should tell him why she couldn't go forward in a relationship with him. Instead, she found that she'd stepped toward him just a couple of inches.

That was all it took for him to move forward and clasp her head in his hands. He covered her lips, kissing her like a starving man finding sustenance. She melted into him, greeting him with softened lips, unable to do anything but encircle his neck with her arms and mold her body to his, matching his ardor with her own. *She shouldn't, she shouldn't.*

She couldn't help herself. His height above her, his body enclosing her in his . . . she felt protected, desired. Found.

She reached up and tangled her fingers through his long curls, pulling him back toward her, needing him. *She shouldn't . . .*

A final inward warning caused her, against every filament in her soul, to pull gently away from him. They stared at each other and she saw the raw longing on his face.

"Bree . . ."

She shook her head slightly. "Travis," she said, her voice broken. "I *really* like you. More than I thought I would. You've surprised me in so many ways since you came. But, well, here's the thing—" Deep inside her something was ripping, something she'd never be able to repair. But it was the right thing, wasn't it? "I don't know how to say this without sounding—" She stopped. Shut her eyes for a moment.

He waited, his face closing.

"I'm not at all a—a holy person," she said. "But I am a person of faith, a follower of Jesus. A long time ago I made myself a promise that if I date someone, he would share the same faith. That's important to me. I like you, but if we don't share this important thing . . ." she shook her head again, even as her eyes began to burn. "I'm afraid it wouldn't work. Although . . . we could still be friends."

He stared silently, his lips partly open as if he wanted to respond. Finally, he gave a small shrug and softly said, "That's too bad, Bree. I was just falling in love with you." He turned and left her alone in the pantry.

She watched his back as he went through the kitchen doorway until his footsteps faded. She cradled her arms in misery, a sudden chill clinging to her skin. Several tears escaped, burning a trail down her cheeks. Into the silence she whispered, "Me too."

C঩ C঩ C঩

Travis avoided the pool area, since Doris and Sarah were swimming, so he began walking. He needed to be alone. His conversation with Bree tasted as sour in his mouth as her kisses had been sweet.

Why hadn't he told her? With just a few words he could have won her. Instead, he felt pummeled and bruised inside. He wanted to throw something, break something. But he couldn't stoop so low. Yes, he had faith, but not the kind she was looking for. She wanted faith that was real, deeply rooted, not in recovery and on life support. She deserved a man she could look up to, trust with her heart *and* spirit. He wasn't sure he was either.

He finally found a bus stop bench to sit on, away from his fellow tourists, from any human contact. A good place to brood. And hurt. To remember how she'd pushed him away.

What else could she have done? He'd given her nothing but the self-sufficient identity he projected. She may have seen other qualities in him, but not a living reliance on God. He'd given up on that so many years ago, it was almost beyond his memory.

Yet, it wasn't. Of course, he remembered those days, sometimes with breathtaking and agonizing clarity. As King David had proclaimed in a Psalm, Travis used to lead the procession to the house of the Lord. Figuratively, at least. And now? The best Travis could do was stop being mad at Him, hoping one day to come back, but giving small, languid efforts when it was convenient. If Bree was a woman of faith, she wouldn't accept him as he was, even with the small but tenacious level of belief he still had.

He'd burned his bridges with Bree Sorenson long before he'd met her.

Travis pulled to his feet and stormed back to the villa. Maybe the pool was empty and he could do laps until his heart didn't hurt as much. Bree. He was pretty sure that he loved her, but—no use thinking of it now. He opened the door and slipped inside.

"What's *that* face about?"

He hadn't seen his mother standing in the foyer as he entered. She surveyed him with crossed arms. Her tone of voice and words reminded him of his adolescence.

"Nothing. It's just time for me to leave Provence."

"Hmm. Someone is feeling sorry for himself, I'm guessing."

He looked down at her and smirked. "How'd you know?"

Turning, he was about to stalk off to his room when he heard her voice again behind him. "Maybe I just need to lock you two in the same room until you work it out."

He snorted a sardonic laugh. At one time he'd have loved that idea. Now he just wanted to get as far away as possible.

Chapter Twelve

The guests were winding down, shifting their focus. Bree could recognize the signs, there under a bright yellow canvas awning on a restaurant terrace in St. Rémy. Soft evening breezes rocked the string of colored lanterns overhead.

At the end of each trip she'd start to hear small references to home . . . some task that had to be done soon after arriving, a phone call to the kids or grandkids, an appointment that needed to be made. Thoughts were shifting away from France, from this temporary sojourn in a far-away, exotic place, and back to the comfortable, the known, the habitual.

"How long a flight is it for you to go home?" Sarah asked Doris.

"Oh, I think it took us about nine hours. The return may be longer because of a longer layover in Chicago. I don't remember. Herb probably won't remember either." She gestured at the empty chair, since Herb had left to use the restroom.

"Let's not talk about this yet," Beverly pleaded. "We still have more than twenty-four hours before we have to leave paradise."

Bree glanced across the café table at Lauren. Her face was impassive, telling Bree nothing of her hours with Jean-Pierre, or her conclusions about their relationship. She'd been gone most of the day and had come back too late for them to talk about it. Whatever had happened that day, Lauren didn't seem ready to discuss it, so Bree would have to stretch her patience ever thinner.

The waiter appeared at the table. "*Est-ce que je vous débarasse?*"

Bree asked around her table, "Everyone finished?" Then she turned back to the waiter. "*Oui, s'il vous plaît.*"

He cleared their plates away. Seconds later he returned and asked again, "*Du café, du dessert?*"

"Oui." Sarah smiled and turned to those at her table. "See, I learned some French this week." Everyone laughed, then gave their dessert orders, either in chopped-up French or English.

They'd just finished their meal under a temperate dusk. Street lamps had begun to glow in the darkness and spread honeyed orbs of light on the pavement below. St. Rémy was the closest town to the villa, where they'd come their second day in Provence, the first day that Bree had talked with Travis like a friend.

A pang hit her near her ribs, cutting her breath. He'd be gone in just two days. He'd sat down for dinner at a different table, probably to stay far away from her. She thought again about his words, *I was just falling in love with you.* Was it a line? Was he truly in love with her? She'd never find out now. She'd also begun falling in love with him the day they walked around St. Rémy together. It didn't matter now. The incident in the pantry and the bitter way it ended had cramped inside her in an ongoing ache. Even her appetite was nearly absent. Wasn't she doing the right thing? Why did it hurt so badly?

She watched him discreetly across the terrace. He interacted with other guests less than usual, letting his mother and the others at his table banter, laugh, and chat while he seemed to half-listen, distracted. After the waiter took their dessert orders, he excused himself and said he'd see them all later. Of all the people present, he likely had the most travel street-smarts to find his way back to the villa.

As she finished licking *mousse au chocolat* off of her spoon, Bree heard Doris say, "Herb is taking an awful long time in the restroom. Could one of the men go check on him for me?"

Bree stilled. She hadn't seen Herb in at least thirty minutes. Doris's face grew taut.

"I'll go check." Alan slid his chair back and went inside the restaurant. Several seconds later he came back out, his face grim. "He's not there. Maybe he went for a walk."

"Oh, Herb!" Doris wailed. "Not again!"

Lauren leaped up and put her hands on Doris's shoulders. "Shhh, Doris. It'll be okay. We'll find him. Maybe he just went for a stroll. It's a nice evening."

"I'll go." Bree rose from her place. "Doris, can I have that photo again?"

Doris hiccupped a sob. She looked older under the terrace lamps. Folds of skin now filled with tears hung around her eyes. She fished the photo from her purse and handed it to Bree. Some of the other diners in the restaurant were looking toward their table, likely startled by the commotion.

Herb had seemed nearly normal that afternoon, but by Doris's and his own admission, he was getting worse. And still subject to gaps of memory big enough to fall into and get lost.

"I'll check inside first then go to nearby stores and streets." Bree pressed an outer layer of calm over the rising panic that filled her chest as she darted toward the front door and slipped inside. She scanned the room, filled with few diners, since most of them had gravitated to the terrace and the balmy summer night. No Herb. Tears pricked her eyes. Not now, not on the next-to-last day of the trip. She could sense what Doris was dreading, not only at that moment but in the months and years to come.

Don't panic. Focus. And lean. The first day she practiced leaning instead of worrying, it had helped, but then she'd forgotten, slipping into the old control and stress mode. If there was any time to lean, it was now—Herb, Travis, Lauren. And her whole future. "Please, Lord." Her quiet prayer emerged through gritted teeth.

"Have you seen this man this evening?" she asked the bartender, holding up the photo. Maybe Herb was still inside somewhere.

"I saw him go to *les toilettes* then outside again." The man jerked his head toward the door.

"*Merci.*" Bree pushed through the door out into the twilight. A few shops were still open for tourists, but many were already dark, metal curtains pulled down in front of the plate glass display windows. She entered one of the boutiques that remained open and repeated her question. Shop after shop, restaurant after restaurant, heads shook. Her hopes began to sag. They *had* to find him. What if they couldn't find him before the day of their departure? What if they didn't find him at all?

She wished Travis were there. His presence calmed her, and he had no trouble leaping into action. But she must have deeply offended him. Regret scraped inside her, leaving a raw ache behind.

Defeated, she sat on the edge of a circular stone fountain, unsure of what else to do. She buried her head in her hands as the helplessness crushed upon her like an avalanche of boulders. "Please, God, I need You. Please lead me to Herb. You know where he is."

Several hot tears squeezed out of clenched eyes, but most were blocked behind what felt like a fist in her throat. She breathed deeply, hoping the temperate night air would allay her panic. The gentle splashing of water whispered in soothing voices. She looked over her shoulder and realized she was at the Nostradamus fountain, the place where she'd sat with Travis earlier that week. It seemed so long ago, instead of only a few days. "And please give me peace about Travis," she added. "Because I miss him already."

Bree looked down glumly at her folded hands, pushing Travis from her thoughts and trying to think of places she hadn't yet tried to find Herb. How could he have just vanished? The crowds had thinned and many stores were closed, so it should have been easier to see him. A faraway shout and some laughter cut through the quiet evening. She decided to follow the sound. She'd tried about everything else.

She continued to hear bursts of sound—laughter, loud masculine conversation—as if coming from a bar. She followed the sound as it grew louder, then she saw its source, a small corner pub with a tattered red awning bearing the words, "*Le Petit Chien Blanc*". A pair of neon beer signs glowed in the dusk, and in the doorway lay what had to be the bar's namesake, a small white terrier. The dog looked up and blinked as Bree approached the threshold, then lowered its head to continue napping. She glanced inside. A row of men sat at the bar talking loudly and guffawing together. She could only imagine the catcalls and comments that would shower down on her as soon as she entered the pub, but she had to find Herb.

Bree squared her shoulders, stepped over the dog, and marched into the bar, photo in hand. Several men were perched on stools along a laminated wood counter, most nursing beers. Behind her a pinball machine made slapping noises and pings, but she kept her eyes ahead of her.

Before she could roll out the phrase she'd prepared, she saw him. Herb sat at the end of the bar surrounded by four or five men of different ages, all grinning or laughing. As she approached, she heard them trying to speak in English.

Herb said loudly, "I live in France."

The man sitting to his left gave a wide, toothy grin and repeated, "I leeve een Frahnce." His buddies laughed and slapped him on the back, and the others tried the phrase then lapsed back to French. An extended wave of laughter followed. Then Herb said another phrase, which the men all repeated between laughter and swigs of beer.

Bree couldn't stifle a smile as she approached the group. "There you are, Herb." She laid a hand on his arm. "I've been looking for you."

His eyes met hers and lit up as a grin spread across his face. "Hello, Bree. These are my new friends. This is Hervé, this is Jean-Christophe, and that's Claude. And Patrick and um . . . yes, and Frédéric. They're learning English." He pointed to each man, who nodded a greeting.

"I see that. Doris is worried about you." She turned to the men and, with a smile, told them in French, "I have to kidnap your English teacher now. I'm sorry!"

She took his arm and asked, "Are you ready, Herb? Say goodbye to your friends."

The men protested in good-natured banter. He went around and shook hands with everyone in the bar. "Au revoir," he called to them, and they responded, "Au revoir, Erb. Salut."

"You remembered so many of their names. I think you're doing better with your memory." She led him out of the bar and into the calm night.

"They taught me that phrase, au revoir. It means good-bye."

"I think you've found a new career. You'd make a good English teacher."

He smiled. "I didn't have to worry about forgetting words. They were happy with the few that I remember."

A wave of relief flooded through Bree and she murmured a silent prayer of thanks. She squeezed Herb's arm as she guided him through the darkened, cobbled alleys back to the restaurant. When they arrived at the terrace Doris ran to him and threw her arms around his shoulders.

That evening might very well have been one of Herb's best memories of the week.

Even if it was one of Bree's worst.

ℭ ℭ ℭ

As soon as Travis had left the saffron-colored lamplight of the restaurant patio, he'd felt as if he'd been let out of a cage. Now he shifted his cumbersome camera bag on his shoulder to continue taking some shots of the picturesque town in the misty calm of twilight. He'd also needed to be alone for a little while. He breathed deeply and strolled through the half-empty cobbled streets, enjoying the caress of the evening breeze, listening to snatches of muffled conversations in French.

He was, in reality, untamed, more at home in a thatched hut in Thailand or a campground in Romania than a fancy villa in France. Soon he'd be back on his own schedule, planning his days, filling them up with his projects. Diving back into his work would channel his sadness, as it always had. In two days he'd exit the Provence parenthesis of his life and return to himself.

But Bree Sorenson had entered his landscape, and he needed to find a way to forget her.

Travis sighed. Just when he thought his heart could heal, that he could stop being so doggone independent and alone, just when he thought he'd found someone who could share life, passion for travel, the future—she'd slipped out of his reach. And her reason was nothing short of ironic, thrusting him back to his past and his falling out with God.

He thought he'd begun a sort of breakthrough in his faith, a tentative new beginning, but once again he'd found himself in no-man's land. Maybe he was fooling himself, thinking he could go back. Or forward. Even Bree had given up on him. Maybe God had too. Travis had just wandered too far and waited too long.

He strolled through one empty street then another, passing sparse groups of tourists or locals. A homey light from the second-floor dwellings spilled onto the worn, square pavers on the road. He adjusted the shutter speed of his camera for evening and took several photos of the nearly empty streets, capturing the golden glow from street lamps melting into the falling daylight. Turning a corner, he found himself facing the Nostradamus fountain where he'd sat with Bree on the second day of their tour. It was the first day they'd been alone, just talking about life together, breaking through the crust of misunderstanding that had begun their relationship. Even that day, he'd known his heart was about to be pulled into an undertow from which he'd struggle to swim away.

A wave of melancholy at the memory of that day blended with the sweet sound of water trickling into the basin. He sat down on the edge of the fountain. He should tell her, shouldn't he? Tell her about his past, the whole ugly story. If she rejected him for not speaking up sooner, he wouldn't be any worse off than he was right now. Tomorrow was their last day.

But it seemed she'd already rejected him, despite her obvious feelings for him. That thought gnawed at him, even if he was slightly gratified when she seemed so dejected that evening. He could hope it was because of him. But if she had a high standard for religious behavior, he'd surely fall short. He'd end up trying to prove himself for her sake. And that would defeat the purpose.

After a few more moments memorizing the soothing sound of the falling drops, he pulled to his feet. May as well find his way back to the villa. He turned and stared at the sculpture of the man reputed to predict the future. "What would you say to me, old man?" he asked aloud. "About Bree? About Clay?" He softly added, "About God?" He knew he should ask God Himself that question, but the words wouldn't come. He wasn't sure they'd even be welcome. Disappointment pooled inside him. He felt more alone than ever.

Travis straightened his shoulders and took a few photos of the fountain before moving on. Enough brooding. Next step, Italy. And after that? The prospect of continuing as Clay's puppet left a sour taste in his mouth, but it *was* his job, and the only network that had given him a chance so far. Maybe his lack of creative control was just a season he had to bear until he built enough credibility to do his own thing. The vague email he'd sent to his boss would only buy time, not replace the inevitable unpleasant conversation. Unless he decided to compromise.

Clay had told him to observe, not necessarily name the company. Travis could write an article without anyone knowing who it was about, though Bree would know. Maybe Clay was right, small group tours had hidden dangers.

Like falling in love with the tour director.

Chapter Thirteen

"On your left is a catapult sling and beyond it is a battering ram used in medieval warfare . . ." The accented voice of their French guide, Christophe, rang out over the ancient ruins of the castle at Les Baux-de-Provence, echoing back through the hollows among the dilapidated walls. Bree half-listened, having heard it all before. Her eyes scanned the members of her group. She hovered a longer yet inconspicuous glance at Travis. He stood near the overlook and gazed across the olive groves and faraway foothills. All day he'd seemed pensive and was frequently on the phone. Probably preparing his departure the next day from the tour and from her life. She'd said they could still be friends, but he didn't seem interested in that. A hollow ache pushed against her insides.

Les Baux-de-Provence was only a short drive from the villa. In Bree's experience, it took less than a day to explore both the village and the château ruins that overshadowed it from a hillside above, so the group hadn't left the villa until after lunch. Bree had hoped to steal a few moments to talk to Lauren about her day with Jean-Pierre, but there were always people around them. Or maybe Lauren was avoiding that discussion. Hopefully there simply wasn't anything to tell.

"A catapult could hurl a two-hundred-pound stone and took over sixty men to operate." Christophe's voice again interrupted Bree's thoughts. "In those days, most of the area we now know as Provence, was controlled, not by the French king, but local warrior knights."

The next day the trip would be over.

"I can't believe we're leaving tomorrow." Sarah's voice came from behind, echoing her own thoughts.

Bree turned and gave her a sad smile. "Me either. I feel like I've known you all for much longer than a week. We'll all go our separate ways."

Sarah's eyes squinted against the sun overhead until she shaded them with one hand. When she did, Bree thought she saw sadness there. "And in a few months, you'll start all over with a new group."

Yes, theoretically. Bree glanced at Lauren and had an uneasy feeling.

"It's been so lovely. Thank you for everything." Sarah's dark eyes shone with sincerity.

"But we aren't finished quite yet. Don't forget, we have our celebration dinner this evening."

"If it's anything like the last special dinner, we'll have a treat from Lauren once again."

They surely would. It had become a tradition on the last evening of the tour to celebrate together around the long dining room table or on the terrace, to reminisce about the highlights of the trip and enjoy a final meal together before departing. Bree knew Lauren enjoyed having a reason to try a new elegant recipe and make sure the evening was superb. And she usually succeeded.

Following the castle tour and a special light show, the group strolled again through the stone alleys of the village then headed back to the van. They were all quiet on the way home, either tired or mentally preparing for their flight the following day and their transition back to the life and people they'd left behind. Bree was relieved to stay tucked away in her own thoughts as well, instead of having to maintain pleasant interaction with her guests.

Back at the villa everyone dispersed. Bree headed toward her bedroom so she could lie down for a few minutes but stopped when she saw Lauren standing in the hallway.

"Bree." Lauren's whisper set Bree's heart pounding. Lauren slipped into Bree's room so Bree followed and closed the door behind them. Bree tensed, waiting for Lauren to speak.

Lauren sat on the edge of the bed. When she looked up, her expression was soft. "I know you've probably wondered what happened yesterday with Jean-Pierre. I'm sorry I was gone so long. Time just flew by without my realizing it, but I shouldn't have left you alone all day."

Bree nodded. She thought about saying it was okay. But it wasn't. Lauren hadn't even called. Something had certainly changed in their relationship, because the old Lauren would never have been gone the day without calling or texting. Bree didn't know if, or how, they'd ever be able to go back to where they had been. "Yes, I was wondering." Like, all day. She shrugged. "You yourself said we were a team."

Lauren lowered her head. "I'm so sorry. It was wrong not to come back sooner or call." She gave no further explanation. "My day with Jean-Pierre was wonderful, but I still don't know what to think. He and I will keep in touch, and I'll try to see him the next time I'm in Provence."

Bree's eyes lifted along with a thread of hope. Lauren was planning on there being a next trip. "That will give you a chance to get back to Mark and see how you feel about him too." When Lauren

162

frowned, Bree added, "Not that I'm pushing you toward Mark, but you should see him again before you make any decisions, don't you think?"

"Yes, that's the least I should do. Of course, I'll pray a lot and take my time. I don't think Jean-Pierre is a practicing believer." Lauren kneaded her hands in her lap. A troubled look hovered in her eyes.

"Do you think that's wise, then?"

Lauren pursed her lips. "He goes to Mass occasionally, and he seems to be open. I know what you're thinking. It's not enough. You're right, we'd need more common ground, spiritually. Maybe I'm just restless about Mark. Maybe I was bored with the relationship and didn't know it until I met Jean-Pierre."

"You'll know in time, Lauren." Bree laid her hand on Lauren's shoulder and was surprised to find tears in her friend's eyes. She sank onto the bed and pulled Lauren into an embrace. Lauren's arms circles tightly around Bree.

"You're a good friend," mumbled Lauren. "Thanks for being patient with me."

Bree chuckled. "Oh, Lauren," she said and hugged Lauren again. She pulled back but kept her hands firmly placed on Lauren's arms. "It's a drop in the bucket compared to how patient you've been with me. I've been a neurotic worrier, afraid to really trust God with my life." Her voice softened. "I'm not a very good example of a woman of faith, but like a good Pharisee, I sure pretend to be."

Lauren's green eyes exuded compassion. "Don't be too hard on yourself, Bree. You've had difficult things to deal with in your past, and you've overcome a lot."

"I guess." Bree swallowed. She shouldn't let herself off so easily. She'd judged Travis for lack of spiritual commitment when he'd been nothing but good-hearted, helpful, and compassionate. In her zeal to protect her heart she'd been distant and rude to him. Yet he'd been the one to walk away. She'd still like to talk to him again before he left. Maybe they could maintain a friendship, at least. If only it could be more.

Two hours later the celebration dinner unfolded on the patio. Lauren put her best culinary skills to work. Candles flickered on each table and colored lanterns overhead lent a festive spirit to their last meal together. Lauren had prepared mixed seafood—filet of sole, prawns, and scallops— accompanied by a vegetable casserole au gratin and braised fennel. During the cheese course, served after the main meal, several people around the table shared their favorite highlights of the trip.

"Why don't we take our dessert inside," Lauren suggested, "since it's gotten a bit chilly?" The evening breeze had become stronger, whipping the umbrella fabric into a flutter and causing the lanterns to sway in a colorful rhythm. Bree helped her bring plates of *Tarte Tatin* from the kitchen into the living room, where they served each guest. On the coffee table Bree set out bowls of vanilla ice cream and crème fraîche to accompany the caramelized apple pie while Lauren brewed a fresh pot of decaf coffee.

After dessert, Herb and Doris stood. "We're retiring early tonight. See you all at breakfast," Doris said.

The Morrisons and Sarah called, "Good night" to them as they disappeared down the hall. Travis had eaten dessert while chatting with the Grahams. As they left the room, he slipped out the back door, Bree guessed to his favorite place by the pool.

Bree sat in a wing chair next to Marcia. She would be sorry to see Marcia leave. "How is your husband doing now, Marcia? I keep forgetting to ask you about him."

"He's coming along after his last surgery. Unfortunately, as soon as I get back, he'll have to prepare for surgery on the other hip, and in a few months, a knee-replacement. He's got a full schedule at the hospital." Marcia finished her last bite of the apple pie. "Mmm. This is such a treat. I'll have ten pounds to lose after this trip."

"Maybe not, with all the walking we've done."

Marcia sipped her decaf. "It was so special for me to have Travis along, since we don't see each other often. At first, he didn't really want to come. I thought it might be nice for him to have some fun, after what he's been through."

"Oh?" Aside from his marriage, was there something Bree didn't know about?

"I'm sure he's already told you about his ministry in the Czech Republic. He went there with his wife when they were in their late twenties."

Bree stilled and her eyes widened. "His *ministry*?" Her voice came out in almost a squeak. Travis, in ministry? "Like a Christian ministry? He was a pastor?"

"No, not a pastor." Marcia tilted her head to the side. "He didn't tell you? He and his wife went there to teach English at the university in hopes that they could eventually start a new church. But his wife ran off with a Czech man. A grad student. It was so sad. Travis took it pretty hard at the time."

Bree's mind was in turmoil. She felt unable to speak as her thoughts ricocheted to random conversations and phrases she and Travis had exchanged over the last several days. He'd made oblique references to the Czech Republic, saying he'd spent time there, but nothing further. Why hadn't he told her? Confusion and frustration frothed inside, creating a hot core of anger.

Marcia stared at her. "Maybe I shouldn't have said anything. I just assumed he'd told you."

"He didn't." The words choked in her throat. "I knew he'd been married, though, and that his wife had been unfaithful."

"It was a shock." Marcia shook her head and frowned. "I knew Lexi for years. Sweet girl. None of us saw it coming." Then Marcia lifted her eyebrows and her eyes connected with Bree's in a direct blue-eyed stare. "He's a good man, my Travis. He deserved better than that. Trying to serve God and look what happened."

Bree tried for what she hoped was a look of sympathy. Was Marcia sending her a message? "That's such a shame," she said. A bland statement to smother her questions. She held herself back from leaping out of the chair and storming to the pool. Her moist hands gripped the wooden handles of the chair, as if that would bind her in place a few moments longer.

Marcia rose. "I'm going to turn in." When Bree stood, Marcia pulled her into a warm hug. Then she pulled back, smiled. "I've loved the chance to get to know you, Bree, and I hope that our paths will cross again. Just wanted to tell you that in case I don't get the opportunity tomorrow."

"I've enjoyed knowing you as well. I'm so glad you were able to come." Bree's words were sincere, even if her thoughts were groping out toward the pool.

Marcia said good-night to those remaining in the *salle de séjour* then disappeared down the hall to her bedroom.

Bree strolled nonchalantly across the room then shot out the back door. She stomped through the moist grass to the pool area, where she could see Travis's silhouette against the setting sun. The colored lanterns danced and spun in the evening breeze.

He looked up as she approached. He didn't seem surprised, even when he saw the scowl on her face. "Nice to see you, Bree." He gestured calmly to the chair beside him.

"I need some answers from you, Travis." She plopped down in the lawn chair and faced him, leaning on her thighs. "You were in ministry. A missionary. You're a Christian but you never told me. Were you just playing with me or—or what? I don't understand."

"My mother told you?"

"Just now. I was shocked, especially after what I said to you yesterday. I can't begin to understand what your reasons could be after—"

"Bree." His voice was quiet but firm. "You'll understand if you let me explain."

Still fuming, she closed her mouth and clasped her hands, kneading them as she waited.

Travis leaned forward, his forearms on his knees, bringing his head close to hers. Shadows of dusk fell over his face but she saw his jaw tighten and his Adam's apple move as he swallowed. "I was raised in a Christian family. I was in church all my life, in Bible studies, in college ministry, everything." His voice was low, with a dull edge. "I was very committed to Christ. I met Lexi in college. We dated for about two years and got married soon after graduating."

He looked beyond her to a place in his memories. As she looked at his face, Bree's angry walls began to crumble. In place of anger, pain for him radiated into her throat, causing an ache. She swallowed it back.

Travis held her eyes in his defeated gaze. "A few years later we moved to the Czech Republic to a city called Brno. We taught English to university students. I didn't realize I was losing Lexi a little bit at a time. She spent more and more time with a grad student named Varoslav. He was spiritually open, she told me. It didn't occur to me how much time she was spending with him because I thought she was meeting a lot with other people as well, mostly women. It all happened right under my nose." His voice had become ragged. "Then she told me she'd fallen in love with him." He looked away from Bree. "She moved out."

He paused for several seconds. Bree didn't dare speak. She could only give him the space to compose his thoughts, his emotions.

Travis shook his head. "The day she left, I remember just sitting there in our living room for hours, like . . . catatonic. I'd tried to convince her to come back, said I'd forgive her. We'd leave the Czech Republic, we'd get counseling. We'd start over." He looked down at his hands. "She never came back. I finally had to tell our ministry team. They were sympathetic, but the leadership said it would be best for me to pack up and leave. Lexi came back to the States months later to sign the divorce papers." He stopped and lifted his face to her, a tortured look painted on it.

Bree didn't speak. As she listened to his words a harsh hand gripped her insides.

"I lost a lot of my faith during that time. I felt like I'd been so diligent all those years. I'd gone into ministry, I'd tried to serve Him. And He dropped me like a brick. The anchor of my life wasn't there anymore."

"He *was*, Travis." Bree's voice was quiet. "He was there all the time, don't you think?"

"I know that now. But back then I felt utterly deserted. I became a lapsed missionary. A lapsed believer." He moved his hand toward hers then settled it back on his knee. "It was easier to present myself to you and everyone else as a nice-guy non-believer than as a completely backslidden, confused Christian. I didn't tell you yesterday because I knew I wasn't a real Christian anymore."

"Of course, you are. Just because you went through a season of distance with God doesn't mean He's rejected you. What about the verse that says no one will snatch you out of his hands?"

He held his palms up, his expression beaten, crushed. "It just didn't seem real to me. I felt like I was in this eternal gray area. Still am, to some degree." He shrugged then let out a deep sigh. "That's the story, Bree. After the divorce I got back into journalism, which I'd done before going overseas. It was all I knew. All that I had left. I've been in a desert since that time, living in the world, far from God. But I'm starting to pull out a little at a time. I'm willing to take a step at a time toward God, if it's not too late."

Bree placed her hand on his arm then slid it down to grasp his hand, warm and dry, in both of hers. He squeezed back and held on. Her hands tingled up to her elbows. In a soft voice she said, "Of course it's not too late. *Nothing* will separate us from His love, Travis. What's the verse again . . . not danger or hardship or death . . ." She caught his gaze in hers, and the intensity and tragedy she saw there momentarily silenced her.

Bree took a deep breath, aching to convince him. "Nothing will separate us from His love," she said slowly, gravely. "Not unfaithful spouses. Not a father who beat us up when we were only six years old. *Nothing* will separate us from Him. Not even our own lack of consistency. And not being a self-righteous hypocrite . . . like me."

He grinned then. "Glad you finally saw that." They both laughed, the soft sound mixing into the night. "Just kidding. You're a good rep for Him. Why do you call yourself a hypocrite?"

She shrugged. "I pretend to be this committed person, but I still have trouble believing God can truly protect me. So, I live in the shadows, not risking very much, counting on my own control methods to protect me. It's hard to walk in joy and live in the moment when I'm doing that."

169

His eyes were gentle as he looked at her, still grasping her hands. "So, you're a kind of prodigal too?"

She nodded, smiling, and their eyes locked together, as her neck became warm and her heart pounded. "I am. We have that in common."

"Bree, are you out there?" A shout from the house shattered the moment. Bree flinched.

"I'm here," she called, hoping she didn't have to leave this haven of honesty with Travis. She looked toward the villa and saw Lauren standing in the doorway, her silhouette etched against the lamplight.

"I just need you for a couple minutes." Lauren's voice rang out toward the pool.

"Must have something to do with our departure tomorrow," she told Travis. "Be right back."

Reluctantly she released his hand and rose from the chair. What terrible timing, right after Travis had opened his heart. Suddenly she understood so many of the enigmas he'd presented since she'd met him. And that understanding completed the partial picture she'd had of him . . . one that had already led her to love him.

She loved him.

She shook her head at the realization, which had finally taken a recognizable form, though she'd suspected as much that day in the pantry. Maybe she should tell him when she returned to the pool. Was it too soon? But they'd be leaving tomorrow. They needed closure. Was she again trying to control everything?

Bree reached the house and stepped into the living room as frustration rumbled deep inside her. Her mind swirled with the feelings she'd identified, the commitment that had lodged deep inside.

Lauren glanced at the pool, apologetic. "I'm sorry to bother you, Bree."

"Bad timing, but you didn't know."

"This won't take a minute, then you can go back. I just wanted to remind you that these forms need to be filled out this evening so we don't forget tomorrow." She held a stack of papers in one hand. "And this one is for the villa. They'll want to do a walk-through tomorrow afternoon when we get back from the train stations. And we need to hand out the evaluations before our guests disperse, because you know, they might not think of it afterward. I wanted to tell you before I went to bed. I'm exhausted."

Bree took the papers and gave Lauren a tight smile. "Wonderful dinner tonight. You outdid yourself." She started back toward the pool, thankful the interruption hadn't taken too long. Before she got out the door, Sarah called, "Bree, could you help us resolve something?"

Bree swallowed and stared at Sarah and Alan, who were standing near the fireplace. *No, I really can't.* The words were on the tip of her tongue, but she couldn't say them. This was her job, and she couldn't brush off her guests on the last evening. Besides, it would be obvious to everyone that she was in a hurry to go back to Travis. She told herself it didn't matter what they thought. Maybe she could dispense with the conversation quickly and slip back out before he left. She glanced at her watch. It was after ten.

"We were discussing the earliest dates of the city of Avignon." Alan perched one elbow on the mantle.

Sarah said, "I don't know if you're well-versed in the history of this area, but we thought you might know whether the Romans were the first to settle Avignon or if there were settlements prior. Alan thinks that there was a prehistoric presence, but I'd heard that the Romans were there first."

Bree wanted to scream, *Who cares*? She quelled her feelings and spoke calmly. "I'm not an expert, but I think Alan is right about that, Sarah. The Romans took over, but there were centuries of civilization before that time."

"I believe it goes clear back to the Neolithic Era," added Alan. "The Romans didn't get there until a century or two before Christ, but ruins show evidence of settlements back to at least the sixth century B.C."

"That's what I've learned as well." Bree smiled and inched toward the back door. "I can't add anything to that. I hope you all sleep well before your big travels tomorrow."

"Are you going to bed now, Bree?" Sarah asked. "You're probably exhausted after all your great organizing this week."

"I have to do some things, paperwork and things but I will see you in the morning."

"Bree, before you go—" Beverly stood up from her seat on the couch.

Bree stifled the urge to scream. Maybe this too wouldn't take very long.

"I'm a member of a bridge group and I think some of them would be interested in a tour like this. Could you send me some brochures once we all get back?"

"I'd be glad to." She inched toward the door again. Normally she'd have stopped everything to promote her company to a potential group of travelers. Now she just wanted to run to the pool.

"Tell, me, what other kinds of tours do you offer? You mentioned wine tastings and cooking groups. Could you do a combination of these things?"

Bree sighed. "Remember the questionnaire you completed when you registered, where you expressed your interests? Each person can indicate what they'd like to do on that form. I'll be happy to talk to you about this after the tour. I still have your contact information. I'll call you and we can discuss it, once we've all gotten settled again—"

"Oh, you're right. We don't have to talk about this now. We can see later on. When I tell them all about it, I'm sure some of them will want more information."

After one or two more questions from Beverly, Bree was finally able to slip back out into the night. As she neared the pool her heart sank. Travis was gone.

Chapter Fourteen

He probably should have waited longer for Bree to return, but she was likely ensnared with myriad details before the departure and would be held up for some time. Maybe she'd even ended up going to bed.

After Travis pulled himself out of the woven lawn chair, he headed toward the front of the villa and the street. He wasn't planning to walk far, but he needed to stretch his legs and breathe in the cool, moist night air before sleeping. He also wanted to spool back through his conversation with Bree. At some point he'd need to shake his memory clear of her large, blue eyes and her scent of honeysuckle enough to remember where he was.

Right. In Provence. On the verge of leaving.

Not far from the villa stood a tiny village church surrounded by a stone fence and wrought iron gate. He'd noticed it several times when they passed by in the van. Each time he'd seen it, the gate was always open. He walked along the uneven road for a few minutes, his sandals crunching on the gravel shoulder. Seeing the little church, he headed around to the side and slipped into the churchyard.

He heard the lyrical sound of trickling water. A fountain? He smiled in the darkness and followed the sound. A welcome thought floated and settled into his mind. Maybe the fountain there was a symbol of divine love still waiting for him to receive, an outstretched hand of invitation.

He reached a fountain darkened by the cloud-covered moon and sat on a stone bench that faced it. Trimmed hedges wreathed around him and a tangle of rose bushes clung to the opposite fence. A trace scent of pine floated on the night air while streams of water splashed down to a basin, performing a symphony with the whispers of branches hovering above.

He'd told Bree everything. Now, he felt clean inside, transparent. There was nothing further hidden between them. Finally, she knew the whole story and she'd responded in a way that could only be called loving. And humble. They had common ground, because she struggled too. But what did it all mean? They were planning to go their separate ways in only a few more hours.

Her words cycled back into his mind. Of course, he knew the verse she'd paraphrased, Romans 8:35. Nothing could separate him from the love of God demonstrated through Christ. He'd even memorized it as a teenager, but had long ago forgotten about it, about its power to bolster his doubt. Instead of letting it rescue him as he drowned, he'd felt forsaken, as if the implosion of his marriage, ministry, and life were signs of God's neglect or indifference. Travis shook his head. Part of him had known better, and the other part hurt too badly to really believe otherwise.

But how to recapture the last five years? He grimaced, then his mother's words drifted back to him. *Don't try to go back. Start where you are.*

Start where he was. Not so hard, was it?

"Father . . ." His voice startled the silence. "I want to take it by faith that You still love me and want me to hang around You. Despite everything. So please help me to start from where I am.

Thanks for not being impatient with me. Thanks for being willing to let me go at my pace, without giving up or going away. I guess you never really did that, even before. I was the one. But thank you that it's not too late."

A gentle peace flowed over him. He relaxed his shoulders. It was okay not to be what he was before. It was a new moment, starting now.

Less clear, however, was Bree Sorenson. Their conversation by the pool left him weak for her, all his barriers crushed on the ground. What had it been to her? Had she merely dispensed her compassion and understanding, as she did to everyone else? Or was she crossing a threshold of self-revelation and emotional intimacy, as well as risk? Had she somehow been reaching out to him? How would he know? In a short time, he'd felt closer to her than anyone since Lexi.

Travis leaned his forehead into his hands and let the night breeze tumble across his back. A few moments passed as peace surged over and through him in steady, reassuring waves.

His cell phone rang into the quiet. He flinched at the sound then sat up and pulled the phone from his pocket. He glanced at the screen. Toby, who'd be giving him a ride to Italy the next day. "Hey, Toby. Are you already in France? Where are you now?"

The voice of his cameraman filled the phone. "I'm not too sure, and if I knew, I probably wouldn't be able to pronounce it. Some town maybe an hour from you."

"You're that close? When did you get to France?"

"A few days ago. I spent a few days in Paris then picked up a car at the airport and headed on out. Man, the tolls were expensive. There was some traffic at first, especially on that beltway around the city, but I'm basically on schedule, if we don't hit any big delays."

"Are you still planning to pick me up tomorrow?"

"That's why I was calling. I'm going to stop at a hotel for the night, but I should be able to pick you up tomorrow around six-thirty."

"Six-thirty a.m.?"

"Of course, a.m." Toby chuckled. "Certainly not p.m. I thought it would be later, but made good time, once I got past the traffic."

Six-thirty. That wouldn't give Travis an opportunity to talk to Bree or say goodbye to anyone in the group. But given the miles they had to drive, he couldn't very well ask Toby to come by later, could he? Have a long breakfast, sleep in . . .

As if reading his mind Toby said, "We have a long drive to the Lakes, so I figure it's a good thing we gained some time."

"I guess so."

"I've got the address and I'll use the GPS to find you. I'll text you if I get off schedule or lost, but I'm not all that far, so it should be fine.'

"Okay, I'll wait for you out front. It'll be a large stone house, slate roof. Just so you know what to look for. Tomorrow. Six-thirty."

A heavy thud dropped inside his chest. Maybe Bree would still be up when he got back to the villa. If not, he'd have to find a way to communicate with her, at least to say goodbye. She'd never said how she felt about him or about staying in touch. He wouldn't read too much into her kisses or her expressions of friendship. From relationships with women in the past, he knew he couldn't assume anything beyond momentary gratification.

Travis walked briskly back to the villa in hopes that Bree would still be up. But when he arrived, only the porch light and the front hall light were on. He glanced at his watch. It was just past eleven. Everyone must have turned in early in preparation for their departure the following day.

Departure. Being in Provence for a week had taken him so far out of his zone of normalcy, it would take a few days to adjust to Italy. He'd been saying for the last few days that he was eager to leave, mostly because of the awkwardness that had developed with Bree after he kissed her . . . twice. He was certainly eager to dive back to his work. But the thought of not seeing Bree each morning caused a hollow ache he wondered if he'd ever get over. Filming a new program at the Italian Lakes might help. Or not.

He went to her hallway and glanced down the darkened tunnel. Looked like everyone was asleep, every room dark, including hers. Even if it were not, what would he tell her, except that he'd be leaving early in the morning? He didn't know how she felt about him after their most recent discussion, didn't know if she'd kept that door open.

Travis returned to his own darkened hallway and approached his room, suddenly tired. A movement in the hall startled him, and he looked up. Alan. Travis nodded toward him and started to open his door. Then he stopped. "Alan?"

Alan stood still, eyebrows raised. Alan was the last person Travis wanted to trust with a message, but there was literally no one else. "Can you do me a favor?"

The man's expression held no more warmth than he'd shown on the first day. "I'll do what I can."

"I've just learned that I need to leave early, about six-thirty. A colleague is picking me up. The problem is, I won't be able to let Bree and Lauren know, and they'll wonder why I'm not at breakfast. Would you mind telling them that I had to leave and that it couldn't be helped? Say good-bye for me? There's no one else awake." He might be able to text his mother, if they weren't in a foreign country. She probably hadn't brought her phone anyway.

He loathed asking a favor of Alan, who seemed to be surveying him as he spoke.

"No problem at all. Good luck to you then." A trace of warmth flitted across his pasty face.

That surprised Travis. Maybe the guy was okay after all. "Thanks, Alan. You too."

He closed the door behind him and stood still a moment. Not a good plan to rely on Alan. Maybe Travis could text Bree, only he didn't have her personal cell number and didn't know if she was using her French cell. Leave a note for her in the kitchen just to say goodbye? He shook his head. She might not see it and a simple goodbye was inadequate. He grimaced. Truth was, he had no idea if she even wanted to keep in touch with him.

He opened his duffle bag and gathered his clothes from the imposing wooden armoire. He laid them out on the bed and smoothed them then rolled them up and stacked them back into the duffle, in order to efficiently transport and wrinkle-proof them. Once he'd zipped the duffel up, he felt ready to leave. But sad to leave. Frustrated by the timing of everything. Frustrated in general. Peaceful with God. So many emotions all at once. He hoped he'd sleep.

Six-thirty was going to come way too soon.

Chapter Fifteen

Bree awoke to a beam of sunshine that sliced through the morning shadows in her room. Still buried in a tangle of sheets, she watched the dancing light for a moment, aware of the absence of tension. A layer of peaceful calm floated over her like a filmy net.

The tour was over. She'd come to know each guest almost as a friend. They'd spent nearly every waking moment together and now they would leave, dispersed to their own homes across the U.S. She always felt a small wave of melancholy at the close of a trip. This one, despite its misadventures, was no exception. She felt the usual satisfaction as well. Another tour successfully completed.

She hugged an armful of sheets to her chest and smiled. Travis Jefferies had surprised her, changed her world, and not just because she now knew he shared her faith. She'd grown to love him even before that. But how could she tell him, with all the hurried bustle that the departure morning always brought? Maybe she'd simply send him a private smile across the breakfast table, catch his eye with a meaningful glance, then try to speak with him after the meal before everything got hectic with organizing luggage and departures.

Bree frowned. What if he thought he'd passed some kind of test, since she knew he had faith? Would he object to that? No, she didn't need to worry about that. She'd seen the raw emotion in his eyes. He felt the same way as she did, regardless of the challenges they'd had in their brief relationship.

Bree pulled herself out of bed and pulled open the curtains, allowing the full sun to soak her for a moment or two. Then she prepared for the day. A day of transition in every area of her life . . . professional, with the successful completion of a tour, and perhaps romantic as well.

She dressed in a flattering cobalt blue top with a scoop neck and matched it with white capris. She wanted to remain in Travis's memory until they met again, whenever that would be. After primping more than usual, selecting matching jewelry, putting on finishing touches, she went down the hall and joined Lauren in the kitchen.

Lauren's eyes widened when she saw Bree, but she said nothing.

"I'll help you." Bree smiled and took two basketfuls of baguette slices to the dining room. Beverly and Michael were settling into their seats at the table, where Alan and Sarah were already serving themselves coffee. One by one, each member of the group arrived, probably with their minds on their flights home. Only Travis was missing.

Throughout the meal Bree kept expecting him to amble in, probably from an early walk or swim, but he didn't come. Marcia seemed unaffected by this. Bree didn't dare ask her.

"Where is Travis?" Lauren finally asked.

Marcia looked up from buttering her croissant. "Oh, I think he had a ride to Italy with a colleague. I didn't think he was planning to leave this early, but that's what must have happened."

"He didn't say anything." Bree couldn't stem the wave that surged over her, though she did her best to look impassive. It was more than disappointment. After what they'd said to each other the night before, after he'd divulged his past to her, he'd left without a word.

She'd known that someone from his team would pick him up that morning, but thought she'd at least have a chance to talk with him. What had he thought as he'd driven away? That he'd never see her again? That it was a nice experience, and on to the next country, the next woman?

Maybe she'd been right about him after all. She was the Provence girl.

Tears pricked her eyes. She looked down and focused on cutting her croissant, unwilling to let anyone see her emotions, the turmoil frothing inside. She'd been a fool.

Breakfast continued with bland conversation around the table. Bree's emotions churned then settled into a dull ache. Two hours later she was again behind the wheel of a van full of luggage and her original passengers as she returned them to the Avignon train station. From there they would take a train to various airports and either travel to another destination or return home.

"Hard to believe we did this just a week ago." Sarah's voice reached Bree from the back of the van.

"It seems like much longer than eight days," Beverly said. "I guess that happens when you're out of your normal environment."

"I think it does us a world of good to have that kind of change." Bree coaxed a bright tone into her voice. The effort was exhausting. "The French have an expression, 'changing the ideas.' That means when you change your context for a period of time, it can refresh the way you look at your whole life."

"Well, this trip certainly changed my ideas," Sarah said with a chuckle. "I think I'm ruined for the ordinary."

The men in the van remained silent. Alan seemed to have given up on his attempts to woo Bree and she was relieved. At the Avignon train station, Bree said good-bye to each guest with hugs and well-wishes. Though she was sincere, she still felt like a machine, her smiles and platitudes a veneer covering the hidden weight inside.

She made her solitary trek back to the villa on the highway she knew so well. A mound of unshed tears hid just behind her eyes, causing an ache in her throat. Several tears squeezed out and moistened her cheeks as they traced a path.

Soon she'd return to her normal life. Only she'd forgotten what normal was supposed to be and, quite honestly, wasn't looking forward to it. Not to her apartment in Virginia, not to planning a new trip. Nothing in her old life appealed to her.

She willed her mind away from Travis Jefferies before new tears could sting her eyes and remind her what an idiot she'd been. So many of life's experiences were painful.

She would chalk this one up to yet one more.

 beta   beta   beta

"Do you really think this is a good idea?" Travis took one look at the endless rows of towering buildings on the Italian horizon as they approached the city of Genoa.

Toby's brow furrowed from behind the wheel of the Fiat, which was beginning to feel to Travis like a small anchovy can. "Why not? Don't you want to eat something before we head north?"

"Looks kind of congested. We could stop at a village somewhere along the way. More local color and fewer traffic jams." Travis unfolded a piece of the map. Genoa looked like a busy, sprawling city. If they got snarled in traffic, it would slow down a trip that was already going to take almost nine hours. But as he considered the thought of staying in the car for even five more minutes, he said, "Never mind. We'll stop, first place you see."

They'd been on the road since six-thirty. Toby had been right on time. With a dismal weight pulling down inside him, Travis had looked wistfully at the darkened villa and climbed into the waiting car. He'd been able to sleep for an hour in the passenger seat, which took a slight edge of sadness off his mood. Several times he'd wondered why they hadn't simply taken a train. Couldn't be too much more expensive, and a lot less exhausting. He'd have to lobby for that with Clay before the next trip. They'd stopped for a coffee and bathroom break in Nice around nine-thirty. Three hours later they found themselves circling the large coastal city of Genoa.

Fortunately, there was a small, rustic trattoria on the city outskirts that was open for lunch. As they tried to decipher the menu, Toby said, "Did you know that Genoa is the birthplace of Christopher Columbus?"

Travis groaned. He didn't need another Alan supplying him with historical trivia wherever they went. Alan. Had he given Bree the message? Probably not, since Travis was the competition. Mr. *Celebrity,* in Alan's words. But there was a slight chance the man had kept his word. In retrospect Travis should have left a note in the kitchen or slipped something under Bree's door. Should have gone against his misgivings. He'd been thinking of Bree constantly throughout the morning. Hopefully by now she knew that he hadn't willingly left without saying goodbye. Without saying anything.

How could he have readily walked away without a word when he had so much he wanted to say?

Travis couldn't stop himself. He pulled his phone out of his canvas backpack, not even sure why. Bree wouldn't be emailing him or texting that day. He looked at the screen. A message from Clay, but none from Bree. Travis glanced at his watch. She would still be running everyone to the train station or airport for their return flights. She might not check her email for several days.

What would he even say, if he wrote to her? Should he just blurt out that he loved her? Maybe now that she knew his story, knew about his faith, however lapsed, she'd be open to him. Travis sighed in frustration. He'd never had to measure up for a woman before. He could pursue her, but given his lifestyle over the last few years, she'd probably reject him. And after Lexi, he didn't know how he'd deal with another rejection from a woman he loved.

"You look just plain aggravated. What's eating you, Travis?" Toby's drawl broke into Travis's mental puzzle.

"Sorry, Tobe. Just lost in my thoughts." He fought the urge to tell Toby he'd met someone. Hadn't finished a conversation. Might be in love. Afraid of being hurt. He liked Toby fine, but they were colleagues, not friends. The more personal information he held back, the better off he was.

"Are you all ready for the shoot?"

Travis hoped he was. He'd made a decision to scout for a few days and then film on the same trip. In the past he'd sometimes made two separate trips, one for research and another for shooting, especially when he was just starting out. "I will be. We'll start out in ritzy Bellagio, a ferry ride from Varenna, where we're staying. But I'll want to include at least some of the local lifestyle."

"Like you always do."

"Yup. Maybe show tourist sites then cut to local people and what their lives are like, then to a new area and do the same thing. It'll remind people there are Italians who have lived there for generations and don't live the way the tourists do."

Toby nodded thoughtfully. "The one's we've met in the past sure don't."

As they finished eating Travis checked his watch. Bree should be back at the villa by now. Maybe he'd email her . . . no, she wouldn't expect anything right now. She knew he was working on a new project.

Three hours later the tired Fiat approached the outskirts of the town of Varenna which they'd use as a home base for the next two weeks. The rest of the camera and technical crew would arrive in a few days, once Travis, Toby, and another cameraman, Ben, made an initial survey of the area and took some background and filler shots.

Clay had promised Travis he could have creative control over the project. On his word, Travis arranged his content without any tourist warnings or scams mentioned. He wouldn't go looking for them, ever again. He'd only include helpful advice, like dodging thieves, avoiding rip offs in pricey tourist traps, and finding smaller crowds in high season. That was reasonable, as well as helpful. Maybe he could convince Clay that this was sufficient and, in fact, what was sought by viewers.

As they entered the town limits Travis caught his breath. Angular, tile-roofed buildings rose in a warm, heady burst of red, orange, yellow, salmon, pink scattered on a steep, evergreen incline. Like a jewel, the town perched on the edge of a vast, pristine lake, sparkling under the deepening twilight. Toby seemed mesmerized by the town's beauty as well, as the car slowed to a crawl. "Wow," he murmured. "This is somethin'."

Toby got back to driving and obeying the British voice of the GPS which led them through narrow cobbled alleys, one after another. They parked on a street adjacent to their hotel.

After unfolding himself from the small car, Travis stretched. Felt good to be back in his routine, back in charge of his work. It might take his mind and heart a while longer to make the transition, since it felt to him like he'd been away for years.

Two hours later he was seated at the table of a local trattoria they'd found squeezed into a narrow alleyway. Among his colleagues, listening to the lyrical sounds of other languages, anticipating his new assignment, he felt his old self returning to him, along with the same purpose and meaning that had driven him over the last several years.

The crew returned to L'Albergo Dante, their hotel for the next two weeks. "Get some rest, guys," he called out as Toby and Ben scattered down the hall. "We'll be starting early." He fished the large metal key from his backpack and mounted the uneven wooden stairs covered with a worn red runner. The room was homey but less luxurious by far than the villa in Provence.

He felt a sharp pinch inside as he thought of it. Only that morning he'd left France, left Bree. He wondered what she was doing, where she was. Had she gone back to the States with the others, or had she and Lauren stayed on for a few days to check out of the villa and regroup? He hadn't had a chance to find out.

A wave of melancholy flowed into his thoughts, despite his elation at being back in his groove, and rolling up his sleeves before the launch of a new project in such a stunning location. He sat down on the edge of the bed and toed off his sandals then pulled his phone from his backpack.

He should email Clay, since he'd gotten the man's mail earlier that day, which meant he'd written yesterday. Travis frowned. He'd get this over with, but first he'd try to touch base with Bree.

He had only the info email address for Le Bon Voyage Travel. Would she even get it? Maybe that inbox was only for the home office, and they might still be in Europe for a while.

Hello, Bree, he wrote. Then he sat frozen for several seconds as phrases hurtled through his mind like asteroids. He typed a line, deleted it. Typed another. No, sounded stupid. He finally settled on, *I'm sorry I wasn't able to say good bye. My ride came too early and I didn't have the chance.* He backspaced over the last line . . . redundant. *My ride came too early.*

He paused again and grimaced. For a published writer he was anything but eloquent at that moment. *I hope we will stay in touch.* Did that sound like *have a nice life*? Or maybe she'd think he was only assuming friendship. He sighed. It was all he could say to her at this point. Maybe friendship was all she wanted anyway.

Shouldn't do this while he was so tired. It would probably end up with the wrong tone and she'd read it wrong. He deleted the email then turned his attention to Clay's. *I trust you are on your way to Italy by now. You likely won't have time to give me a summary of your time in Provence, as you claimed, but it can wait until your return. While in Italy, however, keep in mind the themes we've covered in recent episodes. We'll discuss all of this when you return.*

Travis frowned. What did that mean? Those themes could only be the hazards and scams inherent in popular tourist areas. Was Clay going back on his promise, or just throwing his weight around? Clay had probably reconsidered his agreement with Travis and regretted giving him creative oversight of the next program. Now he sought to backpedal, not caring that the meticulous planning of the program had already been done. Travis was grateful that it was too late to change the program.

Travis jotted a hasty reply. *Just got here today. Everyone is pretty tired, but we'll start tomorrow.* The bare minimum response was all he could muster. And he'd acquiesced to nothing.

Clay had promised to allow Travis creative freedom in the Italy piece, free from warnings and exposés. Before leaving Portland, he'd made sure his boss was in agreement. And that was what Travis planned to do, regardless of any second thoughts Clay might have. It simply wasn't his problem. He'd do things just as he'd planned.

Whether Clay liked it or not.

Chapter Sixteen

Bree hugged her knees into her chest and closed her eyes, savoring the strong but temperate breeze that pushed steadily at her from the sea, ruffling her hair. Sitting atop the stone rampart surrounding the town of Antibes, her rear began to ache, but the view was so peaceful, she couldn't move. Sunlight sparkled across gently undulating waves, cut frequently by a line of small, identical sailboats from a sailing class, following one after another.

Lauren had stayed behind at the café, wanting to finish off lunch with a café au lait while reading her gourmet cuisine magazine. They'd needed some separate space, after twelve days in Provence, then five days together exploring potential sites for future trips on the Côte d'Azur.

Following the formalities of leaving the villa and returning the keys, Bree and Lauren viewed three more properties for future bookings, then headed to St. Tropez for two days. Next on the itinerary were three beach towns relatively close together, Juan les Pins, Nice, and Antibes. A year earlier, Bree and Lauren had discussed adding a Riviera trip to Le Bon Voyage offerings and had chosen the towns then. Bree's notebook was full of prices, ideas, and observations, and her phone was full of photos, which they'd comb through once they'd returned to the States and were back into work mode, planning for the following season. They had one more full day in the busy tourist town before boarding the plane that would return her to Virginia.

Provence now seemed like a filmy dream. Had she really spent a week there, met Travis Jefferies, even fallen in love with him? Maybe she only thought it was love. They didn't know each other well, after all. And what did it matter? She'd never see him again.

Bree winced at the thought. And it didn't stop her from checking her phone email from time to time. He had said he was falling in love with her, but that might have been a line. She frowned. She *had* pushed him away, more than once. Maybe he decided to give her what she'd wanted, space. Only she hadn't really wanted to be left alone, even then.

Since the end of the tour, Lauren's wall of reserve had crept back into place. Once again Bree felt miles away from her friend, incapable of breaking through or understanding what had happened between them. Maybe Lauren was preoccupied by thoughts of Mark and Jean-Pierre. Bree's intuition told her something else was going on, and wondered how she could find out, if Lauren remained closed up like a metal can.

As always, it had been easy to discuss work . . . details, pricing, ideas for excursions. But when it came to the deeper, unguarded layer between two formerly close friends, a quiet awkwardness lay in its place. Pained by Lauren's distance, Bree often ended up cutting away by herself for solitary walks on the beaches of Nice or around the ramparts of Antibes. She hadn't felt so alone since before moving to Virginia three years earlier.

"Lord, I'm glad You're here with me." Her whispered words were nearly lost in the coastal breeze. "I'm not alone, even if I feel like I am. And You understand all that's going on with Lauren and with Travis. Help me to lean on You for all that." She didn't have the strength to figure it all out. Maybe she wasn't supposed to. Not then. Maybe not ever.

Two days later Bree and Lauren boarded a small plane in Marseilles that took them to Paris, where a larger one would carry them back to Dulles Airport in Washington. Back home, back to the same life they'd left. Bree glanced at Lauren's back as the airport employee scanned her boarding pass prior to entering the plane. Bree couldn't shake the feeling that even going back, nothing would ever be the same.

CR   CR   CR

Travis smiled at the shy Italian waitress as she placed a steaming pitcher of dark Lavazza coffee on his table in the breakfast room of the L'Albergo Dante Hotel. "Grazie," he said.

"*Lei vuole un po' di latte freddo*?" she asked, proffering an even smaller metal pitcher of milk.

"Si, Grazie."

The Italian brew slid down like silk. It was his second cup, so he'd be wired that day. He looked over the document covering the small breakfast table . . . the shot list, which would occupy him for the next two weeks. He could visualize the gaps, which he'd need to complete once he'd seen everything he wanted to include in the program. Bellagio, Tremezzo, Menaggio, and, of course, Varenna, around Lake Como, for starters. Then they'd move on to neighboring Lake Maggiore for yet another lineup of stunning locations.

He couldn't possibly cover all six lakes in the region, so he'd chosen two of the most popular, which were also fairly close together. Preproduction would take several days, then they'd shoot for another week. At least over the next few days, with Toby's help, he could shoot the B-roll. With that supplemental footage they could fill in the gaps between primary scenes and interviews. Then by the time the rest of the crew arrived, he'd be ready with the full program. Travis felt a spike in adrenaline as he narrowed his focus on the shoot.

"Excuse me for bothering you." A female voice with an American accent broke through his thoughts. Travis looked up and saw an attractive woman, late twenties, he guessed, standing next to his table. Her auburn hair was caught back by a pair of sunglasses perched on her head. A probing green-eyed stare lowered. "Are you Travis Jefferies?"

"I am." Must be a fan, though he wasn't famous enough for many people to approach him in public.

"I thought it was you. My name is Natalie, and I really enjoy *Planet Discovery*. I try to see all your programs."

He shook her outstretched hand. "I'm glad you like them, Natalie."

"Are you here to film a new program?"

"We're doing a special on the Italian lakes region set to air in the fall. We're just getting started filming today."

Natalie grinned, her white teeth shining against a milky suntan. "Oh, that's so exciting. I don't think I've ever met anyone on television before. I love to travel, so I watch your specials whenever they're on. Have you been to this area before?"

He forced a smile. He needed to finish up and meet Toby at the ferry in about ten minutes. "Yes, I came here a couple of years ago and thought it would be a good place to do a program. And you?"

Natalie glanced over her shoulder at the table where another young woman sat. "My friend Dawn and I are in Varenna for the first time. We were in Rome and Florence before coming here."

"Sounds like a nice trip. Well, enjoy your stay."

"Thanks. See you around." She paused, still smiling for a moment, then turned back to her table. Travis could hear Natalie's friend snicker from across the room. Maybe she had dared Natalie to come over and talk to him. In any case Travis was glad when the woman left without asking to be an extra in his movie. Over the years he'd heard a variety of requests, some hilarious, others indecent. He glanced at his watch and downed his last sip.

The next two days flew by in a blur of breathtaking scenery—plunging cliffs, evergreen-tufted mountains, multicolored clusters of centuries-old dwellings, boardwalks against gently-lapping waves, umbrella-topped cafés, rustic docks. They'd traveled a lot of kilometers. Travis, Toby, and Ben shot footage and scouted locations in several cities surrounding Lake Como.

The pace almost pushed Bree from Travis's thoughts, though not quite. Sometimes at odd moments her face appeared in his imagination, her golden blonde hair, large, blue eyes smoky in the twilight as they'd sat by the pool together, as she connected with his soul—the last time he'd seen her.

He still hadn't contacted her. He didn't fully understand his blockage, but usually ended up telling himself that she'd understand the crazy rhythm of his preproduction phase. She would probably not expect anything immediately. If he were honest with himself he'd admit his hesitation came from uncertainty about her feelings for him. Still, he didn't like having left things so vague, unsure of what she was thinking or if he'd ever see her again. He could simply jot her a note so she'd know he was thinking of her. That wouldn't take too long, would it? But he'd have to decide what to say, and that could take much longer.

Travis sighed. He felt like he was in junior high school, trying to get up the nerve to ask a girl to dance.

The following day was a killer, though Travis reveled in every moment. The crew drove toward Lake Maggiore but encountered Lake Lugano— surrounded by parts of Switzerland— along the way, so he added that to the itinerary. It was well after dark when, following an al fresco meal at a ristorante, they headed back over the hilly highways to Varenna.

Exhausted, Travis climbed the carpeted stairs to his room. As he fished into his backpack for his key he noticed someone in the hallway and turned.

"Oh, hello, Natalie." He kept his voice cool. She'd approached so quietly on the carpeted stairs he hadn't even seen her standing there. Despite the darkened corridor he noticed her sulky beauty, her low-cut tank top.

"I was relaxing in the lounge and saw you come in." Her voice sounded much less nervous than the first day. More self-assured, more familiar. It almost grated on him.

"I guess you've been busy the last couple of days," she said. "I haven't seen you at all."

He snorted softly. If only she knew *how* busy. He felt ragged. "We've covered two lakes and all the little towns along the coastline, all that in two days, so I'd say so." He threw her a bland smile and fumbled with the key.

"Sounds like you need a break. Can I interest you in a drink? Might be relaxing after such a long day." Her tone held a lilt of suggestion, a gentle prodding.

Travis was glad he was too tired to be tempted . . . much. Might be enjoyable to spend time with an attractive woman. And Natalie was right, it would be relaxing. It was just a drink, after all. She smiled coyly at his hesitation.

He shook his head and gave her a tight-lipped smile. "Sounds nice, but we've got an early day tomorrow."

195

"Some other time, maybe."

He noticed how truly beautiful she was, white teeth against a golden tan, large hazel eyes slanted slightly at the corners. If she wanted male company, she wouldn't have any obstacle. Except with him.

He shouldn't look at her for very long, or she'd refuse to believe that he was too tired to go out. The damage was probably done. She'd surely seen the admiring look in his eyes. She'd have easily recognized that look from her extensive experience.

Inside his room he breathed heavily. He had been tempted. It was only a drink but could have consequences he didn't plan or want. Was he just missing Bree? Or was he simply a red-blooded male? A lonely one? Or maybe all of that was an excuse.

At any rate, giving into the *just a little drink* argument would not only increase his exhaustion the following day, making him less sharp, but it would certainly send the wrong message to his fan, Natalie.

He dug into his backpack again and pulled out his cell phone. Threw it on the bed and stared at it. Should he? Would Bree get an email? He suddenly remembered Lauren saying they would be traveling right after the tour. To the coast? He couldn't remember. Bree would be gone for a few days, at least.

He pulled out his digital camera and powered it up. At least he had a few photos of her. He'd wanted to take many more, but he hadn't wanted to appear the lovesick adolescent in front of the other guests. Pretty much what he'd felt like most of the week. Travis found some photos of Bree and clicked slowly through. He'd begun to lose the ability to mentally conjure her face. He'd been able to take her picture several times before she'd realized what he was doing. The candid shots stirred a deep melancholy inside. Maybe he'd find a way to reach out to her sooner or later . . . if she would allow him.

Travis set the alarm on his phone, then set it on the bedside table. He had time to contact Bree after the shoot. Deciding that, he'd be able to focus on his work.

After he slipped into bed, he stared up at the darkened ceiling. The image that floated into his mind wasn't Natalie's sensual appeal. It was the Nostradamus fountain at St. Rémy and Bree sitting on the stone basin beside him, her thick, blond waves curling like ribbons to her shoulders. He mentally caressed the image, trying to keep the memory of her face fresh in his mind. He had to admit, it was fading amidst the many other people and places he'd seen since arriving in Varenna. Each day she slipped a bit further, and even photos wouldn't help. He ached to see her again.

The cell phone beside his bed rang into the quiet and his body jerked. It was after eleven. Travis snatched the phone. Clay. If he was calling and not emailing, maybe it was important.

"Hey, Clay. What's up? I was just about to turn in."

"Travis, I wanted to catch you before you'd gone too far with filming. I've been doing some research on my own. The lakes area in Italy is immensely crowded in summer, so it has huge potential for mishaps, rip-offs, and so on. I'm sure there are things that you can report on, like tourist traps, food poisoning, overbooked tours, capsizing ferries."

"Clay, I thought we—"

"On one hand you'll cover the allure of the Italian lakes, but then at the end, you'll include a segment on things to look out for. People count on you for both sides of the story, the real truth. You can't disappoint them."

Travis sighed. "I told you, if there are warnings that will help tourists enjoy their time better, of course I'll mention them. But I don't want to do the exposé type program like I've done in the past. I want to highlight the positive aspects, not the negative."

"But you're known for this. People expect it when they see *Planet Discovery*."

"We only did one episode like that. And you told me the Italy trip could be on my terms, remember?"

"Did I? Well, the Provence trip was on your terms, wasn't it? How flexible do you expect me to be?" The man's voice had grown sharp.

"The Provence trip was my *personal vacation*. And you signed off on my outline for Italy. I planned the shot list accordingly, and we've just put three full days into scheduling and filming. We can't change now."

"Well, squeeze some time in at the end, then. I'm not saying do a full program on scams. I understand there's research involved there, and you've already started."

Travis wanted to argue, but he had to be careful. "I'm not so sure—"

"Just so you know, after this I have a specific lineup for you. There've been tours in Columbia that have had run-ins with local rebels—"

"How would my program be distinct from Dateline or any other current events program? Mine is primarily a *travel* program. *That* is what people expect from us. We want them to want to travel, right? Not be afraid of it." He seemed to remember Bree saying the same words to him the first night they'd talked in the kitchen.

"This is specifically linked to foreign travel and the victims are innocent tourists. Makes for excellent drama. And that's our focus, Travis. We're not a travel agency. We are primetime television. I've just become aware of small group tours in parts of Africa where people have gone missing—"

"I'm pretty sure I'd have heard about that."

"Or, whatever. These things happen. Our viewers like this." A petulant tone had crept into the man's voice.

"I'm not so sure that they do."

"Need I remind you that you work for *me*?"

"No, Clay." Travis lowered his voice. "Not sure for how long, though."

"What did you say?"

He blew out a breath. "Nothing. We'll talk about this when I come back, okay?"

"Yes, we will. We need to redefine our objectives and make sure we're on the same page. I hope I'm clear."

Clay hung up before Travis could respond. Instead of fatigue his body now tingled with frustration. Wide awake, he replayed the conversation. Had he really warned Clay of a possible parting of company? That had slipped out before Travis could edit his words.

And what had he said about his *special lineup*? Sounded like Clay was planning to close in the walls on Travis's creative license even more, dictating the programs—theme and content— that he would do in the future. If only Travis were better established, he'd simply go independent. He was a maverick anyway and had often chafed under Clay's overbearing ways, not to mention his lack of respect.

But Travis was tied to the public network, an employee of sorts. The very thought rankled him, even if he was thankful for the opportunities they'd given him so far. In the wake of a failed ministry he'd been able to carve a new career, a new identity for himself. He didn't want to lose that, not if he could help it.

But the leash Clay had given him was about to be cut short. Short enough to strangle him.

Chapter Seventeen

The last days of June turned humid, forcing Bree to keep the apartment windows closed and the air conditioner humming. She felt like an insect in an enclosed jar, wanting to be out but having nowhere to go. Seated at her desk, she moved some piles of papers, straightened her post-its and paper clips, and fell back against her chair. Since returning from France a few days ago she just couldn't restart herself, couldn't emerge from her fog.

She didn't really have to be at her desk at all. Following a trip, she and Lauren always allowed themselves a few weeks to catch up on other things or take vacation before starting to plan the next tour. But for once, she wasn't sure what to do with her time. Her thoughts wouldn't stay still. The apprehension that had hovered over her since the early days of their trip had grown tentacles that threatened to choke her.

Because Lauren was coming to *talk*. Finally. About what, Bree dreaded finding out.

Bree opened her computer and was glad to see two inquiries about future tours, though little else for the moment. Against her better judgment, she scrolled through her files from the last trip and found the application she was looking for: Travis Jefferies. She clicked to the last page where his photo stared back at her. Blue eyes, a friendly grin. Sandy curls trapped under the sunglasses perched on his head.

An ache throbbed inside, sending out dull rings of pain. It hadn't been a dream, had it? He had really been a guest on their last trip. She had really spent time with him, kissed him, shared her heart with him. Right before he'd disappeared.

On and off over the previous two weeks she'd gnawed through the question, should she email him? Might not hurt anything, although he was likely still in Italy. She'd probably look as though she were chasing after him. Each time, she'd decided to wait. She'd revisit that decision once she was sure he'd returned to the U.S.

Bree heard the front door open. Lauren. A claw of tension clutched at her insides. "Hi, Lauren," she called, not making an effort this time to sound upbeat. "I'm in the office."

Lauren appeared in the doorway, wearing her hair loose with a headband and a sleeveless cotton blouse. She smiled hesitantly and set a bag on Bree's desk. "I brought a couple of the scones we like from Raphael's. Want one?"

"Sure, thanks." Bree reached into the bag and pulled out the cinnamon scone, her favorite. She wouldn't feel much like eating until this conversation was finished. Her heart thumped so hard, Lauren must surely see her shaking in her chair. She searched her mind for a bland opening, an ice-breaker of sorts, though they'd never needed one in the past. She came up empty. It would just be better to dive into the conversation. Get it over with.

"What's your mind?" She asked. Her voice was soft and she held down a tremble. Tried to sound normal, but it didn't work. "Recently you haven't been the same Lauren I've known for ten years." She managed a half-hearted smile.

Lauren looked stricken. She sat on her chair and wheeled it toward Bree. Then she leaned forward and grasped Bree's hands in hers. Her eyes glistened with gathering tears. She blinked rapidly and swallowed. Her voice emerged in a dry rasp. "I'm *so* sorry, Bree. You are my best friend, and I haven't treated you very well. There was so much I couldn't explain to you during the trip, not until now. I wasn't able to clear the air, because it wasn't a good time to do that. But I couldn't pull off acting normal either. So, I withdrew. It was unkind, and I ask your forgiveness. I didn't know what else to do."

Bree swallowed and moistened her lips. "Of course, I forgive you. But what is it?"

Lauren stared beyond Bree's head toward the window. "I don't know where to start, really. This isn't about Jean-Pierre or about Mark."

Bree tensed. However bad it was, at least the burden of not knowing, which had frozen their friendship into silence, would be finished. She tried to tell herself that this would make it okay.

"When we started this business, I was happy and excited about it. And I loved it at first. But after a while I didn't know for sure if it was—well, if it was my *thing*. I started getting restless."

"When did you start feeling this way?" Bree's voice was quiet, her words slow, though something tore down inside.

"Maybe six months ago. Or maybe more." To her credit, Lauren looked miserable. "I found I wasn't looking forward to the trips as much as I did the first time or two. Truthfully, I think the fact that I love being in France and love having a reason to go several times a year . . . I confused that with loving my job. But the preparation in advance and my role in France, I didn't enjoy them as much as I'd hoped."

Bree's eyes stung. She blinked quickly, wanting Lauren to finish before she dissolved into wails. And she wanted to be alone when that happened. Steeling her voice, she lifted her chin and said, "So you want to leave the company. When will you finish? What will you do?"

Lauren tightened her lips and blinked. Softly she said, "End of the summer. I'll help you with preparations for the tour this fall, but I won't lead it with you. I—I'm still trying to figure out what I'll do afterward. I'm so sorry, Bree."

Bree sat in silence for a moment as the impact of Lauren's words pummeled through layers of denial and pain. She blinked several times. Nodded.

"You can outsource everything I used to do," Lauren insisted with an almost cheerful lilt in her voice. "I know it'll be hard at first to do this alone, but you're *so* good at it. There's no doubt in my mind you can do all of it. *All* of it, Bree. You don't need me at all. You can hire chefs to do my part. Our next trip is a cooking tour, so you'll have less to do on that score. You'll be fine. I'm absolutely sure of that." When Bree didn't speak Lauren said, "Say something, Bree. Please."

Bree's gaze latched onto Lauren's even though she knew her eyes were filling with tears. She shook her head. "If you aren't happy, what else can you do?" Her voice broke. "I'm sorry about that, but I'll be okay. I'll manage." Several tears spilled down her cheeks.

Lauren also began to cry. "I'm so sorry, Bree. I've loved working with you . . . except for your fits of anxiety." She and Bree smiled through their tears. "All the confusion I've had about these men— that wasn't the root issue for me. I was afraid to tell you, so I ended up acting distant."

Both women cried softly for a few minutes in the silence of the apartment. Bree said, "I just want you to be happy, Lauren."

Lauren leaned forward and encircled Bree in her arms, holding her in a tight grip for several minutes. "You're the best friend I've ever had, and I hated hurting you. I hated myself for hurting you." A sob caught in her throat.

"No, don't." Bree pulled back. "You can't make yourself love something. It was a worthy try, and it wasn't a fit for you. You can't blame yourself." Bree believed her words. She wasn't angry at Lauren. She just had no idea where her friend's decision left her. "Have you talked to Mark?"

Lauren nodded. "I told him I needed some space. We didn't break up for good, but we're taking a step back."

"Did you tell him about Jean-Pierre?"

"No. I didn't think it was a good idea, since this isn't really about Jean-Pierre. I think I was restless with Mark before. I do want to go back to France, though I don't know when. I'll have more clarity over there."

"Maybe once you do that, everything will come together about Mark and about what you'll do in the future."

Lauren offered a weak smile. "I hope so. I'm still very confused, but peaceful at the same time."

Bree stood and reached for a tissue to blow her nose and mop her wet cheeks. "I need to get out of the apartment and process all this. But I'll be okay. Please don't worry." She cast a final sad smile at Lauren and squeezed her shoulder. She left the office and grabbed her purse from the kitchen table, then closed the front door of the apartment behind her.

Tears tumbled down her face as she drove toward a local park about two miles from her apartment. Everything outside was blurry from her tears. She wanted to avoid a public place. It was a hot day to be in the park but she couldn't think of any other place where she'd have privacy.

She parked her car and trudged across the crisp, burned grass to a small fountain. She sat on the ground and leaned back against its base, listening to the gurgle of drops hitting the water's surface. A faint chlorine smell wove with the fragrance of dirt and grass. The sound had always calmed her in the past.

But this was something else.

More tears came, stronger and faster, until she was sobbing over her lost dream, as it splintered into a million pieces. Though the park stretched out around her with its wide, open spaces, she may as well have been back at her parents' house, locked in the closet at seven years old. Helpless, trapped, without hope. Alone to fend for herself. The reality crashed down on her as the tears flowed. First Travis, then Lauren, then Le Bon Voyage. What did she have left?

Where was God when she'd been abandoned in that closet? Where was He now?

 C஧   C஧   C஧

By the following week the entire crew was assembled, extra cameramen, audio, and other assorted personnel, and they began filming in earnest. Travis had a varied and interesting lineup of interview candidates, some shopkeepers and other locals who talked about how tourism impacted their lives, both positively and negatively. Travis was back on camera again, talking as if to a friend, and he hoped he came across the same as when he was with his buddy back in Portland.

"Man, that guy at the boat rental kiosk had some choice words about tourists." Toby jammed his fingers through red, wavy hair before depositing his baseball cap backward on his head.

Travis shrugged. "Some people aren't even happy if their income triples during tourist season. All they see is the inconvenience." Though he had disdain for people like that, the man's comments might be enough to placate Clay and his seemingly insatiable thirst for negative commentary.

Travis winced. After that late-night conversation with Clay he'd almost started looking for things that could go wrong, the dark underside of the tourist experience. But it felt like wearing shoes that didn't fit, chafing on every side. In the short term, until he could figure out his next steps, it had to look like he was making an effort to comply with Clay's desire. Then once they were face to face, with the project behind him, they could hopefully negotiate a compromise.

All morning they'd filmed in Lugano. When they broke for lunch an idea occurred to him, maybe something to get Clay off his back or distract him so the Italy program could unfold as planned. He sent a quick email. *Clay, what would you think about a reality show involving a travel destination, like Provence or elsewhere? That might be in line with what you're looking for. We can bounce that idea around once I get back.*

It was just an idea, and he didn't have to follow through on it. If he did, however, he could do it with Bree. A double win. He was gratified by an almost immediate response from Clay: *Great idea. We'll talk more about that when you get back.* How much time Travis had bought, he'd find out soon enough.

For the final two days of the project, Travis planned to film in Varenna. He'd developed an attachment for the place in the two weeks they'd been there.

"Ready, Travis? Take one." The shout came from Bill, the second cameraman. Toby stood on the other side of him, an enormous camera perched on his shoulder. Travis stood on the small boardwalk that hugged the shore of the lake. He was going to walk slowly backward, talking as he went, then the cameras would film various views and pan to the terraced buildings on the hillside as talked. All of this would have to be edited, and if the audio didn't quite meet his expectations, it would be re-recorded.

As usual, Travis ignored the bulk of the camera on the dolly overhead. A small crowd had gathered on the shore to watch. Among the faces Travis spotted Natalie. He grimaced. Hoped she wasn't going to become a pest. Maybe she'd just watch the shoot then go her way. If she had been enamored before with what she'd already seen of him on television, she'd probably start stalking him after seeing a shoot in action. Not that she was unpleasant to look at. But he was not in the market for a new lady friend. He still needed to figure out what to do about Bree, who hovered just beyond all his conscious thoughts.

"Ready, Travis?"

He nodded and when he saw the light on the camera and a small gesture from Bill, he began speaking. "One of the jewels of the Italian lakes region is the town of Varenna. I'm here on the passerella overlooking Lake Como. Just over there . . ." Toby steered his camera toward the hillside, filming over the heads of the gawking tourists, ". . . is the town itself, terraced for centuries up the wooded hillside. This area has drawn celebrities, who have bought sumptuous homes here and in nearby Bellagio, but many of those who arrive are Italian weekenders from the cities of Milan and Verona, less than two hours away."

He talked a few minutes longer about the history of the town and some demographic statistics, then concluded. "There are eight hundred fulltime residents here, and their experiences are as varied as the tourists who flock to these shores every week. We'll meet a few of them. First, you'll meet Marcel, who rents boats to visitors." Of course, the interviews had taken place already, but would be spliced in later, when the editing team got their hands on the film.

Following the segment, the crew collapsed at a lakeside café for a break. It had been a good morning, and Travis figured they would finish on schedule the following day. The cold Italian beer went down easily and slaked the thirst he'd worked up by talking for the better part of the morning. He looked up from his glass and saw Natalie approach wearing a lime green strapless sundress, an impressive cleavage squeezing out at the top. He stifled an inward groan and glanced away.

"Hi, Travis." She sat in an empty chair beside him and pushed up her sunglasses so that her green eyes engaged his. "It was so interesting to watch you all filming this morning. I was fascinated. I'll never watch your program in the same way again. Just to see it actually happen. It was one of the most memorable moments of my trip."

He tried to be cordial without being too inviting. "I'm glad you enjoyed it. We get pretty caught up in it. Nothing glamorous, just hard work." Just in case she was mistakenly star-struck.

"You must have such huge satisfaction, though."

Travis shrugged. "I enjoy watching the end result, after all the hard work. Of course, months of labor go into that finished product."

"And after all that work it must be so rewarding to know you've made an impact on people." She finished with a disarming smile, a smile that nudged his protective wall slightly, though less than her words did. *Impact,* something he hadn't felt in Provence, but now he did, once again. Natalie sat without speaking for a moment while she observed the pedestrians around her.

Travis didn't speak or try to strike up a conversation. It was better that way, even if it felt awkward. And even if he was touched by her comment.

She rose. "Well, I'll let you get back to your work. See you around." She gave a small wave and a promising smile.

When she'd gone several guys on the crew made small hoots and whistles. "Way to go, Romeo. Didn't take too long!"

"Go after her, man. You have time—"

"Some guys have all the luck!"

Travis gave them a dismissive wave. "We have about ten minutes. We need to finish up in Varenna this afternoon and wrap up some nearby sites at dusk. We'll wait until around seven this evening, so we get the reflections and sunsets." He looked around and saw he'd been successful at distracting the crew away from Natalie's attributes and back to their work.

Several hours later, following a twilight filming session, the crew filed into a local trattoria and enjoyed a lengthy meal in rowdy male fashion. High spirits and plenty of laughter with his men felt satisfying after an exhausting day.

Afterward, Travis shuffled through the narrow, cobbled streets instead of returning to his room, to get some time alone in the quiet of evening. Italians and tourists still roamed the streets and he enjoyed the music of varied languages blending together in an understated symphony. Some people wandered through the alleys and others finished their meals on terraces along the water, their conversations and banter rising and dispersing into the night. Across the lake, small lights like fireflies flickered from the houses and buildings as well as the opposite shoreline.

He ended up near the shore where the small boardwalk traced the darkened banks. He'd done one of his film clips there that morning but now the strolling visitors were sparse. The water lapped against the shore in peaceful whispers, low waves blackened in the diluted light.

Travis slipped into an available chair and watched the last breath of the sun stain the sky deep purple. The stars peered through the night and lights from the buildings shimmered off the calm surface of the lake, forming dancing, distorted reflections.

It had been a very good shoot. They'd lost little time and things had gone remarkably smoothly. That wasn't always the case. He pulled his thoughts away from his work. He needed to do that regularly, systematically, to avoid becoming imbalanced or even obsessed by his current project. But that week, whenever he did shift his thoughts, they drifted to Bree. Bree, who he still had not contacted.

He didn't know if he should feel like a heel or if it was simply wise to keep his distance from her. Since he didn't believe he was well-stocked with wisdom, he often felt like the jerk who had blown her off. Yet he couldn't make himself reach out and risk rejection again, so he willingly got swallowed by the project. Excuses, all excuses. He knew it and didn't respect himself for the way he handled it, or his failure day after day to do anything else.

After two weeks he could still conjure her face in his mind, though it was getting harder each day. He missed her. The whole Provence week seemed like a dream. Had it really happened? He recalled their talks, strolling through medieval alleyways together. St. Rémy-de-Provence. Aix-en-Provence. Roussillon . . . He recalled in agonizing detail how she felt in his arms, her soft skin, her floral, feminine scent, how she'd surrendered to him . . . right before pulling away.

She'd never told him how she felt about him, though by her response he would say her feelings were far from neutral. The idea of not seeing her again was simply— unthinkable.

"Mind if I join you?"

Travis looked up. Natalie. Yes, he did mind. She'd changed clothes and now wore a clingy, black top and cut-off jeans.

He gestured to the empty seat beside him, only because it seemed impolite not to. So much for his alone time. The woman hadn't yet taken any hints. She probably thought she could wear him down. Maybe she would. He considered being blunt with her then decided it was too much trouble. Besides that, he didn't want to be rude. Hoped he wouldn't regret it.

"Are you enjoying your vacation?" he asked

"It's been fabulous. My friend Dawn needs more down time than I do, so she went to bed early. I'm a night person, and it's the perfect night for a walk. Looks like you and I had the same idea." Her glance and tone seemed conspiratorial.

Travis shrugged. "We put in long days every day. It isn't vacation for us. Those five guys are my colleagues, but I need a break after ten or twelve hours with them."

Natalie leaned back and encircled her smooth, tanned legs with her arms. "I can so relate. I work in human resources back home in Chicago, and I'm around people all day long. Sometimes I just need to go for a run by myself."

They fell silent for several moments. Travis let his gaze follow the movement of the lights on the water. The air was traced with an evening chill. Reminded him of the barbeque on the terrace in Provence.

"How much longer will you have to film before you're finished?"

He looked at her, then wished he hadn't. Her mouth was plump and pink, and those eyes, green and fringed by thick lashes, slightly tilted for a mysterious, promising look. He turned back to the water. "Tomorrow or the next day should wrap it up." His voice sounded more curt than he'd intended.

"Tomorrow," she softly repeated.

He needed to scoot before he got into trouble. Not that it happened often, compared to the opportunities, though he couldn't claim a stellar record. Travis pulled up from his chair. "Well, Natalie, I'm going to turn in. Enjoy the rest of your visit, okay?"

He pulled himself out of the chair and began walking away when he heard her voice behind him. "I'll walk with you." Then she fell into step beside him. "I need to get some sleep too. We had an early tour this morning, and I'm beat."

They returned along the cobbled path to the hotel, tucked into a side street. He entered the hotel, and she followed behind. He thought she'd turn off somewhere on his route to his room, but either her room was on the same hallway as his, or the woman was following him.

He approached his door and turned to speak to her. When he did she plunged toward him and he found her lips against his, her arms coiled around his neck. He stumbled slightly against the wall as she pressed against him and murmured, "Don't you want this, Travis? I can tell that you like me."

"I—uh—"

Before he had a chance to answer, she pushed toward him and renewed her kiss, pulling him against her until he found himself responding. She did feel good against him, a beautiful woman with soft lips, smelling floral and sweet. Her arms curled tighter around him, pulling him, until they were welded together, leaning against the wall outside his room.

"I can stay with you tonight if you want me to," she whispered into his ear between small kisses she planted on his neck. "I find you so attractive, and I love what you do, it's so interesting. You're such a fascinating and handsome man. I don't think I've ever met anyone like you."

Her words came in breathy succession between kisses. In spite of himself, his blood raced. He should push her away, speak up, do something. He felt himself weakening second by second. He wasn't committed to anyone else, had been alone for a long, long time. He'd never again see Natalie again after tonight. Would it hurt anything, just this once?

Chapter Eighteen

His thoughts were muddy, confused, as Natalie's lips opened against his, as she pressed her chest into him. *Now or never, Travis.* He placed his hands on her shoulders and gently pushed her from him. Once he did, even though she was still only inches away, he felt a new strength fill him. "Natalie, I can't." His voice was ragged. "You're very pretty, but my heart belongs to someone else."

She stumbled backward a step. Her face reddened and her eyes widened. Maybe no one had ever turned her down before. "Oh, I—I must have misunderstood. I'm sorry to have bothered you." Turning she slipped back down the hallway, her head down.

Travis watched her vanish around the corner and turned wearily to unlock his door. He entered his room and sat on the edge of the bed. Close call. *My heart belongs to someone else*, he'd said. Did he mean Bree? Yes and no. He belonged to God. A son. Wayward, yes, but a son nonetheless. There was a time he might have given in to Natalie, excusing it at the moment, though the guilt would have assaulted him the next morning. But not now. Not anymore. He felt clean and something else . . . God's welcome? He smiled, nodded. And not because he'd stood firm just then. God had been reaching out all along, even through his failures.

And what about Bree? She hadn't left his heart or thoughts in the two weeks since he'd seen her. It would have been easy to cut his losses. They'd been separated, couldn't be helped. He lived across the country from her. But those were excuses. He loved her still. It was time to stop waffling and move in her direction.

Travis pulled his phone out of his backpack. Whether she'd agree or not was another question, but he had to try. He didn't plan to give a lot of detail. He wanted to tell her his feelings in person, but he didn't want too much information to go into the Bon Voyage inbox. This was for Bree alone.

Hello, Bree, he wrote. *I'm so sorry I didn't get a chance to say good bye when I left France.* He frowned. So far, it sounded like a good-bye letter. *I want to see you again.* There, that was clear. How? He thought for a minute. He could regroup in Portland for a few weeks then plan some vacation time to see her.

Travis shook his head. He was already flying right over her state, or close to it. If he changed his itinerary, he could stop in D.C. If he did that, he'd see her in less than a week. He closed his eyes for a moment, imagining her face. He'd been working like a dog for two weeks. He could take three or four days before getting back to Portland.

I'll be finished filming here tomorrow. What do you think if I stop over in D.C. on my way back to home? I fly on the 25th. I can get a hotel near you. So that she wouldn't think he was asking her to put him up. *Please let me know the name of your town and if it's okay for me to come. Thanks, Travis.*

He pushed send and leaned back on the bed, satisfied. Satisfied that he'd finally made a move toward Bree. And satisfied to have escaped a dicey predicament with Natalie, which would surely have shadowed his chances with Bree, not to mention his fledgling attempts to get back with God. God had given him the strength he wouldn't have had alone.

As he drifted off to sleep he imagined Bree in her green tank top and painted toenails, laughing, her left arm out the car window. She'd looked at him, inviting him with her wide, blue eyes, snagging a soft, pink lip with her white teeth, and reached for his hand . . .

The following morning Travis sat at the same café table as he had throughout his visit and sipped the rich, chocolaty coffee he would miss. He'd tucked a few packages of the delicious ground beans in his duffle. No sign of Natalie today. He doubted he'd see her again.

He'd wanted to start early so they could wrap up filming. They'd see if anything had to be re-filmed, then begin the journey home. A couple of months ago he'd booked a flight from Milan to Paris for two days, then on to JFK. Though he was eager to see Bree sooner, the extra days might give her more time to respond. That morning he'd sent an email to change the ticket from JFK to Dulles. Back to the States. Back to Bree Sorenson. He grinned in anticipation but hoped his decision would meet a warm welcome. He probably should have awaited her reply before changing the ticket. But he knew regardless of her response, he had to see her.

Long bands of sunlight spilled in through tall windows. A hush of conversation in various languages drifted around the dining room, and the scent of baked bread floated from the kitchen. The same Italian waitress brought him more coffee and milk without being asked. She was used to him by now. She smiled shyly. "*Signore . . . ancora . . . ?*"

"*Si. Grazie mille.*"

His phone beeped indicating a new email. From Bree? He glanced at the phone. Not yet. His travel agent had responded to him about the change.

Below the email from his travel agent sat one from Clay he hadn't seen that morning. What did he want now? Travis read, *I'm giving you a choice. You do what you want with Italy, but you do it my way for Provence. Of course, since you're still in Italy, it'll be easier to adapt the Italy content. Just giving you advance notice before you launch into a new project. Clay.*

Travis was beginning to wonder if Clay had early dementia. The man had already agreed to leave Travis alone to work on the Italy project. Since Travis' arrival in Italy Clay had gone back on his promise and now had brought up the Provence idea—again. Apparently, the reality show idea didn't placate him. Clay wasn't giving up.

There was no way he could change his position on Provence. Not only because he didn't want to, but he couldn't possibly betray Bree. Not to mention he had no footage. Travis hit "reply" and responded slowly and carefully. *Clay, I understand your concerns, but you did agree to allow me creative oversight of this project. The Provence trip was my personal vacation time, so naturally, I have no data or footage. I think it's best that we honor those discussions and start fresh when I return. I can hear your ideas at that time and we'll decide on a plan. I cannot do otherwise at this point.*

He re-read the email and pushed send.

Travis breathed deeply and prayed, *Lord, your will on this. Help me to have integrity in this job You have given me. Help me know what to do.*

Only minutes later an email returned to him. Clay had written, *Don't forget, you work for me. I want part of the program to cover what we discussed, since that is what people expect. Or the Provence group, which I'd actually prefer. Try to make this happen. We cannot change our branding and suddenly offer a new type of program. I'm off to a meeting now.*

Frustration ate at his bones. This had been going on for too long. He chafed at this feeling, like a puppet on Clay's string. He had to respond. *It is far too late to change the Italy program. I'm sure you understand this. We complete filming tomorrow.* He was struggling to remain polite. But he knew it wasn't simply a matter of it being too late. He was opposed to Clay's agenda, opposed to sensationalism built from peoples' disasters. How had he landed in this position?

Travis stared down at the phone. *Or the Provence group.* Out of the question. He wouldn't betray Bree. He typed, *I can't comply with the Provence trip. And I don't agree that viewers will be disappointed by a well-done program without warnings. I need to work with clear expectations before a project begins.* He held his breath then hit send.

The next day went by with no word from Clay. Travis took that as a good sign. He also had not heard from Bree, but he didn't know if there was a reason to be concerned. He could contact her again that evening. It would be morning for her, and she'd be more likely to respond.

The last morning in Italy, Travis took a long look around the town, mentally recording the pink cast on the buildings, the reflection on the water, the stalwart evergreens staggered up the hillside. He'd try to return one day.

During an afternoon break Travis look over his emails and saw a response from Clay. It said simply, *Okay.* He cocked his head, perplexed. Okay? Sounded like Clay was in agreement. And that was nothing like Clay.

Just to make sure, Travis shot off a response. *Okay, what?*

The afternoon went by quickly, absorbing him into the final aspects of filming and organizing the work. Travis forgot about Clay. The final hours were the most critical, a time to make sure the check list was complete.

At four he finally proclaimed it a 'wrap'. The film would be sent back to Portland and once he returned, he and the editing team would plunge into their piece of the project, under his supervision.

He returned to his room to organize his things for an early departure the following day. He'd meet the crew for a celebratory dinner in a couple of hours at one of their favorite trattorias. After he packed, he pulled out his phone to see if Bree had responded.

He frowned. She hadn't. Maybe she was still traveling and hadn't received his message. It was possible, but not likely. A self-proclaimed control freak, she'd check her phone regularly. He hoped she wasn't angry that he had left too early to say goodbye. He regretted not contacting her sooner and hoped that was not the reason she hadn't responded. He could always phone her if necessary, but he still had a couple of days. And he'd rather her respond on her own.

Travis jotted off another message. *Hello, Bree. I sent you a note a few days back. Did you receive that? I'd like to come see you and wanted to ask if that was convenient for you. I hope to hear from you. Travis.* He re-read it. Sounded kind of cold to him, but for a second contact, it would do.

In his inbox sat a new mail from Clay. Travis looked at his watch. It would be eight a.m. for him. He opened it. *Okay means I understand you refuse to change either program. I'm tired of this discussion, so I guess we're finished here.*

Travis felt a thud like a small cannon ball hitting his stomach. He wrinkled his brow. Finished? Was Clay *firing* him? A chill rippled along his scalp and down his spine. He'd pushed the man too far. Maybe Clay was bluffing, manipulating. Maybe not.

Travis re-read his message to Clay. It did look something like an ultimatum. Had he intended that? His jaw tightened. For months Clay had been pressuring him in a direction he objected to going. Maybe it was better this way. He wouldn't beg for his job, apologize, or hang his head, although it would do more than sadden him to leave television. It would send him back to zero.

Travis sank down on the bed and let Clay's response and its implications wash over him. Fired, because he refused to do things Clay's way, refused to compromise. It was the moment now to think about options, to brainstorm a new career plan, no longer theoretically or wishfully.

This time it was for real.

Chapter Nineteen

Four days after the conversation that had tossed her future firmly into mid-air, Bree dragged herself back into the office. She'd kept the office door closed as if the room were not there, avoiding emails, shunning anything that reminded her of the company. Soon to be *her* company—alone. She knew she had to face it sooner or later. Especially if she were going to ask herself that difficult question: Did she *want* to run Le Bon Voyage alone? Another question that hid not far behind, *could* she do it without Lauren's help?

She sat at her desk and stared at the tidy workspace. Her eyes fell on the small, round stone she always kept on her desk where she could see it. She picked it up and rolled it in her palm, squeezed it, then held it up so that she could read it. "Nothing will happen today that you and I can't handle.—God"

She let it sink in a word at a time. Reread it. Twice. She listened to her breath, stilled her thoughts. She was not going to move until she'd received that message like an arrow into the soft tissue of her heart. She chose to receive it. No longer would she run about like a hamster on a wheel. Things needed to change and now was the time. It all boiled down to one thing: There was nothing He could not handle. Including her safety, her career, and her heart.

After a few moments of focused concentration, a tiny smile crept up Bree's face. Yes, and even this. Even Lauren leaving their company and everything that had happened with Travis. God already knew these things, and nothing took Him by surprise. Just because she didn't know what lay around the corner didn't mean *He* didn't. Everything was not up to her.

She laughed aloud and shook her head. "Lord, I've been trying to take Your place for too long. How about if I let You handle everything?"

Her gaze panned the small office and swept across Lauren's corner desk. Could Bree outsource Lauren's role? Probably. Bree was organized, had plenty of contacts in France. They'd broken through the hardest part of starting a business, the first three years. They weren't solid yet, but a lot of things were routine by now. Maybe she could do it. With God's help. And His protection.

A small hum began inside that radiated wider and wider. A splash of joy and anticipation became a wellspring. Lauren had assured Bree the other day that she was capable of doing the job alone. She'd been sincere, Bree knew, since Lauren was not inclined to flattery. And she was right. Bree *could* do it alone. It might be more nerve-wracking than usual the first time or would have been before she'd learned to *really* lean on God. And she was confident she'd get the hang of it.

And as Lauren had also said, the fact that the next trip was a cooking tour would take some effort off of Bree's plate. It would enable her to transition gradually to her new role. The cooking classes had already been reserved for several months. Bree only needed to book chefs for the at-home meals, or enlist the guests themselves since, she'd been surprised to learn, they enjoyed helping with some of the cooking.

The front door opened. "Knock-knock. It's me," Lauren called.

"In here."

Lauren appeared in the doorway, looking worried. "How are you doing, Bree? I'm surprised to see you back at your desk."

Bree swiveled her chair to face Lauren. "I'm good. Really."

"Really?" Lauren's brows arched. "Oh, I'm so glad." She grabbed her own desk chair and faced Bree. "You know, I'll still be around for a couple months. We'll transition together."

"Thanks. It's going to be okay. I think God is showing me that I can do this with His help, and I can entrust everything to Him." She added with a grin, "Sure is a lot easier that way."

Lauren laughed. "So, I've been saying! I'm so grateful. You seem so—balanced and mature about this. I'm seeing a new Bree, too, trusting more than before. I don't know what to say. It's lovely."

"That means a lot. I really want you to be happy and I do hope you'll find your niche. I'll be fine, though. Do you want to stay for lunch?"

"I can't today. Rain check? I have a hair appointment in a little while but wanted to stop by and check in on you."

"This is the first day I've been in the office since our chat. I needed some time away and it was helpful. It gave me perspective. Now I have to regroup and catch up on the—on my business."

Lauren and Bree stood and reached for each other, holding in a tight squeeze. Tears pricked Bree's eyes. Things were different in their business, but they were back to normal in their friendship. Bree was immensely grateful for that.

After Lauren left, Bree sat again, feeling thankful and ready to begin a new chapter. She turned on her computer and waited as numerous emails downloaded. She scanned the list and her eyes widened when she saw not one, but two messages from Travis.

She clicked the earlier one and read his message. He wanted to see her, to come to her town and stay a few days. *She* wanted to see

223

him, for many reasons. One reason was that she was a better Bree than she had been before. She felt lighter, free of tension, despite what had happened with Lauren. And she wanted to test her feelings for him, be with him again. She'd learn why he hadn't written to her sooner. Surely, he had a good reason.

Bree glanced at the date of the mail. It had been sent two days earlier, but she hadn't responded. What must he be thinking? She looked up at her desk calendar. In four days, she'd see Travis. She read the second mail, which he'd sent yesterday, repeating the same request. She hoped he hadn't changed his mind, thinking she didn't want to see him.

She hit *reply*, in a hurry to compose a message to him. *Hi Travis.* What to say? If she had more time, she'd try to be eloquent but not overdo it. *I was happy to receive your mail. I'd like to see you, too.* That was an understatement. Bree laughed aloud, feeling giddy and lighthearted.

She shook her head, aware of the need to think clearly. *I live in a Virginia suburb of D.C. called Benson, about a half-hour drive from the airport.* She listed a few hotels near her home and gave him her personal email and cell phone number. She added, *I'm glad you're able to come.* She hoped she wasn't too late.

On impulse she phoned Lauren to give her the news about Travis. It rang and rang. She must be in her hair appointment or driving and unable to answer. Bree left a message. "Travis is coming here to see me. Just thought you'd be interested to know."

She hung up, a wide grin on her face.

Minutes later her phone rang. "That's great news, Bree." Lauren's voice was jubilant, though Bree heard traffic noise in the background. "I'm saying that because I know you really like him. And I think he could be good for you. He's a good guy."

Yes, he was that and more.

After lunch, her cell phone beeped with a new message. She snatched up her phone and read the screen. Travis. Clicked on his text. He'd gotten her response. He was coming to see her.

Her heart raced, hope exploding like fireworks. Her head told her to tread cautiously. After all, he'd left without a word and not contacted her in weeks.

She quickly skimmed his message, which included his flight details. He'd concluded, *Can't wait to see you. T.*

He'd signed 'T'. That was kind of intimate, wasn't it? At least like a good friend. And he couldn't wait to see her. Well, the sentiment was completely mutual.

଼   ଼   ଼

"I wanted us to have breakfast together before we all head out," Travis explained to the five men seated around the table on the final morning of their stay in Varenna. L'Albergo Dante had become a homey Italian nest for over two weeks, but that day they'd all fly away to the four winds. A wisp of melancholy blew by as Travis considered that thought, and as he understood that it might be the last time for him to be in front of a camera . . . anywhere.

He swallowed his emotions and downed his last sip of Lavazza coffee, which sweetened this bitter moment just slightly. What sweetened it much more was Bree's response, which he'd received the previous evening. He'd see her in only three days.

He'd had one additional exchange with Clay since then as well. He'd asked Clay to allow him to complete and air the Italy program before parting company, since they'd put so much into it and it only needed editing. The man had responded simply, *Agreed.* Must be Clay's new method, these one-word answers. But this one was crystal clear. His executive producer wasn't budging on his decision,

225

nor telling Travis he'd been impulsive when he'd fired him. No, Travis had the distinct impression that he himself had burned all his bridges.

Travis cleared his throat and said, "Guys, I need to update you all on something." The men around the table quieted their conversations and turned their attention to Travis.

"In the near future, maybe within the next six months, I am considering starting an independent film company. Most of you work freelance, so I wanted to let you know I'll be looking for skilled people, as you all are, to help me out. I'll send you all updates from time to time and if you think you'd like to join me, just let me know, either now or later."

The questions began. "Will you do the same type of programs that you've been doing?"

"Do you have investors already?"

"How long have you planned going indie?"

Travis held up his hand. "I appreciate your interest, guys, really. First, I want to say I enjoyed working with every one of you and hope at least a few of you will be able to work with the new company. It would be a privilege to continue with you. I plan to get away from the scam and exposé-type journalism and do programs like what we've done here. This project has been the epitome of what I want to do in the future. I've been feeling a lack of freedom in creativity and doing things as I feel—" he searched for a word, "—compelled to present them. I want people to fall in love with the other countries and peoples of the world. I think that has the power to break down barriers but also bring enjoyment of our fellow human beings. That's my aim." He was gratified to see nods and smiles around the table. "If that's your vision too, I hope you'll join me. And either way, I hope we'll stay in touch."

A hard lump remained in his throat and continued during the well-wishes and hugs at departure. Nearly every man said he'd consider it a privilege to continue working with Travis and appreciated his integrity and vision. A very good start to a new business.

As he boarded the plane in Milan with Toby, Travis realized he wasn't thinking of his next two days in Paris, one of his favorite cities, as much as he was thinking of Benson, Virginia and Bree Sorenson.

∞   ∞   ∞

It had been a productive morning. In the last two days Bree had gotten back into the groove, but with a new sense of ownership. She was the boss now.

She sent information to several people who had inquired about tours and wrote to the guests of the recent trip to ask them for referrals. Making a few more advance reservations for the coming trip helped her feel more on top of things, even though it was months away. She booked a new villa as well. And she'd sent several email inquiries to chefs that Lauren had recommended, ones who worked in the Luberon region, as a first step in setting up the at-home meals for the coming tour.

She didn't need to work full-time yet, but as the new sole owner of Le Bon Voyage, she'd need to think on her own about every aspect, possibly even changing a few procedures. She felt ready, as she took one small step at a time.

At noon she was about to quit for the day. She arranged papers and post-its that were scattered across her desk, even though she'd be returning to it later. She was about to leave the office when the phone rang. "Le Bon Voyage, Bree Sorenson speaking," she answered in her "official" voice. Might be a new potential traveler.

"Hello, Miss Sorenson. My name is Will Spence, and I work with the PNC Network."

"Hello. What is this about, Mr. Spence?" Bree frowned. Wasn't PNC Network the company Travis worked for?

"I'm calling about a program we're considering on tours in a small-group context. Travis Jefferies spoke to us about that possibility. It isn't definitely on the schedule, but we'd like to talk to you more at length to see if there is potential. You do know Mr. Jefferies, don't you?"

Bree sank down to her chair, perplexed. "Yes, I know him. Is this call about the reality show idea?" Her scalp prickled. Had Travis done a report after all on the Provence trip?

"Maybe. We were interested in that idea. That's why we wanted to speak with you and hopefully arrange a conference call with our executive producer as well as some other staff here at the station. When would be a good time to do that?"

Her head was spinning. Travis had spoken about the reality show idea to his network *before* confirming it with her? She'd told him she might be interested in the future, but certainly not yet. And he'd assured her that she could think about it and let him know if she wanted to discuss it further. No pressure, he'd said. Yet he'd already scheduled it.

"Hello?"

"I'm not ready to set a date just now, Mr. Spence. I'll be in a better position to schedule something in a week or two. Would that work for you?" She'd buy some time until after she spoke with Travis.

He had a lot to answer for.

"No rush, although we'd like to start well in advance of airing the program, as I'm sure you can understand."

She took the man's number and hung up, then fell back against her chair. Was *that* the reason for Travis's visit?

Bree couldn't believe it. For two days she'd been excited about spending time with Travis, to pick up where they left off in Provence. To see if there was something between them that they could build on.

But her buoyancy evaporated like vapor over a stove. He wanted to use her and her company to further *his* career. What about hers? What about the feelings he seemed to have for her? Was this all wrapped up in the program? A means to an end?

She would still see him the following day. She looked at her watch. In just over twenty-four hours. Despite his betrayal, there was still a giddy flutter inside. Despite her anger, she'd let him explain himself. Despite everything, she wanted to see him.

Even if it was for the last time.

Chapter Twenty

The text message arrived at three in the afternoon. Restless, Bree was on her knees with a sponge in her hand cleaning the refrigerator when she heard her phone beep. She snatched it off the kitchen table. Her heartbeat ratcheted up several notches when she saw Travis's name pop up. He had arrived.

He'd just gotten through customs and was on his way to the hotel. *I'll be waiting outside the hotel at 5, if that's good for you. I'd like to take you out to dinner.*

Bree couldn't suppress a smile, even though she was technically still angry at him. How to stay angry, though, when she only wanted to pick up where they'd left off and enclose him in her arms? If only she hadn't learned his true motivation. Why should she be so surprised and hurt?

Later as she drove in the direction of his hotel, a tug of war between excitement and frustration yanked around inside her. She wore a cotton dress in deep turquoise, casual yet flattering against her hair and eye color, and had spent longer than usual in front of the mirror. She'd left her hair loose, brushed to a golden sheen and tucked behind her ears. It had only been three weeks since she'd seen him, but it felt like months.

Oh, how she wanted to believe the best about him. But what else could she conclude? Travis had talked about his idea to his boss before talking to her. Maybe he planned on doing a reality show with someone else, but the network was the one who had made the mistake. Maybe there was a logical reason for the misunderstanding. Maybe he was innocent.

And so it went, back and forth in her mind, all the way to the hotel. She followed her GPS, relieved to have the clipped voice instructing her, in light of her distraction. Finally, the hotel came into view.

Bree turned into the driveway and saw him leaning against a column under the covered portico of the hotel, fiddling with his phone. He looked dressier than she'd seen him in Provence, wearing long pants, a plaid button-down shirt rolled up to his elbows, and sandals. His curly hair fell nearly to his shoulders and was tacked into place by his sunglasses on top of his head. Even from a distance he was striking. Tall, well-built, well-dressed. Something warm and fluttery stirred inside her. She took a long breath and blew it out in a puff, trying to calm her hammering heart.

Not the time to get weak. As her Honda approached the overhang, he looked up and grinned, then tucked his phone away in his backpack. Some of her defenses fell then, but she'd try hard to keep the rest from sliding away.

Travis pulled the passenger door open and slipped inside, filling up the car with his nearness. "It's *so* good to see you." His eyes roved over her appreciatively. "You look—beautiful."

Okay, the anger was going to be really tough to hold with him staring at her as if she were the most gorgeous creature he'd ever seen. And to have him sitting so close, close enough to touch. "How was your flight?" Sounded cordial, aloof. Not at all what she'd choose to say, if the circumstances were different.

"It was direct, so not long. I was anxious to get here."

She focused on driving but glanced at him. "Did your shoot in Italy go well?"

His eyes narrowed slightly. "Perfectly. I missed you, but otherwise everything was fine." He gave her a lopsided grin, and she had to smile back.

Bree was thankful she could keep her eyes on the road. Looking at him too long would surely melt her anger and then she'd get hurt all over again.

"Where are we headed for dinner?"

"There's a place I thought you'd like, just casual cuisine, but there's a terrace and—" she glanced at him, "—a fountain." She'd planned it before the phone call from Will Spence.

"Excellent choice." His eyebrows lifted, and his tone was almost sensual. The focus in his eyes told her this wasn't purely business.

After a few seconds of silence, his tone shifted. "Bree, I'm getting the distinct impression that you're irritated about something. I should know, since I've been the object of your irritation more than once. Want to tell me what's going on?"

She sighed. At least they'd get the hard part over with. She shot him a glare. "Yesterday I received a call from a certain Will Spence from your network. He told me they were preparing for a reality show that you talked to them about, and they wanted to set up a conference call with me and your executive producer." She glanced at his face and saw furrowed brows. His mouth hung slightly open in what could only be described as bewildered.

"What?" He sounded genuinely astonished, then sat still for a moment, as if in deep thought. Suddenly he jerked his head up. "Oh, I think I understand what happened." He turned back to her. "Can you please pull over somewhere so we can talk about this for a minute?" His tone was firm.

Bree turned on her blinker and scanned the side of the road for a turnoff. She pulled into a shopping center lot and parked on its perimeter under some trees. After cutting off the engine, she turned toward him, bracing for his response. "I'm listening."

"This is a bit complex, so bear with me." He took a deep breath. "My boss, Clay, is the executive director of the network. He knew that Provence was vacation for me, but he still pressured me to dig for something to expose, since I was already there."

"Doesn't sound fair. That was *your* vacation time." So, there *was* some thought about using the tour negatively in a program.

"I said the same thing and told him no. I wouldn't have betrayed you, Bree." His eyes latched onto hers.

She swallowed, feeling her defenses begin to melt. "I know." she whispered. "What else happened?"

"He kept pestering me about it while I was in Italy too, even though he'd already agreed to let me do that project my way, just a normal travel program. I guess he'd changed his mind. He wanted to keep the same focus I was known for, scams and warnings, even though I kept *telling* him I want to change directions."

He leaned back against the seat, looking stormy. "I wanted to throw him a bone so he'd leave me alone so I mentioned the reality show idea. I said we could discuss it when I got back, never dreaming he'd do anything about it before then. I never told him your name or your company's name. I really doubted that I'd ever follow through on it with the network, because I don't have the same vision anymore." He looked apologetic. "I don't know how they found your name or contact, Bree. Honestly."

She was flooded with relief at his explanation. "I understand. And I believe you." She hadn't realized she'd been holding her breath. She let it out slowly

"I'm glad you believe me. At any rate, there's no worry about him because I don't work for him anymore."

Bree's eyes widened. "What? You quit? Or were you fired?"

"Kind of both. He kept pressuring me to do things his way." Travis looked away. "This has been coming for a while. It's for the best."

"I wonder why they contacted me about the show, then."

"I can't imagine, unless Will didn't know I wasn't with the network anymore. It's recent. Or it's possible that they want to do a program with you but not me."

"Why would I do that? I'd only do it with you."

He smiled then, with the same warmth she'd been craving since their parting in France.

"What are you going to do now?" She couldn't imagine that he'd stay unemployed for very long. "Of course, you have magazine articles, books, interviews. You'll be in demand, that's for sure."

"Thanks for your confidence. I'm not worried. I'd like to start an independent film company. It's harder than working for an established network, but at least I'll be my own boss."

"I can see you doing that." She nodded with certainty then combed one hand through her hair. "We'll have something in common. Lauren quit Le Bon Voyage right after we got back to the States. It's all mine from now on. I'm the boss." Like it or not.

"Was—that hard for you?" His voice was gentle as his gaze found hers.

"Yes, at first." She shrugged. "But it's growing on me, the idea that I'm in charge and can do things my own way."

He laughed. "Exactly. The beauty of being the boss. Of course, there are negatives too, like lots of responsibility, the finances."

"I already had those, so there's just more of it."

234

He cocked his head as he looked at her. She was aware of his nearness and the familiar scent of his cologne. He said, "We could join forces and make that reality show ourselves, like we talked about in France."

She stilled. Frowned. "Is that why you came here? To talk about the show?" Bree braced for his answer.

He stared at her. Blinked. Slowly, and with surprising firmness he said, "Didn't even cross my mind. I don't even want to talk about it now."

She swallowed. Heart hammering, she ventured with a voice that sounded small to her ears. "What do you want to talk about?"

He had unhooked his seatbelt and slid one arm along the back of the seat. He leaned toward her, tightening the space between them. His gaze held fast to hers, then wandered around her face, down to her lips, then back to her eyes. She couldn't look away. The car seemed warm as heat crept up her neck.

"I wanted to see you again." His voice was soft. "We never finished that conversation by the pool. You didn't come back—"

"I did, but you'd already left."

"I thought you'd been pulled into some of your last-minute duties, so I went for a walk, figuring we'd have a chance to talk the following day. But my colleague arrived to pick me up too early the next morning. I would have told you, but everyone was in bed. I ran into Alan and asked him to tell you what had happened and that I had to leave early."

"He didn't."

"I figured as much. He had his eyes on you the whole trip, so I knew I had a slim chance of him doing any favors for me."

"I was glad to get rid of him, though it's unkind to say."

Travis chuckled, then sobered. "Must have seemed cold to you when I left without saying anything."

Bree looked at her hands. "I was kind of hurt. I really wanted to talk to you more, but everyone kept asking me questions. I couldn't get away. Then when I didn't see you the next day—" She looked at him. "You could have emailed, couldn't you?"

"I should have. I knew you were traveling so I figured I'd wait. Mistake, huh?"

She managed a half-smile and shrugged. "It's all right."

"Besides that—and this is really the more honest reason—I didn't know how you were feeling about"—he tightened his lips and gave a one-shouldered shrug— "about me."

Joy and love unfurled inside her, like the opening of a long-sealed gift box. She wanted to reach out, to touch him, and ached to respond to his uncertainty about her feelings.

Before she could gather her words, he said, "Bree—" He stared out the front windshield at the shade tree, which cast angular shadows on the hood of the car. "I'm not a godly man. In some ways I'm still kind of a prodigal. But I think I'm pointed in the right direction. So, I want to ask you—"

"Travis."

He turned back to her, his face masked in what appeared to be sadness and resignation as he awaited her response. "Travis," she said again, more softly. "I love you."

She watched his face then as her words registered. The blink, the slow smile. Slowly, he leaned toward her and coiled his arms around her, pulling her close. He covered her lips with his, pressing her against the seat, holding nothing back. Hungrily he kissed her, his pent-up longings seeming to match her own.

Bree detached her seatbelt and curled toward him, wrapping her arms around his neck and sinking into him, savoring the smell and taste of him, wanting to draw him nearer, wanting to surrender.

A tiny sound escaped her throat as he tightened his arms around her waist.

Everything else dropped away—her fears, the past, and currently, the upheavals in the company. All of it faded until there was only this man, a man who wrestled with his own questions but courageously moved ahead, a man who, surprisingly, seemed to complete her in so many ways. Travis . . .

He kept his hands clasped around her waist and pulled his head back. His eyes searched her face as if memorizing everything he saw. Longing and raw emotion beamed from his expression. His clear blue eyes didn't waver.

He leaned forward again, tilting his head to angle toward her. He brushed her lips, softly, sweetly this time, then lingered there, renewing his kiss. When he pulled away from her this time, he whispered, "I love you, Bree Sorenson. I was meant to meet you." He smiled then. "To lock horns with you—"

They both chuckled, their foreheads touching, as she stared right into those clear blue eyes, feeling as though she were falling into him. "I'm sorry I was so hard on you. I didn't know . . ."

"We can thank my mom. She wanted to go to Provence and I couldn't disappoint her."

"Oh, we have more than that to thank her for." Bree gave a throaty chuckle. "I wonder if she was planting seeds."

"Definitely." His voice was gentle. The tiny lines around his eyes deepened as he grinned at her. He ran the tips of his fingers down the curve of her cheek then twirled them through a lock of hair on her shoulder.

"You should call her and let her know about . . . the new developments."

"I will," Travis said. "She'll be happy. She likes you."

"I like her too. But I especially like her son."

Travis swooped in to kiss her again, taking her breath away. Bree was lost, unable to think clearly as she melted into him.

He murmured against her ear, "Thanks for not pushing me away this time when I kissed you. That's a new experience." He pulled back, his eyes teasing her. "Though next time won't be in a car, I promise."

"That's good news." She grinned, feeling buoyant. "So, where do you live? Oregon, right?"

"Yeah, we need to talk about that. What do you think if I move here? I have to edit the Italy project for a month or so, then I can close out and move."

Her eyes widened. "You're willing to move here from Oregon?"

"Of course. How do you expect me to court you from across the country? I want to be able to see you. A lot. And I could use a change of scenery." He stared at her, an inviting smile pulling at his lips.

She gazed at him in wonder. "You're serious, aren't you?"

He nodded, holding her gaze. "I told you I love you. I think I started loving you the moment I saw you in the villa." He grinned then. "Even though you weren't very nice." They laughed.

"I hope you'll let me make it up to you."

"Absolutely. For as long as you like—"

She leaned toward him and caressed his lips with hers. At this rate they'd never get to the restaurant. And she didn't care.

"I'll look for a place to live during my visit this week. You can advise me about neighborhoods."

She just shook her head, a smile of wonder spreading on her lips. How quickly things could change. Two weeks ago, she was in business with Lauren and Travis was a faraway dream she thought never to see again. But now Lauren was gone, and here was Travis, his arms wrapped around her, wanting to move across the country to be near her. "The east coast makes for shorter flights to Europe, too."

"Another bonus." Travis slid back to the passenger seat. "Are you ready to go on our first date?"

She cast him a smile she hoped was full of promise. "I'm ready for everything the future holds, starting with tonight." And she was. She'd been freed from her fears before this moment, and now, this.

He linked his fingers through hers and squeezed. The look in his eyes and the smile tugging his lips told her he felt the same.

Epilogue

"If you don't hurry, there won't be any pizza left for you," Travis called from the couch.

"Don't you dare. I'll be right there." Bree closed the kitchen cupboards and glanced at her watch. The program wasn't airing until eight. They still had a few minutes.

Since moving into the new house last month, she had trouble finding nearly everything. Of course, several boxes were still stacked in the dining room waiting until she had time to go through them.

Where had she put the paper plates? They would be more practical for a pizza dinner in front of the TV as they watched the pilot documentary, the first they'd done together as a couple. Bree peered into a drawer and finally found the plates. Before leaving the kitchen, she looked around at pans stacked inside one another, cartons of table linens, assorted glassware, and plastics bins of unknown contents . . . her beloved mess. What a year it had been, culminating in that evening.

As if the beautiful wedding and spectacular honeymoon in Varenna, Italy, hadn't been enough to fill up her heart full for some

240

time to come, she and Travis had launched their own independent film company.

The travel film world had been a leap for Bree. Although she still planned to lead several tours a year with Travis's help, she also wanted to travel with him and help with his projects. *Their* projects. Especially in the organization category, he had certainly benefitted from her neurotic perfectionism.

Only she didn't feel so neurotic anymore.

Bree went to the den and tossed the plates on the ottoman, then slid onto the couch beside Travis. She nestled into his arms, which encircled her like a warm blanket. She looked up at him, her face close to his. "Ready?"

He stared down at her and murmured, "'Bout time. I missed you," then leaned forward for a lingering kiss.

"Thought you were hungry for pizza—" She giggled when he kissed her neck. "Stop, we won't have time to eat before the show starts."

"You sure it was pizza I was hungry for?" A mischievous twinkle danced in his eyes just before he placed a final kiss on her brow and reopened the pizza box.

Bree curled her arms around her knees and let out a contented sigh as she watched Travis pull slices of pizza from the box. She lived for these moments, when the world felt so right, as though all the frayed pieces had been magically sewn together.

When she mentally paged through the previous year, she felt simply . . . awed. Awed by how much had happened, how much they'd accomplished, how many doors had opened. It had taken most of the previous year to establish the new indie company, Small World Productions, and complete their first project. They'd participated in a film festival, gathered investors, and found a network willing to air the pilot.

And of course, they'd gotten married.

Bree and Travis carefully guarded evenings like this one. They grouped filming and travel projects together, so they wouldn't spend too much time away from home. Their new home was a bungalow on the outskirts of D.C., not far from the airport, the new studio they'd begun working with, and their new home church.

Familiar music filled the living room. Travis handed her a slice of pizza. "We'll have to eat our pizza while we watch, since you didn't let me eat any first." A smile played on his lips. "This woman is always all over me. Can't get anything done."

She nudged him and grinned. "Shhh. It's starting. Eat your pizza."

The cable network had been willing, no, eager, to air the reality show. Travis had expected obstacles in changing networks but found that his reputation had prepared the way. He hardly had to introduce himself, thanks to the stunning success of the Denmark-Italy program, which had aired the previous fall.

A month after moving from Portland to Virginia, Travis accompanied Bree back to Provence for a cooking tour. Of course, the guests were thrilled to have a TV travel personality in their midst, but mostly Travis stayed behind the scenes, helping out as Bree led the group for the first time without Lauren.

"This is your baby," he'd insisted. "But I'm here for whatever you need."

She'd been immensely relieved to have his steady presence. Of course, by then, they'd become inseparable. From that group they were able to recruit some of the participants for the reality show, which they filmed the following spring.

"I think Jenny and Nate have good stage presence, don't you?" Bree bit into her pizza as she watched the opening scene. The characters showed up in different vignettes prior to coming together at the villa, some in a state of conflict, others with differing issues that would explode onto the screen in later scenes.

"Hmm. This pizza is lukewarm." She set it down and leaned back to watch the program, which she'd seen a half dozen times already, having also participated in the editing with Travis. Another brand-new experience.

"They did a good job and look great on camera. Geoff is kind of stiff, but he reminds me of Alan, so I guess in that sense he fits right in." They laughed.

They were pulled into the show and watched the rest in silence. The final credits scrolled down the screen. "That was really fun," Bree said, "but I'm glad we won't be doing reality all the time. I loved what you did in Italy. I really prefer the classic travel and discovery shows, with the interviews of locals too, of course."

"Always." Travis gathered the paper plates and stood. "Oh, I want to tell you about the phone call I got today."

Bree leaned back and looked at him expectantly.

He sat down on the ottoman, facing her. "You're gonna love this. A call from the PNC Network. First, Clay is no longer employed with them. Not sure what happened there. They have a new guy, Adam, I think. Seemed nice enough. He was eager to get me back on the network. Told me he wouldn't take no for an answer."

Bree's eyes widened. "Really? Did you tell him you're already set?"

He grinned. "I did. I invited him to view the program tonight. He told me he was aware of it and that he'd watch it. He said he'd wait until I was ready."

"Sounds like you're in demand. I'm not surprised."

"*We're* in demand, my love. *We* are Small Planet. You and me."

"And Le Bon Voyage."

"Of course." His eyes latched onto hers as he became serious. "What a *bon voyage* it was. Where it all began."

She couldn't help herself. She plunged back into his arms, her voice muffled against his shirt. "Yes, where it all began. But this one won't ever end."

Travis flicked the pizza box aside and once again pulled Bree into his arms.

I hope you enjoyed reading *Prodigals in Provence*! If you did, please consider leaving a review on Amazon and/or Goodreads for me. It would help other readers discover my books and be encouraged by their inspiring truths. You can also sign up to receive news and updates about new books at www.Kyle-Hunter.com

The story doesn't end here. You may be wondering what happens with Lauren, Bree's friend, whose life is hanging in mid-air.

Her story is told in the sequel

A Promise in Provence.

Lauren is at a turning point. If only she knew *where* to turn. Her long-term relationship with Mark is fading fast. Instead, she feels drawn to Jean-Pierre, an attractive Frenchman she'd met the previous summer. When she's laid off from her job as a chef, she decides to go see him in Provence, France.

Mark can't get Lauren out of his heart, even though it's been close to a year since she asked him to give her space. When she goes to France, he's afraid he'll lose her for good. That is, until he decides to go there, too, as a last-ditch effort to win her back.

At first, Lauren is angry that Mark follows her to France. But a joint desire to help a young refugee boy leads them to work together. Lauren finds herself torn between the two men. Worse, she's confronted with obstacles in helping the boy and even greater obstacles within herself.

More Romantic Stories that Take You Places...

Circle Back Around

Hailey and her father haven't always seen eye to eye, especially in running the failing family textile mill. Frustrated, Hailey leaves the mill and her hometown in North Carolina to start a new life near her sister in Colorado. Only months later her father calls to ask a special favor. He needs heart surgery and asks Hailey to run the mill in his place.

Moving back would devastate Hailey's sister, Hope. Yet Hailey would have an opportunity to possibly save the mill, and at a time when her father needs her most. And maybe he'd even approve of her for the first time in her life.

Filled with self-doubt, Hailey returns to North Carolina and struggles to make a difference at the mill, facing more challenges than she bargained for. Her attractive neighbor, Alex, is almost enough to outweigh the difficulties, but she doesn't know that in the shadows lurks someone who wants to destroy both her *and* the mill.

One December

Is there any way to recapture what happened under the moon one December?

Nikki has loved Mike for as long as she can remember. Mike has his own past hurts to resolve, having lost both parents when he was fourteen. He's tried to escape the memories by starting a new life on the West Coast.

At Christmas, he comes back to New York for the first time in three years. He and Nikki rekindle the friendship they had as children and share their newfound faith. Under a Christmas moon, romantic sparks fly . . . but their mutual attraction takes an unexpected detour.

Nikki is devastated, believing the romance is over. She impulsively takes a one-year teaching opportunity in Paris to face her own fears and to get over Mike.

If they think they can run away from each other, they'd better think again.

"*One December* sizzles with romantic tension, taking the reader on a roller-coaster ride from New York to San Francisco, with a delightful detour in Paris. I couldn't put it down!" – Elizabeth Musser, author of *The Secrets of the Cross* trilogy and *The Swan House.*

Second Chance Series

In **The Second Chance Series**, you'll meet Marissa, Julia, Sydney, and Eden, four college friends who, twenty-five years later, renew their friendships as they find themselves empty nesters and single again. You'll love getting to know these women and following each one in her own book.

Marissa Rewritten (A Novella: Book 1)

Author Marissa Thompson has had a writer's block since her husband died almost two years earlier. Her three closest friends are a comfort. Despite this, things are getting urgent as her career hangs by a thread and repairs on her historic home mount up. Prodded by desperation, Marissa heads to Wilmington, North Carolina for a Civil War research trip. She hopes for inspiration, but receives support from a surprising source, a feisty character from her last novel.

Jarrod Lambert has already lost his wife. He's always been close with his only daughter, a college student, but she seems to be slipping further away from him. In an effort to reconnect with her, he makes an impulsive trip to see her in Wilmington.

Through an accident, Marissa and Jarrod meet and discover common ground. Will it be enough to overcome the obstacles standing between them?

Julia Redesigned (Book 2)

Can a stack of letters provide clues to an age-old conflict and a doorway to a new family?

For the last three years, Julia De Luca has juggled her successful interior design business with caring for her elderly mother. Following her mother's death, Julia finds old letters from distant relatives in Italy. They remind her of visits she and her mother made when Julia was a child. Could these letters hold the answer to why their trips to Italy ended abruptly when she was ten years old?

These people whose names she's forgotten are the only family Julia has left on earth. How can she reconnect with them after so many years? Would it be crazy to try?

Her compelling desire to locate her distant family leads Julia on an impulsive trip to Florence, Italy. Along with savoring the sights and flavors of Florence, Julia discovers that families can be messy, that it's not too late to fall in love, and that there's more to Julia De Luca than she ever knew.

Kyle Hunter writes inspirational romance and women's fiction that sometimes take her characters to faraway places. She lived in France for thirteen years. Currently she lives in North Carolina where she writes fiction, non-fiction (under the pen name K. B. Oliver and blogs for Oliversfrance.com), and teaches French to adults.